DEAD BELOW DECK

JAN GANGSEI

DEAD BELOW DECK

HARPER
An Imprint of HarperCollins*Publishers*

Library of Congress Control Number: 2023948470

ISBN 978-0-06-331044-5

Typography by Julia Feingold

24 25 26 27 28 LBC 5 4 3 2 1

First Edition

For my mom

DEAD
BELOW
DECK

ITINERARY

DAY ONE:
DEPARTURE!

 ### DAY TWO:
AT SEA (SWIM, SUN, CHILL!)

DAY THREE:
NASSAU, BAHAMAS (PLACE YOUR BETS!)

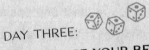
KEY WEST, FLORIDA (CHEERS TO THE SUN!)

 ### DAY FIVE:
ARRIVE AT GRAND CAYMAN

BREAKING NEWS ALERT—4/16, 10:08 A.M.

AN UNFOLDING TRAGEDY AT SEA

We have just learned in an exclusive report that Giselle Haverford, the eighteen-year-old daughter of Senator and likely presidential candidate Robert Haverford and stepdaughter of popular lifestyle blogger Britney Michel Haverford, has gone missing from the family yacht, *The Escape*. Giselle Haverford reportedly went overboard under suspicious circumstances late last night or early this morning after departing Key West, Florida. The yacht is currently en route to Grand Cayman, where our sources tell us at least one passenger is expected to be taken into custody. More on this story as it develops.

DAY 5

Latitude, longitude: 19.952696, -82.953878

80 nautical miles off the coast of Grand Cayman

What have I done?

"Don't leave this room." The first mate releases the arm he's been using to keep me steady on the long, vertigo-inducing walk back to my stateroom from *The Escape*'s bridge, where I sat and listened in shock as Captain Hjelkrem radioed the Coast Guard to report Giselle overboard. *Overboard.* This can't be real. Can it? My pounding hangover is suddenly gone, replaced by something else. Something far worse. Confusion. Disbelief. Horror.

I nod, throat tight, doing my best to stay upright as the Haverford family's yacht thuds across the churning waves. "I won't," I manage to croak out. Where would I go, anyway? We're in the middle of the Gulf of Mexico, miles from shore. There's nowhere to go except straight down into the water.

I'm struck with a horrifying image of Giselle, hair floating on the surface as she disappears beneath the dark waves. A slender hand, reaching out and grasping the empty air for help that isn't coming.

A memory? Or just my imagination?

3

Does it even matter?

Because Giselle is gone, and I'm to blame.

My eyes well with tears.

The first mate backs into the hallway with a sad shake of his head and clicks the door shut. An eerie silence fills the room, save for the sound of my ragged breathing. I am completely and utterly alone, trapped in a prison of my own making.

I sink onto the edge of my bed, staring in disbelief at my trembling hands. Hands I thought I knew. Pale and freckled. Long fingers, thick like Mom's. Chewed-down nails. I try to picture these hands, placed squarely on Giselle's back, and I don't know what to think.

What if they were right about me? What if I'll do anything to get what I want?

The mahogany walls of my stateroom begin to close in around me like a fist squeezing shut. In less than two hours we'll arrive in Grand Cayman, where Giselle's family—and the police—will be waiting. For me.

I try my best to conjure up an image of what went down on the top deck last night. But there's nothing. Just a black hole where a memory should be, and a persistent, nagging guilt that chews at my core. An unspoken truth, gnawing me from the inside out.

We take a wave, hard, and the Egyptian cotton robe next to my bed sways ominously on its gold hook. Another wave and the tray of cold coffee and stale croissants on my night-stand crashes to the floor. I jolt, heart pounding against my rib cage like a spooked horse trying to bust free of its stall. Something inside me breaks along with the coffee cup; the last bit of hope that this has all been a bad dream. That I'll wake up and discover Giselle reclining on a lounger under the bright blue Caribbean sky, green eyes dancing with mischief, a dazzling smile lighting up her suntanned face.

Tears roll down my cheeks as the cold reality of what's happened sinks in. I swipe them away and hobble to the veranda in search of air, wincing with each step on my freshly bandaged foot. I fix my eyes on the distant horizon, a curved line of deep blue that divides the sky from ocean, life from death. It's the only thing keeping me oriented now that up has swapped places with down, left with right.

A flurry of activity and voices erupt on the deck above me. I can hear the other girls, their words carrying on the breeze from the open balcony doors of the primary suite. I strain to listen, hoping desperately for good news. Some sort of miracle. Reports of a fishing boat that happened by and plucked Giselle from the deep water, and now she's wrapped in a thick towel drinking warm coffee from a metal thermos with a gruff old fisherman, laughing and plotting her revenge.

"Look at these Polaroids. I can't believe she kept them," I hear Vivian say. "Oh, I remember this. See?" Her voice cracks. "Last year when we dressed like M&M's for Spring Spirit Week. Giselle had to be different and be a peanut one, and—" She chokes back a sob.

"They'll find her, Viv," Emi says. "They have to. She's

Giselle Haverford. I bet every Coast Guard boat and helicopter in a hundred-mile radius is out there now, circling the last place her cell phone pinged."

"Yeah, you're right." Vivian sniffles. "We can't give up hope. She's always been so strong. If anyone could survive this, it's Giselle."

I want to shout up to them, tell them how sorry I am. How I'd do anything—*anything*—to make this right. But the words sound hollow, even in my own mind. I can't make this right. Maybe if I hadn't always been so busy trying to make things right, this never would have happened in the first place.

"I have her necklace," Vivian says, her voice cracking again, and I picture the gold heart-locket necklace that always dangled from Giselle's neck. The crew found it this morning, broken and snagged on the dented third-deck railing. Ripped away as she'd tumbled into the water from the deck above.

I swallow hard to keep myself from throwing up.

"Let's go upstairs and start the vigil," Emi says.

"What about Maggie?" Vivian asks, and my back stiffens at my name.

Emi scoffs. "What about her?"

"Never mind," Vivian says. "I don't know what I meant. I guess I'm still in shock. I can't believe she'd do something like this. I liked Maggie, you know?"

"Yeah, well, so did Giselle," Emi answers. "And look how that worked out."

An automatic bubble of annoyance springs up in my chest,

because of course Emi would say that. She's never liked me. But I push it back down, along with a deep sense of shame. Because this time, Emi's right.

"She really had me fooled," Vivian says, then pauses. "Hey, what are you looking for?"

"Giselle's journal," Emi answers. "I saw her put it under here, and now it's gone."

Icy terror spikes through my veins.

The journal!

I hurry back into my room, heart stuttering as their voices fade away, and punch in the combination to the small safe in my closet. The metal door springs open like an old-fashioned jack-in-the-box, minus the creepy clown. I jolt back in horror.

There's the journal, still locked tight, just like it was when I stuffed it inside two days ago. It sits right on top of two freshly bundled stacks of hundred-dollar bills that I also shouldn't have. The corner of a fake passport pokes out from beneath the cash.

And underneath that, a letter written on elegant cream linen stationery, carefully folded in thirds, tucked into a matching envelope with a broken wax seal. If only I had left that stupid thing alone. Now it sits there like a bomb on its final count-down to detonation.

Ticktock. Ticktock.

My head feels like it's detached from my body and is floating away. A tiny balloon in the big blue sky. A tiny person in the big, wide ocean. I should dump this all overboard. Destroy the evidence.

But I can't. Not without knowing what Giselle wrote.

I yank the journal from the safe. The pink sequined cover is rough against my palms, and I try to imagine Giselle buying this thing on purpose. It reminds me of something that twelve-year-old me would have picked up at a buy-three-get-three-free sale at Claire's. Back when I'd save up my chore money to get myself some cheap lip gloss, scrunchies, and unicorn jewelry that turned my skin green after three days.

I slump onto the bed, journal dropping onto my lap, and put my head in my hands.

I wish I could go back in time. Be the person I used to be. Before Giselle. Before Prep. Before this trip. Riding my bike up and down the country roads, slaying imaginary dragons with my foam sword and plastic shield, fighting evil to protect my kingdom. Stretched out in the back of my truck with Allison, fingers entwined, the starlit sky above us a canvas of infinite possibilities. The places we'd go. The people we'd become.

I don't know you anymore, Allison said when I ran into her last fall, the first time I'd seen her in months. Tears shimmered in her blue-green eyes. *You've changed. The hair, the clothes . . . everything. You've become a totally different person.*

Maybe I have. But people don't really change overnight, do they? It happens in degrees, so small you barely realize what's going on. Until before you know it, that foam sword is shoved away in the closet, dented and chipped, lost beneath the broken Barbie dolls and clothes that don't fit anymore. And the one person you swore you'd never be without is somewhere, alone, on the other side of a wide ocean.

Or what if we don't really change at all? What if growing up is little more than a peeling away of our protective layers, bit by bit, to get at our true selves?

What if this is who I really am?

A liar.

A thief.

A killer.

I tug at the journal's lock, desperate for answers. It doesn't give. I grit my teeth in frustration. There has to be some way to get this open.

Wait! The bobby pins Emi used to secure my updo back in Nassau . . .

I rush into the bathroom, ignoring the stabbing pain in my foot, and grab one from the discarded pile on the counter. The thin metal easily yields as I bend the pin open. I snap it in half and peel away the plastic coating, then sit on my bed and shove both points into the lock.

Scrape, twist, scrape, twist.

Nothing happens.

I wiggle the pins harder, sweat beading along my hairline as I struggle to find the internal latch.

Scrape, twist, scrape, twist.

I'm about to give up when it finally catches. The lock pops open with a *click*, and I blow out an anxious breath. I press the journal open and start to read.

Dear Mom . . .

Mom? I swallow down the lump in my throat. I shouldn't be invading Giselle's private thoughts like this. Haven't I done enough already? But no, I need to carry on. I need to know what Giselle knew.

Who she told.

Dear Mom,

I'm not exactly sure where to start. This journal was Dr. Richard's idea. He handed it to me during our last session before school started. Said I could write to anyone. Myself. You. An imaginary friend. Just let it all out, tell my story. If you swallow a secret, he said, it will slowly eat you away from the inside.

I'm afraid it's too late for that, though, isn't it?

What I really need is YOU, not step-monster Britney. I don't understand how Dad could replace you so quickly. Not even a year and he already has a whole new family—new wife, baby—POOF! As if the first family never existed. Never even counted. How does someone do that?

It's September and I'm back at school, which is a relief after spending the summer "bonding" with Britney at that wellness spa in Colorado. It was fucking awful. Meditating and daily breathing exercises with Miss New Age has got to be its own special brand of hell. She even got Dad to do some sort of healing cleanse with crystals, which is totally ridiculous, right? This is DAD we're talking about. I mean, c'mon, if he really thinks some hot blonde half his age loves him for his glowing aura (and not because she can totally picture herself as First Lady), well, he's even further gone than I thought.

For the first time ever, I drove myself to Prep. Five long hours from Manhattan to New Hampshire alone with my thoughts. Dad had gone back to DC early to meet with his advisers. Step-monster Britney stayed home (thank God!) because she was too exhausted from her so-called work and taking care of the new baby (despite the fact that Knox's nanny, Josie, does everything from feeding him to putting him to bed to waking up at night when he cries).

When I got here, I unloaded the car on my own, hauled my bags inside and up three flights of stairs. It was weird. No Dad giving me a hearty slap on the back as we dumped my things in the dorm with a "Give 'em hell, Giselle!" No you, dabbing your eyes with a tissue, telling me how proud you were of me and to not forget to call and write back!

Why didn't I ever write back?

I've saved them all, you know. Your letters. The ones you sent every week, written on your special linen stationery with your initials monogrammed on top, envelopes closed with a red wax seal. It was so old-fashioned and corny, but you said there was something special about a real letter. Something you could hold on to, not like an email or text.

So, I've put them all into a drawer in my desk here at school. That way I can read them whenever I want. And maybe even pretend you're still here. I wear your locket every day. You know, the special one Abuelo gave you for your quinceañera, mi corazón— my heart—engraved inside. I'll never take it off.

Anyway, after I finished putting my things in my room, I went down the hall to Emiene's. Viv was already there, flopped on a fuzzy turquoise papasan chair, her suntanned legs slung over the edge. Emi was unpacking her camera gear from a huge Louis Vuitton suitcase and piling it on her desk.

Giselle! Emi said, arms loaded with camera lenses. *You're here, finally!*

Vivian popped out of the chair and wrapped me in a hug. I couldn't help but stiffen a little as the last year came back to me in a rush.

OmigodGiselleLookAtYou, Viv said, her words gushing out in one breath. *You look ah-mazing! AH-MAZING!! Like, I think you lost fifteen pounds this summer. I mean, not that you didn't look incredible before, but wow.*

Emi set down her camera gear and came in for a hug, too.

I missed you, she breathed into my ear. *The Hamptons sucked without you. I can't believe you left me on our last summer together, bitch.*

I know. I missed you, too, I said, voice catching in my throat. She had no idea how much I would have preferred a carefree summer of bonfires on the beach and lazy days in the sunshine. Instead of . . . ugh, I don't even want to think about it, let alone put it in writing.

When Em released me from her iron grip and went back to unpacking, I squished in next to Viv on the papasan. *Okay,* I said. *Let's hear about Paris!*

Viv launched into a tale of her summer spent hooking up with this hot Parisian guy named Raphael who zipped her around the cobblestone streets on his Peugeot and introduced her to baba au rhum and took her to the French countryside (all documented in loving, sunlit detail for her gazillion Instagram followers, of course).

Emi filled me in on everything I'd missed—the new summer people who'd moved in and how a candle shop (seriously, candles?!) had taken the place of our favorite ice cream parlor. The only good thing about the summer, she said, was that she'd had a lot of free time to compile footage for her film school application to USC.

I know you'd laugh, Mom, because when I was little, I always said I couldn't wait to grow up and be bigger, faster, FREE (like that time I ran off in the park chasing a butterfly when your back was turned, and you were so mad but crying with happiness when you found me, remember??). Still, as soon as Emi mentioned college, this unexpected sense of bittersweet longing tugged at me, knowing that next year everything would change. Even more than it already had, which was saying something. No more huddling in our rooms together on the first day of school, complaining about our dorky uniforms and talking about our crushes. No more us—me, Em, Viv—the three amigos, the three musketeers, or whatever it was our teachers called us over the years. Three best friends, always and forever: Emi, the filmmaking and loyal-as-hell daughter of a Nigerian supermodel and Greek shipping magnate; Viv, the blond bombshell with brains and a talent for documenting her extraordinary life for maximum likes.

And me, Giselle Haverford.

The princess. The queen bee. The perfect smiling face in Dad's campaign commercials. The girl whose eleventh birthday was featured in a four-page spread in People magazine, radiant as she blew out the candles on her giant (but tasteful!) eleven-tiered cake and hugged her celebrity godparents. The girl who is envied—and maybe even a little feared—as she looks down from her perch atop Andover Prep's glittering social heap.

Of course, that's all a lie, isn't it?

I'm not that person anymore.

I'm not sure I ever was.

And let's face it, the three amigos began to splinter apart the day Britney stepped into my life and took over yours.

I really wish I could have known you better, Mom. I wish I'd asked you more when I had the chance. About my grandparents and the uncle who died before I was born. About your childhood in Miami and my abuelo's life in Cuba. About your hopes and dreams and the design career you gave up so you could play the role of the perfect political wife and be my mom. Now it's too late. All I can do is write these pretend letters.

Letters that no one will ever answer.

But maybe that's for the best.

Because two can keep a secret if one of them is dead.

DAY 5

APRIL 16—MORNING

Latitude, longitude: 19.808054, -82.601259

90 nautical miles off the coast of Grand Cayman

Never again.

I know, famous last words and all that. But seriously. I never want to see another bottle of Cristal in my life. I don't care how fancy it is or how many "notes of pear" it contains or how effervescent the bubbles might be. After last night, I'm swearing off champagne for good. My head pounds. I can hardly remember coming back to my room and climbing into bed. Still in my bathing suit and cover-up, apparently.

My stomach heaves. I throw back the covers and rush to the bathroom, attempting to steady myself over the toilet as I regurgitate last night's mistakes. I wipe my mouth with the back of my hand, fairly certain I just barfed up my spleen and flushed it out to sea.

I slump to the floor. I've never felt anything like this. Not even the morning after that all-night party in the field behind Kyle Parker's house, which is the only other time I've gotten drunk. It was mud season, that glorious time of year when every dirt road in Vermont turns to quicksand. Allison and I got stuck three times driving to that party, and I worried we might have even worse luck trying to get home. We were already going to have a hard enough time explaining the mud splatters on Alli's jeans from when she tried to push my truck free while I stepped on the gas (an idea that seemed a lot better *before* we tried it). But having to explain to Alli's control-freak parents what we were doing with a bunch of camping gear and a cooler filled with cheap wine five miles outside town—instead of sleeping over at each other's houses like we said we'd be doing—would be far, far worse.

As it turned out, Allison's parents wound up being the least of my worries.

I shake my head.

Bigger and better things, I tell myself.

Bigger and better things.

But first, I've got to make it off this yacht in one piece, which seems pretty questionable at the moment. I drag both hands over my face, trying to wake up. I swear, it's like I've been drugged or something. Then I remember the rounds upon rounds of sickly sweet rum runners back in Key West that came *before* the champagne. How many of those did I knock back? At least three. What on earth was I thinking? I never should have let myself lose control like that. Especially around Giselle. Did I do anything stupid?

A chill creeps up my spine as little snippets of last night's debauchery flit across my mind—*Giselle, champagne bottles, smashing glass.* All at once I go from cold to hot, then cold again, and a pounding starts up in my head like someone's cracking a mallet against my skull. From the inside.

Bam, bam, bam.

Ugh, make it stop.

Bam, bam, bam.

"Maggie! Are you in there?"

It takes a minute to realize that the pounding is actually coming from the door to my cabin. And it's not my cabin steward, Marina, dropping off the morning coffee and croissants. Those are already on the nightstand, getting colder and staler by the minute. I can hardly bear to look at them, let alone put any of it in my mouth.

"Maggie!" the voice yells again, more urgently this time.

I swallow the bubble in my throat and creak open the cabin door, wincing. Vivian stands on the other side, dressed in purple-and-black Lululemon yoga pants and a matching sports bra. Her shiny blond hair is pulled into a high ponytail, and there's not a hint of dark or puffy beneath her clear blue eyes. I honestly don't know how she does it. But then, maybe I do. I'm pretty sure those two-hundred-dollar bottles of moisturizer lining her bathroom counter don't hurt the cause.

"Ouch," Vivian says, scanning my face. "I don't know what you and Giselle did after Emi and I went to bed, but you look like you got dropped in a blender. Maybe you should consider going vegan. You'd be amazed what cleansing your body of animal fat would do for you. I mean, I feel fine today! Great, even!"

I swallow hard and shrug. "And give up this body built by

cheeseburgers?" I try to smile, parched lips sticking to my dry teeth.

Vivian doesn't laugh. She cranes her neck, peering over my shoulder and into my stateroom. "So, where is she?"

"Who?" I have no idea what Vivian is talking about.

"Giselle," Vivian says, and continues to look past me. "Didn't she crash in here?"

"No," I say. But I look behind myself and check anyway. I was so out of it last night, for all I know Giselle is asleep on my floor and I stepped right over her in the five minutes I've been borderline conscious.

"She's not?" Vivian's voice rises. "When did you see her last?"

"Up on the deck. She didn't come down here." I begin to close the door as a wave rolls the yacht, bringing another wave of nausea over me. "If you don't mind, I need to lie down. For a couple of weeks. Or at least until we dock."

Vivian jams the toe of her Marc Jacobs sneaker in front of the door. "Actually, I do mind," she clucks. "Giselle didn't show for sunrise yoga this morning, which is totally not like her. And Emi said she never came back to their room last night. We can't find her. Anywhere."

"Hey, don't worry, okay?" I say. "If she feels half as crappy as I do, I'm sure she's just dead to the world somewhere right now."

Vivian cocks an eyebrow.

"*Sleeping*," I say. "I'm sure she's sleeping it off somewhere we

19

won't hassle her. So maybe we shouldn't."

I try to close the door again.

"That won't do," Vivian says with a bouncy headshake. "We have to find her and sober her up before we get to Grand Cayman and her dad gets on board and grounds her for the rest of senior year. You have no idea how uptight Giselle's dad can get. He took away her car once for getting a B on an exam. And, I mean, you know how he is about his image? Forget it. You saw how freaked Giselle got when those people took our picture in Key West, and we weren't even doing anything wrong!"

And I thought Allison's parents were bad. At least I didn't have to sign a nondisclosure agreement before spending a weekend with them at Six Flags like I did to go on this trip. But then, a photo of Allison pounding a hurricane while underage isn't likely to snag a six-figure payout from TMZ like it is with Giselle.

"All right, just give me a second." I dodge into the bathroom, get dressed, and swish some Listerine in a feeble attempt to rinse the taste of last night out of my mouth. I run my fingers through my tangled hair, not even attempting to tame the curls I've been working so hard to straighten these past several months. My face is ghostly pale, freckles in stark contrast against my white skin. My eyes look more red than blue. Vivian was right. I'm a mess. I splash cold water on my face, pat it dry, then follow Vivian's perky blond ponytail as it bounces its way to the upper deck.

The sundeck is at the top and very back—I mean *aft*—of the

yacht, opposite the helipad and overlooking the infinity pool on the deck below. An eight-person hot tub sits in the center, surrounded by two built-in seating areas that run along the deck rails. A large bar outfitted with a flat-screen television, high-back stools, and the finest collection of top-shelf liquor money can buy rounds out the front. This place is bananas, really. Like something straight out of a movie.

It's midmorning, and the sun is a burst of gold in the clear blue sky. It would be lovely, really, if my pounding head and the endless rocking of this boat weren't making me want to curl into a ball and die right here on the deck floor.

Emi is sitting at the bar—the same bar where we all sat swigging Cristal last night. I can practically hear the popping corks, feel the foaming champagne as it spills over the rim of my glass and down my fingers. My stomach heaves a little.

Emi twists in her chair, swinging her long legs to the front and crossing them at the ankles. I'm taken aback, because Emiene looks like shit. Her hair is all messed up, and not in that good way she's perfected with tousled curls and a wispy fringe. More in a tossed-and-turned-all-night kind of way. She hasn't bothered with her usual black eyeliner, either, making the dark shadows beneath her eyes look more pronounced.

I glance past her, noticing the empty tray of snacks and small plates from last night are still sitting on the marble bar top. Weird. I can't believe the staff hasn't cleared that by now. There's usually at least one uniformed crew member—if not more—milling about silently like ghosts, polishing and shining the already gleaming surfaces.

Emi's eyes dart between me and Vivian. "Where's Giselle? She wasn't in Maggie's room?"

Vivian shakes her head. "You couldn't find her, either?"

"Nope," she says, eyebrows bunching with concern. "I've checked everywhere."

"Well, obviously not everywhere," Vivian answers, then launches into one of her good-old-days-before-Maggie-arrived stories. "It's like that time freshman year, remember? When she fell asleep in the laundry cart hiding from us and got rolled down to the laundry room and didn't wake up until the cleaning staff almost dumped her in the washing machine. Remember how freaked out everyone got? She thought it was hilarious."

I force a chuckle, even though I'm not part of their inside joke. I never am. I tamp down the sting of resentment and remind myself that next year it won't matter. If all goes as planned, I'll be at Pratt in Brooklyn, finally realizing my dream of studying architecture, and whatever a bunch of high school girls think of me will be irrelevant.

"Okay, so the last time anyone saw her was here," Emi says. "And the last person to see her was Maggie." She narrows her gaze at me. My hackles go straight up. It would be totally like Emi to blame me for not effectively babysitting Giselle in my drunken stupor.

As if any of us could tell Giselle what to do. I may have only known these girls for eight months, but it took me about eight seconds to figure that one out.

"So what happened after we left, Maggie?" Vivian says in her sweet, breezy way. "Did you guys stay here or go somewhere else?"

"W-W-W-Well," I stammer. I wish my headache would ease up. Every word is painful. I almost look forward to waking Giselle up, wherever she's passed out, so she can join me in the suffering. She kind of deserves it. The last thing I really remember is her dumping the last of the champagne into my glass, despite my objections, and practically forcing it down my throat.

"Well?" Emi says. "Spit it out already."

"After you left—" I do my best to draw each word out and pronounce it clearly like I've practiced over and over with my speech therapist. But I immediately trip up. Nothing like stress, lack of sleep, and a nasty hangover to trigger my stutter. I take a deep breath, annoyed with myself. I don't like to stutter in front of people like Emi. She's the sort who would try to finish my sentences for me. Or worse, think I'm stupid when I'm not.

I may be many things, but stupid is not one of them.

"After you left," I repeat, slowly, "we moved over here." I walk to the built-in loungers along the thick fiberglass railing, stopping short as a stab of pain shoots through my right foot. I stumble back onto the blue-cushioned seat, eyes welling with tears, and look down. The deck is covered with shards of glass, sparkling like spilled jewels.

I pull my leg across my knee, feeling light-headed as I extract a jagged piece from my foot. Blood trickles onto the deck, hitting the white surface in bright red splats. I breathe through my nose as a fresh wave of nausea rolls over me and the edges of my vision begin to blur. Pain I can handle. The sight of blood is a whole different story.

"Maggie!" Emi says sharply. "What's your problem?"

"Stepped in broken glass," I manage to say, my voice thick.

"Wow, what did you and Giselle get up to after we went to bed?" Vivian asks, tossing me a towel from the stack by the hot tub.

I press the towel to my foot, trying to keep myself from fainting. That's the last thing I need. "Nothing," I answer. "We hung out. And then I, uh . . . fell asleep, I guess. Woke up here. Alone. So I got up and went to bed."

"That's it?" Emi says. "You didn't see Giselle leave? Or which way she went?"

I shake my head.

"Some help you are," Emi says, and she and Vivian train their eyes on me. A familiar feeling inches its way up the back of my neck and down my arms like gooseflesh. It's a feeling I know all too well. I'm back at my old high school, reliving that moment in the locker room. That split second in time when I knew that I was on the outside, looking in. No longer part of the team. The circle had closed without me in it.

Bigger and better things, I tell myself again.

Bigger and better things.

For a moment, there's just the sound of the waves as *The Escape* slices through the water. Then Emi snaps her fingers.

"I know," she says. "We can check the video!"

"The what?" Vivian asks.

"Security footage," Emi says. "Giselle's dad installed security cameras a couple of years ago. Was supposed to stop her from swiping the liquor or something. But Giselle would delete the footage before he could check it, so whatever. Also, it's kind of disgusting. I mean, you don't want to see what some people get up to in the hot tub . . ." Emi groans. "Anyway, the computer is below deck in the equipment room. We can look and maybe it will give us a clue which way Giselle went. Worth a try, yeah?"

We follow Emi down four flights of narrow steps, her flip-flops smacking against her heels as she goes. I hobble along with the towel tied around my foot. We exit the stairs into a narrow corridor somewhere deep within the bowels of the ship, below the waterline.

It's darker down here and claustrophobic. No natural light. Rows of florescent tubes flicker and pop overhead, and a strip of emergency lighting snakes along the floor. The sound of the yacht's engine is louder, a persistent hum that vibrates underfoot and rattles the walls. The air is stale and smells like a pungent combination of fuel and window cleaner. This whole place feels off-limits.

"Should we even be down here?" I ask.

"It's Giselle's boat," Emi answers. "We can do what we want."

"Yeah, okay." I fold my arms across my chest, feeling trapped, suddenly imagining a rush of water coming down the hall. I want to get this over with quickly and get back upstairs, where I can see daylight.

As we walk, we pass several narrow doors, about half the size of the stateroom doors upstairs. I peek inside an open one. A bunk bed and dresser occupy most of the small room, and a porthole-shaped picture of the ocean hangs on the back wall where a window should be, like some sort of consolation prize. A pair of uniforms on a metal rack sway back and forth with the ship's motion. This must be the quarters for the dozen or so crew members who prepare our meals, clean the yacht, and keep it running.

A door behind me opens and quickly clicks shut.

I look over my shoulder and spot our deck steward, Christopher, rushing in the opposite direction toward the stairs we just came down. I should really give him the heads-up about the mess on the top deck so he can clean before Giselle sees it and gives him hell. I think it's safe to say he's endured enough of her wrath on this trip.

I dodge down the hall and tap his back. He turns, nearly jumping out of his skin. He looks exhausted, shadows beneath his hazel eyes, dark hair mussed and no longer slicked back with gel. Even his golden tan seems faded somehow against his crisp white uniform. I can't help but wonder if he still feels like this job was a great way to see the world between college and grad school, because he looks like he's aged twenty years in the last twelve hours alone. I think of Giselle, forcing him to work last night when he was supposed to be off duty, and I feel his pain.

"Sorry," I say. "Didn't mean to sneak up on you."

"It's okay," he says, pasting a smile on his face and wiping a bead of sweat from his forehead. His eyes dart toward his closed stateroom door, then back at me. "What can I do for you?"

"Just wanted to let you know there's a bunch of broken glass on the upper deck. Stepped in it a few minutes ago." I lift my towel-wrapped foot in demonstration, relieved the bleeding has stopped. "And there are dirty plates and stuff on the bar. Didn't want you to get in trouble over it. I, uh . . . well, I know Giselle can be kind of particular."

"Thanks." Christopher blows out a breath. "I'll get right on it. I'm really sorry about your foot."

"Don't worry, I'll survive."

He begins to turn away, but I stop him.

"Yes?"

"You haven't seen Giselle, have you?"

"Not since last night on the deck," he answers, rubbing the back of his neck, not really looking at me. "Why?"

"We're not sure where she went," I say. "Don't worry about it. I'm sure we'll track her down. We're going to check the video."

"Video?" Christopher swallows hard. His eyes rove past me, down the hallway, and his mouth presses into a thin line. I glance back to see the girls disappearing into the equipment room. Christopher's eyes meet mine, a flicker of something dark crossing them, and goose bumps prickle across my arms.

"Yeah," I say quickly. "So we can see where she went last night. That's all."

"Right. Of course," Christopher answers. "I'd better go and clean the deck. Thanks for letting me know."

He scurries up the stairs, and I head the other way, feeling strangely unsettled. The boat rocks. I stop and reach for the wall to steady myself, swallowing my nausea, and begin walking again. As I pass the laundry, I half expect Giselle to pop out of a basket with someone's dirty shorts on her head, laughing. Another one of her pranks. But the only noise is the rhythmic whir of the oversized washing machines, towels and linens spinning in the sudsy water.

Swish, thump, swish, thump.

I find the girls in the equipment room, standing shoulder to shoulder in front of a desktop computer monitor. I squeeze in next to Vivian as Emi logs in using Giselle's credentials and pulls up the video feed.

The screen fills with thumbnail video clips. Emi scrolls past the ones of the four of us in the hot tub, then at the bar, and then clicks on one with just me and Giselle sitting on the loungers, talking and drinking. But nothing is really happening. I'm barely lucid, head lolling back onto the chair and snapping forward again. God, how embarrassing. Why didn't I go to bed when I'd wanted to?

Right. Because Giselle told me not to.

And we all obey our queen.

Emi skips forward until the video shows me, alone, carefully swinging my feet to the side of my lounger and staggering away. She backs up a few videos, hand trembling slightly on the mouse, and clicks. This time, it's me and Giselle again, huddled closer together like a couple of old pals sharing secrets. I'm stretched out on the lounger with my bare feet crossed at the ankles, cover-up hood pulled tight over my ears.

Onscreen, Giselle inches closer, her fingers curled around the neck of a Cristal bottle. She dumps champagne into my glass until it spills, then pulls back slightly. Her head lingers next to mine, lips moving.

I feel the memory of her hot breath on my cheek, and all at once I hear her words as she whispers them into my ear.

Oh no. Oh no. Oh no.

I break into a cold sweat and my mouth goes dry. The room suddenly feels too hot, too small, too crowded. I really want to leave. Get far, far away.

I take a careful step back, toward the door. The hum of the engines grows louder. Or is that the rush of my own blood pulsing through my ears? I can't tell anymore. All I know is that this is bad. Really, really bad. My breath stutters. I need to get out of here.

Onscreen, I jolt quickly away. The glass in my hand tumbles to the deck and smashes. The clip ends.

The next clip starts and Giselle is standing on the lounger, camera zoomed in on her. I'm not in the frame anymore. She sways, swinging the champagne bottle back and forth.

Wait, I don't remember this. Do I?

Emi taps a key, turning the volume all the way up.

Giselle's laughter carries over the sound of wind and waves. She turns and puts one foot on the thick fiberglass railing. Then she hoists her other foot up and stands, swaying like a drunken ballerina, suspended in midair. A puppet held by invisible strings.

There's a collective gasp in the tiny room.

I wait to hear my voice, telling her to get down, stop being ridiculous. Because of course I did that, right? But there's nothing. Just the thrum of waves rising and falling. The wind whistling. Was I passed out already? Trying to speech-therapy my way into coherently shouting "Stop!"

Where am I?

Onscreen, Giselle spreads her arms to the sides and tilts her face skyward, auburn hair tumbling down her back in waves, the champagne bottle dangling from her hand. "Hey, Maggie!" she yells. "Look at me! I'm the queen of the world!"

Vivian lets out a nervous laugh. "She always did have a thing for young Leo in that old *Titanic* movie. Way less creepy than middle-aged Leo and his baby model girlfriends."

Suddenly I'm in the shot again—moving slowly toward Giselle, hand raised.

I'm going to pull her down, right? What else would I be doing?

I hold my breath.

Giselle looks over her shoulder and her eyes widen in horror.

30

Her arms spin in circles, off balance. The champagne bottle flies backward and crashes onto the deck.

"Maggie?" she says. "Maggie! NO!"

I reach toward her . . .

And push.

All the air feels like it's been sucked from the room as Giselle lurches forward over the edge into the dark.

"No!" Emi shouts, clasping her hand over her mouth.

"Oh my God," Vivian whimpers.

I forget how to breathe completely.

"It's n-n-n-not—I d-d-d-don't . . ." I say, trying to make sense of what I just saw.

I will my figure onscreen to do something. Run for help. Scream. *Anything.*

Instead, I watch—transfixed and horrified—as my dark outline leans over the railing, looks down, then straightens and slowly walks out of the frame, shoulders hunched and head bowed.

The pitch-black night and whistling wind are all that remain.

Dear Mom,

A new girl showed up at school today.

Her name is Maggie Mitchell.

She arrived this morning with a literal bang. As in, her rusty old pickup truck actually backfired when she sped into the student lot just a few minutes before the first bell. Everyone on the quad stopped and stared as she climbed out of the driver's seat, red hair springing in wild curls around her head, a pair of oversized black sunglasses covering half her face.

As soon as her beat-up Converse hit the pavement, she rolled up the too-short sleeves of her uniform blazer, slung an old messenger bag across one shoulder, and strode toward the admin building without a single glance in our direction.

I couldn't decide if she was actually an edgy Prepper or trying to be what she THOUGHT an edgy Prepper should be.

Dammmmmmmn, Emi said next to me. Who the hell is that?

Vivian craned her neck and squinted toward the truck. From our seats in the courtyard, we could just make out the Vermont tags and a half-peeled-away Bernie sticker on the bumper.

The bell rang.

We gathered up our stuff and headed to first-period literature. The new girl showed up a few minutes later, just after the second bell. She slipped into a seat in the back, pulled out a notebook, and buried her face in it.

I cast a glance over my shoulder.

The new girl was peeking over the top of her notebook.

Right at me.

I turned back to my desk. What was that about? I mean, I'm used to getting stared at all the time. But this felt different somehow. Color me intrigued.

Later at lunch, Emi, Viv, and I were sitting outside again at a picnic table by Haverford Hall, under a huge willow tree that swayed in the breeze. It was one of those perfect New England fall days, the kind you always loved so much. When the sun is bright and warm, but the air is still cool enough for a light sweater.

The new girl walked outside holding a lunch tray and looking around for somewhere to sit. As she paused on the brick steps, her eyes caught mine. So I waved her over.

A bunch of juniors at the next table swiveled their heads, curious to see who had scored an invite to my table.

What are you doing? Emi asked under her breath.

Being friendly, I said.

I gestured toward the empty seat next to Viv, and the new girl sat down, opposite me and Em. I could feel Emi squirm next to me. Heaven forbid I invite someone new into the fold, right?

I introduced myself and Viv and Em.

The new girl said her name was Maggie and gave us a shy smile, revealing front teeth that overlapped just slightly. She was pretty, in a fresh-scrubbed, small-town sort of way, with a smattering of freckles across her nose, fair skin, and blue eyes. Her fingernails were painted with chipping black polish and chewed to the quick. She noticed me looking and tucked her hands away.

I asked her where she'd transferred from. Maybe Choate

or Phillips Exeter? She looked kinda familiar in a way I couldn't place. I was sure I'd seen her somewhere.

Have we met before? I asked.

Maggie's cheeks flushed. Nah, I just have one of those faces, she said, speaking slowly and carefully pronouncing each word. I've been in Europe for the last year. My dad is posted overseas.

Really? Where? Viv asked. I spent my summer in France! Met this ah-mazing guy in Paris. Raphael. He was so hotttttt. Hold on, I have pictures . . .

She scrabbled around in the crocheted handbag she'd bought on Etsy (to feature in her grandma-chic aesthetic posts). Emi gave her the side-eye. At this point, we'd already been treated to about a hundred-too-many showings of Vivian's extensive Raphael photo collection. (And I still can't decide if he's a real person or a model Viv hired to pose shirtless with an armful of baguettes to up her follower count.)

I think you were asking Maggie a question, Viv? Emi said.

Oh yeah, right. Vivian dropped her bag. Where in Europe?

Maggie said she'd been at a small school in Switzerland. Mostly expats. Not very well known outside Europe.

What are you doing here, then? I asked.

Long story, Maggie answered.

Viv told her we had time.

Well, I agreed not to talk about it, Maggie said—if they agreed to let me leave without "incident." She made little air quotes with her fingers, picked up her sandwich, and took a bite. I mean, personally, I don't see a problem with standing up to the patriarchy.

But whatever, I got sent to live with my grandmother in Vermont, and here I am.

My face brightened. I told her all about our ski chalet near the resort in Westville and how much you loved it.

Cool, Maggie said, eyes darting quickly away. I've heard it's nice there. Never been, though. I don't ski. She looked back at me and shrugged.

So where is your dad posted? I asked.

I can't really say. It's kind of . . . classified, Maggie answered. Sorry.

You mean, like, he's a spy? Viv said, her eyes wide.

If I told you, I'd have to kill you, Maggie answered with an exaggerated wink, and we all cracked up. Well, all of us except Emi. She elbowed me.

Don't look now, she said with a tilt of her chin. Creeper alert at ten o'clock.

Oh no, Vivian said. Still?

Still what? Maggie asked. She turned and followed our line of sight across the green, to where Wyatt Garcia sat on a bench at the edge of the playing field, rolling a well-worn soccer ball beneath his foot and not-so-subtly watching our table. He reached up and ran his fingers through his thick, dark curls, and for a brief moment, I could imagine doing the same. My cheeks burned. What was the matter with me?

Wyatt caught Maggie's eye, and she gave him a small wave.

Wait, you know him? Vivian said, whipping her head around to face Maggie.

Yeah, Maggie answered. I mean, no, not really. He was in my art class this morning. Loaned me a charcoal pencil. He seemed okay. What's his deal?

He's nice enough, I guess, Vivian said. I've never really talked to him. His mom is our dorm housekeeper. Oh, and he's sort of got this . . . thing for Giselle.

A thing?? Emi said. More like he's OBSESSED. Spent most of junior year staring at her. I bet he has one of those stalker walls covered with Giselle's photos in his room, too.

C'mon, I said, looking down at the table and trying to swallow back the lump in my throat. It's not that bad . . .

Out of the corner of my eye, I saw Wyatt scoop up his ball and stand. I could have sworn he shook his head before walking away, but I refused to look.

Maggie dropped her half-eaten sandwich onto her tray and gathered her things. It's been cool meeting you guys, she said. I'm supposed to do a little more paperwork in the headmaster's office, so I'd better run. See you guys later?

She looked right at me when she said that, then walked away.

Emi watched her go. That was . . . interesting, she said.

Interesting? I asked. What do you mean?

I don't know, she said. Just seemed a little dodgy with all that stuff about getting kicked out of some unnamed boarding school and her dad's foreign posting she can't tell us about, don't you think?

He's totally a spy, Vivian said. That is sooooo cool. I've never met a spy. At least, I don't think I have. I guess I could have.

They don't really come right out and tell you, though, do they? You think she would actually kill me if I posted a picture of her on my Insta, ha ha . . . ?

Definitely, I said, laughing along. Probably has a poison-tipped umbrella in the back of her truck. Viv cracked up.

Or the more likely scenario is that she's full of shit, Emi said, scowling.

Omigod, Emi, I said. Just chill. Does it really matter? So what if she made up that story? Like you never lie? I kind of like her. She's funny. And we could use a little shaking-up around here. We've been going to school with, like, the same hundred people since freshman year. Gets a little dull.

Yeah, well, that's what you said about Beatrice sophomore year, and look how that turned out, Emi countered. Nearly got yourself expelled.

Oh c'mon, I said. Be real. Nobody's expelling me. I jutted my thumb over my shoulder at the cavernous student center behind us named in honor of Great-Great-Great-(something-) Grandfather Senator Robert Haverford the first (and his ten-million-dollar bequest).

Whatever, Emi said. There's still something off about her. If her parents have enough money to send her to boarding school in Switzerland, why don't they get her some braces and fix those crooked front teeth?

That was sort of an ironic statement coming from someone whose supermodel mother is famous for her tooth gap. Honestly, I was getting a little sick of Emi always trying to get between me and anyone who might be a new friend. Like remember back in preschool when she'd "accidentally" spill juice on anyone who tried to sit next to me?

Eh, as long as she doesn't really plan to kill us, I'm cool with her, Vivian said. She pulled out a huge SAT prep book and plunked it on the table.

What, a 1490 wasn't good enough for you? Emi teased as Viv flipped the book open.

Well, Dartmouth doesn't admit just anyone. Unless you're a Haverford, Vivian said. She laughed, but there was an edge to her voice that wasn't there a year ago.

Ha ha, I said, and laughed back, even though there was an edge to my voice now, too.

Viv kept her eyes cast down on her study guide, acting busy, and I was reminded, once again, that nothing was ever going to be the same between us. How could it?

Okay, I know what happened last year wasn't technically Vivian's fault. Even so, the whole chain of events started with her, didn't it?

And let's face it, when push came to shove, she chose her side.

And it wasn't mine.

Subject: VIVIAN PAGE (VP)
Interviewer: Detective Rebecca Bennett, RCIPS
Date: 4/16

RCIPS: Thank you for speaking with us. For the record, this is Detective Rebecca Bennett of the Royal Cayman Islands Police Service, speaking with Vivian Page, eighteen, of New York, New York. You understand this interview is voluntary, correct, Miss Page? And you are choosing of your own free will to answer our questions in an effort to determine what happened on *The Escape* the early morning of April 16 that led to Giselle Haverford being pushed overboard.

VP: Yes, ma'am. That's correct. [takes deep breath]

RCIPS: Thank you, Miss Page. Let's start at the beginning. How long have you known Giselle Haverford?

VP: Oh, wow. Since forever, it feels like?

We've been at Prep together almost four years. Andover Preparatory, I mean. It's a boarding school in New Hampshire. We've all been best friends since the very beginning.

RCIPS: So, by "all" of you, you mean you, Emiene Karousos, and Margot Mitchell?

VP: Margot? Oh, you mean Maggie, right? I didn't know that was her actual name. It's pretty. She should've used it. But yeah, we were all best friends since the beginning, except for Maggie. She was new this year. We haven't known her for long.

RCIPS: So how long have you known Miss Mitchell?

VP: Let me see, seven, eight months, I guess? And, uh— [stops abruptly]

RCIPS: Yes?

VP: No, it's nothing. Never mind.

RCIPS: It sounded like something. Why don't you continue?

VP: It's just . . . all things considered, I guess maybe we didn't really know Maggie at all, did we? Not in the way we believed. I mean, I didn't even know her real name! [exhales loudly]

RCIPS: Are you okay, Miss Page?

VP: Yeah, yeah. Sure. I'm okay. This whole thing feels unreal, you know? Like, this isn't how things were supposed to go. None of it. We were supposed to be having fun, celebrating the end of our senior year. We've all grown up together, me, Em, and Giselle, and this was going to be our last big thing before we go our separate ways to college and . . . [indistinguishable mumbling, sniffling]

RCIPS: Miss Page? Can we get you some coffee or tea? Water?

VP: No. I'm okay. It's just . . . is it hot in here? I'm really hot. Is there, like, a window we could open somewhere? I'm finding it kind of hard to breathe.

DAY 4
APRIL 15—NIGHT

Latitude, longitude: 24.246965, -83.238892

180 nautical miles off the coast of Grand Cayman

The Escape's engines grow louder as we pick up speed, pulling away from our last port stop in the colorful island city of Key West. We're sitting in the hot tub on the yacht's top deck, chin-deep in bubbles, champagne flutes in hand.

"To our last night!" Giselle exclaims, hoisting her glass high in the air.

Emi, Vivian, and I raise our glasses in return. *Clink.* I take a sip, cool bubbles sliding down my throat. My cheeks are tight and warm from a day of sun, sand, and a few too many frozen rum runners with dark rum sloshing on top.

"This can't be our last night!" Vivian says with a groan. "I'm not ready for this trip to end. School. Finals. Ugh. It's like saying goodbye to Raphael when I left Paris. He held me so tight, as though he could stop time with his strong arms."

"Oh, please." Emi rolls her eyes. "It's been, like, nine months since Paris. Enough about Raphael, already. I think you really spent the whole summer making out with that dorky junior with the big trust fund and even bigger nose—what's his name, Albert?—who's been following you around all year, lovestruck."

"Shut up," Vivian says. "I have a hundred Instagram pics that prove Raphael's existence, not that I need to prove anything to you. Albert, seriously. As if."

"Huh. That's funny," Giselle says. "Because I'm pretty sure I saw you smashing lips with Albert behind the field house after cheerleading practice. You aren't nearly as sneaky as you think." She grins and takes a swig of her champagne.

Vivian's face turns bright pink. "He's nice, okay?" she says. "And his nose isn't big. It's Romanesque."

"Don't worry," Giselle says with a sly grin. "You're hardly the only one around here who's into kissing people in secret."

I angle sideways, hoping nobody can see the heat rising in my own cheeks.

"You just don't know when to stop, do you?" Emi says, slamming her barely touched glass of champagne down on the edge of the hot tub. I flinch, surprised.

"You okay, Em?" Giselle asks, all wide-eyed innocence. "I didn't say something to upset you, did I?"

Emi ignores her and sinks into the water with a huff, tilting her head back and closing her eyes. I don't know what's going on between her and Giselle, but at least for once Emi's not paying attention to me. Most of the time she's like Giselle's own personal guard dog, and I've got the little nips around my ankles to prove it.

Rita, the chief steward, appears a few minutes later and sets a tray of snacks on the bar. She lingers, fussing over their placement. Giselle watches her every movement, lips pursed.

"Excuse me, Rita?" Giselle says as Rita adjusts the snack tray for the third time, even though I'm pretty sure they were perfect already.

"Yes, Miss Haverford?" Rita stands at attention, shoulders squared and hands behind her back. Rita is probably in her late twenties, with smooth black hair cut in a bob and a no-nonsense demeanor. I'm not a hundred percent sure what her duties are as chief steward, save lurking around constantly and making sure the other stewards are doing their jobs. Emphasis on the lurking.

Giselle gives her a pointed look. "Why are you working the deck tonight? I thought Christopher was on duty."

Rita clears her throat. "We have a lot to do early in the morning to prepare for our arrival in Grand Cayman. I gave him the evening off to rest."

"I don't recall you clearing that with me," Giselle says. "I'd like Christopher to tend to us for the remainder of the evening, not you."

"Of course, Miss Haverford," Rita says, flushing. "I will send him to check on you in a bit."

"Thank you," Giselle answers. "Have a good night."

Rita nods and scurries back down the stairs and out of sight.

"Good call," Vivian says, watching her go. "That woman creeps me out. You know the other day, I came out of my stateroom, and she was just standing in the hallway, staring at your door and messing with her phone? Was weird as hell."

"Huh," Giselle says. She grabs the champagne bottle and

refills our glasses with a breezy smile. But her hand shakes, just slightly, and her gaze drifts toward the stairs as though Rita might still be there. Watching. "Well, tomorrow we'll be in George Town, and she won't be our problem anymore. So there's that."

We drink and soak a while longer. Once we've gotten good and pruny, we dry off and move to the bar. Christopher silently appears to scoop up our pile of discarded wet towels, T-shirts, the random cover-up, and shorts from next to the hot tub. Tomorrow morning, everything will be clean and neatly folded and returned to our staterooms like magic.

"May I do anything else for you this evening, Miss Haverford?" Christopher asks, making sure not to look at her directly. He keeps his voice professional. But I can hear the exhaustion beneath his words. And irritation. Maybe even hate. Though, who can blame him?

"I think we're all set," Giselle says with a dismissive little wave, and I can't help myself, for a brief but intense moment, I hate her, too. As much as I've tried to see the good in her, there's this little nagging voice that won't stop whispering in my ear: *It isn't fair.* Does she really think owning a yacht makes her superior to everyone else? Drill down beneath the surface, and I'd say we have a lot more in common than she would probably care to acknowledge.

"Okay, then. Have a good night, Miss Haverford," Christopher says, and heads back toward the stairs. Vivian's eyes trail after him, no doubt admiring the view. But she doesn't try to get him to stay this time. Girls like Vivian don't do sloppy seconds.

I pop a tiny pastry into my mouth from the tray on the bar. A mini key lime pie with a dollop of fresh whipped cream on top melts on my tongue. I do have to appreciate the attention to detail around here, right down to the delectable treats that match the theme of our latest stop. I squint back toward the port.

We've made it far enough away now that the Florida Keys are little more than a tiny collection of twinkling lights on the horizon. The dark expanse of open ocean stretches ahead, nudging against infinity. The star-covered sky seems endless. This yacht, which felt so huge the day I stepped on board, suddenly feels small. A miniature dot being swallowed by the darkness.

Emi clunks the remaining bottles of the Cristal she bought last night in Nassau onto the bar top.

"Okay, bitches. We need to finish this before we hit Grand Cayman and Giselle's dad gets on board," she says. "So let's drink up and destroy the evidence!"

A cork pops. And another. Champagne fizzes, sticky on my fingers as it spills over the top of my glass. My head floats like it's bobbing in the water below. I'm not used to drinking like this, but I'm trying to keep up. Running as fast as I can for that homestretch. Still, I'm two paces behind. Always two paces behind. The story of my life.

But dammit, I've made it this far and I'm going to cross that finish line, whatever it takes.

Giselle has abandoned the entire concept of a glass and is swigging straight from a bottle, champagne dribbling from her lips and down her chin. She sways to the beat of the music coming from a tiny speaker above the bar, eyes closed. Vivian and Emi are huddled together, each with their own bottles of Cristal.

"Oh! I was so excited for this trip, I totally forgot to tell you who I bumped into before we left school for break!" Vivian says.

"Who?" Emi asks.

"Wyatt Garcia," Vivian says, voice low.

Giselle's eyes snap open. I tense.

"He's still around?" Emi says. "Thought he'd be in juvie by now or something."

"Yep. Saw him in town at the CVS," Vivian says. "Awkward."

"Did you talk to him?" Emi asks.

"Nah," Vivian says. "I just picked up my stuff and left. But I could feel him watching me the entire time, like he wanted to say something. It was the worst. I mean, it's not like I had anything to do with what happened, but still."

I grab another pastry and nibble the edge, the flaky crust suddenly dry and flavorless. I set it down and pick invisible crumbs off my fingers, doing my best to ignore this entire conversation. I don't want to open my mouth and say something I'll regret.

"Honestly," Giselle says, and I feel the burn of her stare. "Who cares anymore? That's old news. Right, Maggie?"

I nod slightly, careful to avoid making eye contact.

"Good!" Giselle says. "Let's talk about something else, then. Like . . . how about the merits of a good film school?"

Emi shakes her champagne bottle and sets it on the bar, glaring at Giselle for a brief moment. So brief, I think I'm the only one who saw it. "You know," she says. "I think I've had enough. I don't want to be hungover tomorrow. See you bitches later. I'm going to bed."

"Oh! I have some special green tea on my dresser," Vivian says. "Prevents hangovers. Help yourself. You'll thank me in the morning, I promise."

"Don't do it," Giselle says. "You'll be pooping for the next three hours. That's all Vivian's special teas make you do."

"Ha ha." Vivian rolls her eyes. "Don't listen to her. Cleansing the toxins from your system is great for your health and your complexion, too. When was the last time you saw me with a pimple?"

"When your tretinoin prescription ran out?" Giselle says.

"Oh stop, you know I don't believe in using anything nonorganic," Vivian says. At that, I have to do a double take, because I saw what she had in her makeup bag our first night on board. Vivian ignores me and keeps talking. "Grab the tea, Em. And don't forget to post and tag me about it tomorrow when we dock!"

"Yeah, sure," Emi says. "Good night." She disappears down the stairs. Vivian yawns.

"You know, you should probably go with her, Viv," Giselle says as Emi's footsteps fade away. She smiles sweetly, but there's a trace of something else in her voice. Threatening almost. Vivian's mouth opens and closes, clearly unsure what to make of being tossed out. Everybody loves Vivian. At least that's the role she's carefully tried to carve out for herself. The nice one. Well, until you see her in a CVS and she pretends you don't exist.

Vivian blinks. "But—"

"Get some *sleep*, m'kay?" Giselle says, cutting her off. "I need you fresh for sunrise yoga. Feeling a little bloated." She pats her stomach. "I can't believe I ate a whole plate of conch fritters in one sitting. If I'm not careful, I'll turn into junior-year Giselle 2.0."

"Right, yeah," Vivian says. "Those things looked pretty greasy. Delicious, but greasy! Glad I don't eat anything with a face. I am a little tired anyway. See you in the morning." She takes a gulp of champagne and sets her glass on the bar, hand trembling slightly, and follows the path Emi just took. She casts one last concerned look back at us over her shoulder before she goes downstairs and out of sight.

Now it's just me. And Giselle.

Finally.

I've got nearly a full glass left, but I can barely keep myself upright. I force the rest down my throat, eyes watering, and try to work up my courage. I've got to do this before it's too late.

"More?" Giselle says, holding up a champagne bottle.

I shake my head.

"What, don't quit now!" Giselle says. "We've still got a full bottle left. We owe it to Emi to finish. She blew, like, two grand on this crap, remember?"

Of course I remember. How could I forget? Emi practically shoved the receipt into my face.

"Maybe we should dump it overboard instead," I quip.

"Ooh, now, that's a side of Maggie I don't see often," Giselle says. "I appreciate a little snark."

"Yeah, I . . ." I try to stand, and my head spins. Not my best plan. I grip the edge of the bar to steady myself.

"Easy there," Giselle says, grabbing my hand. "Why don't we get comfy?" She pulls me toward the big, cushy built-in loungers by the railing and shoves me onto one. I sink into the thick cushions. "Better, right?" She flops onto the lounger next to mine. "Now, give me that glass."

"Um-hmm," I say, handing her the empty flute. There's really no point in arguing with Giselle. Her boat. Her friends. Her rules.

She overfills my glass with champagne and hands it back to me, then sinks into the lounger and extends her tanned legs. I've spent most of my life wishing for a bronzed glow like hers, instead of my pale, freckled skin that burns at the mere suggestion of sunshine. There's a streak of red right down the middle of my shin where I missed with the sunscreen earlier today. I cross my other leg on top of it. At least it's better than that time I rubbed sunscreen on my own back a couple of summers ago and wound up with one sunburn-free spot on my shoulder blade in the shape of a hand.

I take a small sip of champagne. My stomach rolls along with the ship. My vision begins to blur. I want to get up, but I'm not even sure I can anymore.

"I've always loved the open sea," Giselle says dreamily. "The horizon. The endless sky. I'm really going to miss this boat."

"What's that?" I ask, wondering if I zoned out and missed some key part of this conversation.

"Dad's selling her," Giselle says.

"Who?"

"*The Escape*," Giselle explains. "The step-monster gets seasick. More like she hates this boat because Mom designed the interior. Whatever. This is our final voyage. We're delivering her to the new owner in Grand Cayman. Once we reach George Town, she'll officially be the property of some billionaire investor."

"Oh, I'm sorry," I say, even though I'm not sure selling a yacht—probably to buy another house or plane or some other fancy toy—ranks all that high on the problem-meter. I should know.

"Yeah, it sucks." Giselle sighs. "I haven't told the other girls yet, so you won't say anything, will you?"

"Of course not." I may not be any good at keeping friends, but I sure as hell can keep a secret.

"At least I convinced Dad to let me bring you guys along," Giselle says. "I'm glad you could come, even though it was last minute. You're having fun?"

"Yeah, of course. This has been . . ." I search for the right word. "Incredible." I smile.

"Good. I'm glad to hear that." Giselle tilts her head to the side and inspects me with a quizzical look as she twirls her necklace around her finger. The shiny gold heart dangling from the end flips, over and over, like she's trying to hypnotize me with it.

"Okaaaay?" What does she want?

"Sorry, I don't mean to sound weird," she says, leaning forward and letting go of the necklace. "I've just had the feeling you had something on your mind. If there's anything you need to get off your chest, you can tell me, you know."

I suck in a deep breath. Here's my chance. I should do it. But something about Giselle's smile makes the skin prickle on the back of my neck. This isn't the Giselle I remember from the chalet. Or school. The one I thought I knew. My stomach clenches. Why can't I open my mouth and spit it out?

The truth will set you free, right?

Damned if I know.

Maybe the truth is more like a match. Light it and wait to see what burns. Hope you don't torch yourself in the process. I chicken out completely.

"Nothing I can think of," I say. But the words twist at me, slowly, like a knife in the gut.

I take another gulp of champagne. A strange sensation washes over me, like I'm sinking and floating at the same time. I shiver.

"Cold?" Giselle asks.

"A little. And more than a little wasted. Too much champagne.

I should go back to my room. It's late."

"Don't be silly! There's no such thing as late when you're on vacation. Or too much champagne."

She raises her Cristal and flashes her dazzling smile. The smile that mesmerized me the first time I saw her. The smile that made me believe if you had enough—boats, cars, designer clothes—it was possible to blunt life's sharp edges, file them down into a pill, easy to swallow.

But I'm beginning to wonder if those edges just keep getting sharper. Until you're the point of a knife. Stabbing at the world around you.

I sip my drink. Time begins to take on a strange shape, like an accordion compressing and expanding, breathing the night in and out. I don't know how many minutes have passed or how many times Giselle has refilled my glass or if I've been awake the whole time. The boat sways gently. I open my eyes to discover Giselle pushed up next to me, grinning. How long has she been here? How long have *I* been here? I shiver again and pull the cover-up hood over my ears, wishing I could disappear into it completely.

There's a thudding noise from somewhere behind us, almost like footsteps. Followed by the howl of the wind. And a door slamming?

"What was that?" I say, looking back with a shudder. "Did you hear something?"

Giselle shrugs. "Probably just the boat, creaking. Or Emi sleepwalking again, ha ha. Don't worry about it."

She waves the Cristal bottle back and forth in front of my face. I'm dizzy watching it. All I want to do is sink back into the cushions and sleep. Why can't Giselle just leave me alone? "Time for a refill!" She tilts the bottle toward me.

"I don't think I can," I slur, trying without much success to focus. One Giselle, two Giselles, three Giselles, four. No matter how hard I squint, I can't stitch all the Giselles blurring in front of me back into a single person.

"Sure you can." She dumps the rest of the champagne into my glass. "You want to be one of us, right? Isn't that why you're here?" The weirdly menacing tone has returned. I slowly lift the glass to my lips, unable to taste the bubbly liquid as it slides down my throat, my stomach in knots. My tongue feels too big for my mouth, my fingers too thick and clumsy around my glass. I just want to sleep.

Giselle leans closer, breath hot on my cheek.

"You never will be, though," she whispers. "One of us."

"Excuse me?"

"It's too bad. For a while there, I actually thought you were different. Not like the rest of them. I thought you were my friend."

My back stiffens. "I am. Your friend, I mean."

"Don't," Giselle says bluntly. "Don't lie to me. I've had enough of your lies."

I swallow hard. Try to sort out what Giselle is getting at. She can't know. Can she?

Giselle grins wickedly.

"The name Allison Couture mean anything to you?"

What? My mouth opens and snaps shut. How does Giselle know about freaking Allison?

"Yeah, I thought so," she says, low and threatening. "You really thought you could fool me?"

"Listen," I say, trying to keep the tremble from my voice. "Whatever it is, it's not what you think. I can explain."

"Just stop," she says. "I know the truth. I know what you did, and tomorrow everyone else will, too. You can kiss your free ride goodbye, fraud."

The glass slips from my hand, shattering on the deck below. Giselle pulls away, eyes like daggers. I'm acutely aware of my heartbeat thrumming in my ears, the blood coursing through my veins. Something simmers deep in my gut, long pushed down—a mix of fear, anger, anguish, desperation—and threatens to erupt, burst to the surface. I can't let it. I can't. I can't. I can't. I have to hold on. I can't let go. Not now. Not when I have nothing else left.

"I . . . I . . . I . . ."

The world turns upside down, and I'm drifting above myself, untethered, watching Giselle as she stands on the lounger, swaying and laughing, swinging the empty bottle of Cristal. Her words ricochet around my brain.

I know the truth . . . I know what you did.

I know the truth . . . I know what you did.

I know the truth . . . I know what you did.

I know the truth . . .

Everything goes fuzzy and fades to black, like that day I've tried so hard to forget. *Escape.* Time disappears, the night sky folds on top of me. The next thing I know, my eyes blink open and I'm curled on my side, an eerie blanket of silence draped across my shivering body, shattered glass at my feet. The deck is empty.

Giselle is gone.

Subject: EMIENE KAROUSOS (EK)
Interviewer: Detective Rebecca Bennett, RCIPS
Date: 4/16

RCIPS: Beginning recording. This is Detective Rebecca Bennett of the Royal Cayman Islands Police Service. Can you state your name, age, and residence for the record, please?

EK: Emiene Karousos, eighteen, of New York, New York.

RCIPS: Thank you, Miss Karousos. And you are participating in this interview voluntarily, correct? [pause] I know this is difficult, but if you could please answer verbally.

EK: Yes, I am.

RCIPS: Thank you. You were a passenger on *The Escape* as it traveled from New York to George Town, with stops in the Bahamas and Key West, Florida?

EK: Yes, I was a passenger. Um, should I be speaking to you without my parents? Or a lawyer?

RCIPS: You are eighteen, no? Your parents do not have to be present. Our discussion here is purely informational to help us establish a timeline of the events on board. I have already spoken with your friend Miss Vivian Page. But if you feel you need a lawyer . . .

EK: No, no, it's okay. I don't need a lawyer. [exhales loudly]

RCIPS: Let's continue, then. Was this your first trip on *The Escape*?

EK: No. I've been on Giselle's yacht before.

RCIPS: Once or twice?

EK: More than that. A lot. Giselle and I have been friends forever. Best friends.

RCIPS: Okay, so let's talk about your most recent trip. The yacht's log indicates you departed Key West, Florida, shortly after nine p.m., correct?

EK: If you say so. I wasn't checking the time. Is this really important?

RCIPS: We are simply looking to establish a timeline of events, as I've explained.

EK: Okay.

RCIPS: So, let me see. As I understand,

after the yacht departed, you and the other passengers were together on the top deck continuing to cele-brate.

EK: That's correct.

RCIPS: I also understand that you were the first to go to bed. What time was that?

EK: What time? I don't know exactly. Like I told you, I wasn't watching the time. We were on vacation. Maybe one a.m.?

RCIPS: And that was the last time you saw Miss Haverford?

EK: [clears throat] Yes, it was.

RCIPS: And Miss Page and Miss Mitchell were still with her?

EK: I've already explained this, and I don't see why it matters. We all saw what happened. Why aren't you focused on Maggie right now?

RCIPS: Okay, let's talk about Miss Mitchell a bit, then. What can you tell me about her?

EK: [incoherent mumbling]

RCIPS: I could not hear your answer. Can you please speak up and speak clearly?

EK: Where should I even start? She's a

liar, for one. I'm pretty sure nothing she ever told us was true.

RCIPS: Meaning?

EK: Meaning she just sorta appeared out
of nowhere on the first day of school.
I tried to find her online, but there
was nothing. No Insta. No Snapchat.
No TikTok. She was like a ghost.

RCIPS: This bothered you?

EK: Yes, it bothered me! Giselle is—well,
she is who she is, and she always
attracts these clingers who just
want to be around her. She never
does anything about it, though. In
fact, she seems to kind of encourage
it sometimes.

RCIPS: So none of what you're saying bothered Miss Haverford?

EK: No. She didn't seem to care at all
until—

RCIPS: Until?

EK: Well, until the last few months. She
and Maggie didn't seem to be that
close anymore. Not like they had been
when school started. I assume something happened. It was weird when I
found out Maggie was coming with us

for spring break. I didn't expect
that.

RCIPS: Interesting. Were they getting along
on this trip?

EK: I guess.

RCIPS: Did you ever see them arguing?

EK: No, I don't think so.

RCIPS: How about you and Miss Haverford?

EK: What do you mean?

RCIPS: Did the two of you ever fight?

EK: Wait, what? Why are you asking ME
that? I loved—I mean I love—Giselle.
I would do anything for her. She's my
best friend, and you've got to find
her, please. [begins to sob]

Dear Mom,

I've been hanging out with Maggie a bunch these days. Out on the quad between classes, in the library, during lunch. She's a lot of fun. She's kind and pretty chill and super funny. Like yesterday, she pretended to sneeze every time our lit teacher said the word "perseverance" while talking about The Old Man and the Sea. I don't know how she kept a straight face. I sure couldn't. By the time Miss Lively had to stop class and offer Maggie a box of tissues (twenty-something sneezes in), I was shaking so hard from trying to hold back my laughter, I'd nearly vibrated out of my chair.

Maggie doesn't spend a lot of time talking about herself nonstop, either, which is sort of . . . refreshing? And she seems genuinely interested in me and not all the famous people I know. She even told me I reminded her of her roommate at her old school back in Switzerland, who'd been her best friend. When I asked more about her, Maggie's face kind of fell. She said they'd lost touch after she left. I could tell it made her sad, so I didn't push for details.

It's been cool having Maggie around, especially since, get this—Emi has a boyfriend now. His name is Zane, and I know I should be happy for her since she's been crushing on him since freshman year. But I hardly see Emi anymore. Which is annoying, right? I never expected Emi to be one of those people who ditches her friends because she's got a hot date. I miss our late-night chats, when we used to whisper for hours after lights-out, sharing our secrets and dreams. Now I could probably explode right in front of her and she wouldn't even notice.

You know what's ironic, though? Emi has the nerve to get all jealous of the time I've been spending with Maggie! She likes to say she's just "looking out for me," but I call BS on that.

Like last night, Zane was away on some football team thing, so Emi came to my room after dinner to study with me and Viv. Well, Viv was the only one studying. Em still managed to text Zane the whole time. As for me, I was totally procrastinating my essay on the alternate ending to Great Expectations for AP Lit (wouldn't that be nice, to rewrite your own ending?) and trying to think up a good senior prank for homecoming.

(You know how I love a good prank. Like remember that April Fools' Day when I covered our toilet seats with cling wrap—hilarious!—okay, maybe Dad didn't think so when he peed down his leg before a big campaign meeting, ha ha. Or that time I programmed your phone so that whenever you typed my name it switched it to "OH GLORIOUS PERFECT DAUGHTER." You never did switch that back, though . . .)

Anyway, that's when I came up with an AWESOME prank idea: instead of sneaking into Chester and decorating the pissing-boy statue the night before the homecoming game (like we do every year), we'd swipe the whole thing! Then we'd hide it in the stands, all dressed in Prep gear and unveil it when the teams marched onto the field. Can you imagine the Chester team's faces when they spotted it? It would be EPIC!!! Right???

I slapped my book shut and told Em and Viv what I was thinking.

I dunno, was Emi's unenthusiastic response. *We should probably stick with tradition.*

Then she went right back to texting Zane.

Yeah, it's a cool idea, Viv said. *But how do we get it back here?
It'll never fit in your car.*

We could ask Maggie! I said, thinking out loud. *She has a truck!*

Well, that was enough to get Emi to put down her phone. Just
like that, she launched into this whole big thing about how we still
don't really know anything about Maggie, except her story about
getting kicked out of some probably made-up boarding school in
Europe.

Who says she's making it up? I countered. *You have some sort
of proof?*

C'mon, Emi said. *It's so clearly bogus! I've searched everywhere for her and nothing! It's like she's a completely made-up
person.*

Em, I said. *She already told us she's not allowed to use social
media. Besides, do you actually think Prep admits made-up people?*

Spy, Vivian said, glancing up from her calc book with a smirk.
One hundred percent, her dad's a spy. Maybe she's one, too!

No, she's CREEPY, Emi said. *Haven't you noticed how she's
always watching Giselle? And lately it's almost like she's . . .
imitating her. The new blowout, the Docs that look like Giselle's—*

Or, I cut Emi off. *She only wants to fit in.*

Whatever. I thought one stalker would be enough for you, Emi
answered. *But maybe you just like the attention.*

I felt my cheeks burning.

Maybe I do, I said, giving Emi a pointed look. (Not like I'd been getting much from her, right?)

She rolled her eyes at me and went back to texting Zane.

So I texted Maggie.

She was all in, of course. Just like I knew she would be.

We have a truck! I told Em and Viv with a huge smile on my face.

Emi shook her head and gathered her things.

Yeah, okay, she said as she walked out the door to meet Zane's bus. Have it your way. But when this all blows up in your face, don't say I didn't warn you.

DAY 4

APRIL 15—EVENING

Mallory Square
Key West, Florida

As we walk down Duval Street toward the sunset celebration on Mallory Square, my calves are still twitching from crouching on the toilet seat back in Sloppy Joe's. I can't shake the image of Giselle's eyes locked briefly on something behind her in the mirror.

Me?

I play the scene like a video in my head, over and over. Rewind. Repeat. Rewind. Repeat.

Did she see me? I can't be sure.

If she did, she's doing a pretty good job of hiding it. But then, you'd never know anything was bothering Giselle at all. She's flouncing through the crowd, half walking, half dance-shimmying with her suntanned arms above her head. It's hard to keep up with her as she weaves through the sweaty bodies pushing their way toward the end of the street. I wish I had that ability to completely shove what's bothering me out of my head. With Giselle, it's like some sort of superpower.

Emi's hanging back, a few paces away from Giselle. The air still feels charged between them.

We reach Mallory Square, a brick-laid pier overlooking the turquoise waters of the Gulf of Mexico. The square is jam-packed with artisans and performers. Vivian watches, mouth agape, as a bulky-armed man with a long, scraggly beard juggles bowling balls.

"That's got to be terrible for your core," she whispers under her breath.

A slender woman next to him swallows fiery swords, which I imagine is even worse for your digestive tract. Farther down, trained cats jump through hoops and walk tightropes while the crowd cheers and hoots.

Vivian spots a vendor braiding hair with colorful beads. "Ooh!" she says. "I'm going to get some to match my nails!" She disappears into the crowd.

"I feel like dancing!" Giselle says. "Who's with me? Em?" She doesn't ask me. It's like I'm suddenly invisible.

Instead of answering, Emi pulls out her phone and taps it. Two seconds later her boyfriend, Zane's, face fills the screen, all golden curls and toothy smile.

"Hey, babe!" he says.

Giselle rolls her eyes and dances over to a group of guys wearing Virginia Tech sweatshirts. She grabs a tall guy with floppy blond hair by the hand and grooves with him to the beat of a nearby steel drum band playing "Cheeseburger in Paradise." From the smitten look on his face, I'd say he considers himself the cheeseburger right about now.

I wander over to a small makeshift booth covered with

trinkets and knickknacks. I pick up a piece of driftwood painted with an island street scene, a rooster strutting down the center of a narrow road lined with colorful cottages and palm trees.

"That's Bahama Village," the girl manning the stand says. She's about my age and wears a simple white T-shirt streaked with paint, cutoff jean shorts, and flip-flops. Her hair is braided into tightly beaded corn rows. "The real part. Not the touristy one."

"It's really pretty," I say. "Did you paint it?"

"Thank you," she says. "Yes, I did. I made everything here. It's all stuff I've found on the beach or that people throw away. I clean it up and make it beautiful." She runs a hand, fingernails splattered with paint, over the collection of random items on the table—seashells, ceramic tiles, jewelry. I like that idea. Making treasure out of trash. If only I could do the same.

I set down the driftwood and pick up a piece of brilliant blue-green sea glass that has been artfully wrapped in metal wire and hung as a pendant from a black leather cord. It matches Allison's eyes perfectly. I frown, my chest tight.

"You don't like it?" the girl says. "I have others."

"No," I say, snapping out of my funk. "This is beautiful. Perfect. I'll take it. How much?"

She says ten dollars. I hand her a twenty and tell her to keep the change. I slip the pendant over my head and look for the girls. The crowd has grown, and I've briefly lost sight of them among the revelers.

Finally, I spot them near an ice cream stand. They're clustered together, admiring the single beaded braid in Vivian's hair. For a fleeting moment, it feels like we're back at school in the courtyard. Fussing over Giselle's new earrings or watching one of Emi's videos through the tiny screen on her camera.

It feels so very normal.

Deceptively so.

Because nothing about this trip has been normal.

Goose bumps prick my skin, and I rub them away, shivering.

Suddenly, the steel-drum music twangs to a stop, and the crowd stills and quiets. Giselle stands on her tiptoes and waves me over, then ushers us wordlessly through the throng of people to the water's edge. Before I can ask what's happening, Giselle puts her finger to her lips, mouths *Shhhhh*, and says quietly, "Wait for it . . ."

Emi points her camera at the horizon and hits record.

The sun is now a golden coin, sinking slowly into the water. As the last bit of orange disappears and streaks of red and purple shoot across the sky, the crowd erupts into a boisterous cheer. Giselle throws her arms into the air and whoops. I join in the applause, swept up in the moment, as though enough cheering might coax the sun right back out of the ocean to perform an encore.

"This is amazing!" I say to no one in particular.

"Yeah, my favorite part," Giselle says. "'Do not go gentle into that good night . . . Rage, rage against the dying of the light.'"

"Dylan Thomas, right?" I say.

A small, sad smile crosses her face as her hand reaches up to touch the gold heart dangling from her necklace. "I read that at my mom's funeral," she says. "Doesn't matter how hard you rage, though, does it? The sun still sets. Day still turns to night. Might as well clap and cheer. Go out with a *bang*."

I'm trying to formulate something to say in response, my thoughts automatically dragged to Dad. Not everybody goes out with a bang. Some slowly disappear, like a fire burning out. But before I can speak, Giselle has turned and begun to shimmy her way through the crowd. The rest of us follow in line like a bunch of baby ducklings back to the limo that waits on Duval Street to return us to the yacht.

We reach the marina, twilight yielding to inky black sky. *The Escape* looms at the end of the long pier, bobbing gently in the water. Waiting to swallow us up like a monster. So different from the day we boarded in New York, full of hope and promise. I can't shake the feeling of dread inching down my spine as we traverse the dock, wood planks groaning beneath our feet with every step. I want to turn around. Disappear back into the crowd and catch a flight home. Or just stay forever in this tiny island town where nobody cares who you are or where you've come from.

Or why.

I hang back as the girls cross the gangplank onto the yacht. Giselle casts a look over her shoulder. "You coming, Mags?"

"Yeah." I nod. "I think I dropped my necklace in the limo. I'll be right there."

"Okay, but hurry!"

70

"I will."

The girls disappear inside.

I make a show of walking back toward the limo, even though the necklace is still tucked safely beneath my shirt. I just need a minute here in the parking lot, away from the girls, to collect myself. It's our last night, and I can feel the time slipping away. *Ticktock. Ticktock.*

I watch as a white-feathered egret lands near a tangled patch of mangroves along the shore, pecking its yellow beak between the gnarled branches in search of dinner. Somewhere else, there's a splash. A fish jumping maybe.

And then a woman's voice coming toward me.

"I think she's getting suspicious," the voice says in hushed tones.

Quickly, I step out of sight behind a large palm tree.

A shadowy figure crosses the lot, head bowed and phone clutched to her ear.

"Yeah, well, I'm the one taking all the risks," the voice continues, then pauses. "So I'll be the one to call the shots, got it?"

The woman crosses onto the dock toward *The Escape*, the tall lights illuminating her dark hair, crisp white uniform, and navy Top-Siders. I catch my breath.

Rita.

She jams her phone in her pocket and boards, muttering to herself.

What was that about?

Do I even want to know?

Not really, I decide. I have enough problems of my own.

I stand there a moment longer, thinking. It would be so easy to turn around. Walk away from this whole thing. I have enough money now to buy a ticket and fly home. All I need to do is keep my head down, finish my senior year, and leave for college. Forget all this.

But then I picture Sophie—small arms wrapped around Nana's legs, big blue eyes watching me as I pulled away from the house four days ago. I picture Mom, lines of worry etched deep into her face. And Dad. The shadow in the room that grows longer and darker with every passing minute.

I can't turn back.

I need to finish what I've started.

See this thing through to the bitter end.

Even if it kills me.

Dear Mom,

I called Dad tonight right before lights-out. I guess I was feeling sort of lonely. Em was busy (again) with Zane. Viv has kinda been avoiding me whenever Emi isn't around, saying she has to study and work on her college essays. The dorm was quiet, just random voices and footsteps in the hallway as people got ready for bed. Suddenly, I didn't want to be here anymore. I wanted to be home. With you. And since I couldn't be, I called Dad. It took like five rings before he even answered.

Giselle, he said. This is a surprise. How are you?

Fine, I answered. Just wanted to say hi.

Well, hi to you, too, he said. But he sounded distracted. I could hear a keyboard clicking, like he was on his computer at the same time. I felt myself tensing. Typical Dad. Multitasking is what he'd call it. More like, always focusing on something more interesting than your own kid.

So yeah, I said. I'm excited about homecoming this weekend! When are you getting here? I can't wait to see you.

There was silence on the other end. Even the clicking stopped. Dad cleared his throat.

About that, he said. I don't think I'm going to be able to make it. My advisers need me in DC. You understand, don't you?

I mumbled something as he kept talking, making excuses. The truth is, I'd tuned him out. You and Dad always came to homecoming, no matter what. But maybe he only bothered because of YOU, not me. I know I've been a huge disappointment to Dad this

73

last year—my grades, image, everything.

The thing is, I'm starting to think I've ALWAYS been a disappointment to Dad. Remember when I was little, back when you and Dad still seemed happy together, and I found the two of you giggling over breakfast one morning? When I asked what was so funny, you flushed, and said with a grin that it might be a good time for a baby brother (or sister). Brother, Dad said. Someone to carry on the Haverford name!

I thought it would be fun to be a big sister!

So I waited. And waited. And waited some more. No brother (or sister) ever came.

After that, something changed in Dad. I'm sure you must have seen it, too. The way he looked at me. The way he acted when we were together. Stiff. Formal. And I think I knew in my gut, even then, that no matter how hard I worked and how perfect I became, I'd never be the son he really wanted.

And now? Well, he has that son he always wanted, doesn't he? His little heir to the throne.

What does he need me for?

Before I hung up with Dad, I asked how Knox was doing. I purposely didn't ask about Britney, but he told me anyway. All about her new yoga class and daily meditations, and I mean, c'mon, I can't even deal anymore with her (and Viv, too) and all their lifestyle guru crap. Like a kale smoothie can fix anything. Ha, right.

I ended the call, feeling even worse than I had before.

But then my screen lit up.

A text. From Maggie.

It was a goofy .5 selfie of her face, forehead huge and distorted, eyes wide like an alien. No message, just the silly picture.

I laughed and took an even sillier one of myself and sent it back.

That started a volley of progressively ridiculous selfies, and then I was laughing so hard I actually forgot all about the phone call with Dad. I didn't even care if an image of me with a pencil stuck in my nose turned up on TMZ.com and embarrassed Dad.

In fact, there was a not-so-little part of me that hoped it would.

DAY 4

APRIL 15—MORNING

Mile Marker 0
Key West, Florida

I have never been so happy to have both feet planted on solid ground.

The Escape slid into port this morning in the Florida Keys, a chain of islands that dangle from the tip of southern Florida like a strand of broken pearls. After a breakfast of granola and fruit and mimosas (made with Cristal, of course), we hopped in a limo to Key West.

Now we're standing in front of the Southernmost Point monument, which is not really much of a monument at all but a giant concrete buoy painted black, red, and yellow. My legs sway beneath me, still trying to compensate for the rough seas they're no longer struggling against. I'd mentally prepared myself for a lot of things before this trip. Somehow the endless motion of the boat was not one of them.

Giselle pops her iPhone on the end of a selfie stick and stretches her arm as she, Vivian, Emi, and I smoosh our heads together beneath a painting of a conch shell.

"Say 'rum runner'!" Giselle shouts.

"Rum runner!" we sing in unison. Vivian throws a peace

sign. I smile. *Click.* We make goofy faces, tongues jutting out, and Giselle snaps another picture. We erupt into giggles and head back toward the waiting limo, passing a huddle of sunburned tourists in Bermuda shorts and knee-high socks commiserating in German. For a moment, that exhilaration I'd felt when we started this voyage a few days ago returns in a rush, and I forget everything else.

Almost.

One of the tourists loudly says, "Haverford?"

Giselle stiffens next to me. I look back over my shoulder to see a middle-aged woman holding her phone out, taking a photo. Or video. The breezy smile has fallen completely from Giselle's face. She scowls as we settle into the limo's smooth leather seats.

"I can't believe it," she says. "We haven't even been here for five minutes!"

She stares out the window, frowning. I sneak a glance at my phone, that single SeaChat message from YouCantRun still hanging in the air above my head like a guillotine ready to drop. I can't decide what's worse: that one of them sent the message in the first place, or the twenty-four painfully long hours of dead silence since then. All I can do now is try to shove the whole thing out of my mind and worry about it later.

I turn off airplane mode and my phone immediately buzzes with a new message notification, this time from Striker29.

My stomach churns. I don't have time for this.

I quickly angle my phone away, feeling Giselle's eyes on me. "Everything okay?" she says sweetly. But something about the way her lips curve into a tight smile, like they're stretched over a set of fangs, makes me shudder.

"Yeah, just got a message from my mom. My little sister finally learned how to tie her shoes," I say, even though I taught Soph to tie her shoes last year. "A little sad I missed it. I'm kind of like her second mom. You know how it is."

"Mmmm, I hear you. Those bonus babies have a way of worming their way into your heart, don't they?" Her face goes soft for a moment, and my heart aches for her a little. I've seen firsthand how much Giselle adores her baby half brother, Knox. She's like a different person around him. Sweet and genuine, without this need to always be . . . perfect, like school Giselle. School Giselle would just as soon die than get a blob of mashed banana in her hair.

"Tell Sophie she's awesome," she says.

"Will do." I type out a quick message to my mom letting her know I'm in Florida and doing fine. I leave the other message unread. I don't want to know what it says. Not right now. It can wait until tomorrow when this is all over and done. I power down my phone and shove it into my pocket, neck sweating.

I glance at the other girls to see if they've been watching. But Emi is busy pointing her camera out the window at the passing scenery—palm trees and colorful scooters and people riding beach cruisers with wicker baskets on the handlebars. Vivian is pursing her lips and taking selfies from every angle possible. *#LimoLife #DreamVacation #LookAtMe!!!*

We take a sharp right turn, and the limo pulls into the

palm-tree-lined drive of a grand hotel built from white stucco and red tile roofing that seems to stretch on forever. I crane my neck and stare out the window in awe, admiring the Spanish architecture.

They don't build 'em like this anymore is what Dad would say. What he always said when we'd go for walks and admire the woodwork of some grand old Victorian. Or in his workshop when he'd let me help guide the saw along the grain of the wood, teasing out the object hidden inside.

Well, maybe I'll design something like this, Dad. Someday. I'll make you proud. I'll help you get better.

We roll to a stop under a portico. A white-gloved valet opens the back door and extends his hand.

"Welcome to the Casa Marina," he says with a Spanish accent and an elegant bow. "Checking in?"

"Si, nos estamos registrando," Giselle answers, taking his hand and swinging her sandaled feet out of the car onto the pavement. She stands. Everything about her glistens in the midday sun, like a sparkling jewel spilled from a velvet bag.

The girls and I climb out behind her as the valet loads our day bags onto a gold luggage cart. His name tag reads: *Ivan, Cuba.*

Giselle tilts her head. "De dónde es usted en Cuba?"

"Baracoa," Ivan answers.

"Ah! Mi abuelo era de San Luis. My grandfather was from Cuba," she says over her shoulder.

"No kidding? That's cool," I say. Even though I knew that

already. I've done my homework. I know all about Giselle's maternal grandfather, Osvaldo Fleitas Hernández, the legendary businessman who came to the United States on a raft from Cuba as a young man with just the clothes on his back. In less than ten years, he'd turned a small corner market in Miami into the country's most successful Hispanic specialty food chain. He died one of the richest men in America, leaving a fortune to his only living child—Giselle's mother.

"Muy bien. Tierra hermosa," Ivan says. He smiles. "Let me show you to your room."

We follow Ivan into the high-ceilinged lobby. It's all dark mahogany and white-cushioned furniture and rows of tall arched windows, with a registration desk at the back and a concierge station off to the side. I could spend a whole day in here with my sketch pad just studying the intricate details of the dark wood beams that cross the ceiling.

"This is so awesome," Vivian says, snapping pictures with her phone as we walk across the polished wood floors. "I can't believe you got us a room here for the day!"

"Yeah, well, the public beach is full of sand fleas. And they definitely don't offer oceanside massages or cabana service," Giselle says.

"Yeah, and hopefully the staff here keeps the paparazzi at bay," Emi adds.

"Truth," Giselle answers.

Ivan shares key facts about the resort as we walk.

"Henry Flagler." He points at a portrait of a stern-looking

white-haired man hanging by the front desk. "Flagler was the oil magnate who brought the railroad—and tourism—to Key West. This hotel was part of his vision. Though he didn't live to see it built, when the Casa Marina opened in 1920, it quickly became *the* place to visit, attracting presidents and celebrities and titans of industry."

I can totally picture it—men in top hats and glamorous women in long dresses gliding through this very lobby, where a whiff of old money still mingles with the scent of cocoa butter, sunscreen, and warm, salty air. We exit through the back doors and cross the manicured grounds, dotted with palm trees and bright flowers.

Our room, as it turns out, isn't really a room at all. Instead, it's an open-air suite facing the ocean with tile floors and a private beachfront lanai. It's breathtaking. Ivan unloads our bags in the spacious living area. Giselle shoves a wad of cash into his palm, says "Gracias," and takes off through the back door. I stand there a minute, stunned at just how easily Giselle tosses money around. Envy, the sharp-fanged monster that perpetually lives on my shoulder, takes another little bite of my soul.

"C'mon, Emi!" Giselle shouts over her shoulder as she peels away her sundress to reveal the pink bikini beneath. She runs across the beach toward the ocean, sand flying around her feet. "Last one in is a rotten egg!"

Emi strips down to her bathing suit and runs after her, grabbing a float along the way. She paddles out to Giselle. While they bob in the water, Vivian stretches out on a lounger in the sun and angles herself for more prime photo ops.

I find a secluded spot farther down the beach and stretch out on a towel beneath a deep blue umbrella. I pull out my sketchbook and begin to outline the stuccoed architecture of the grand hotel behind me. But my eyelids grow heavy. I set my pencil down and lean back. The heat radiating from the sand and the soft tropical breeze quickly lull me to sleep, and soon I'm drifting gently across the waves in my dreams.

Suddenly, the water turns rough. I'm thrashing, going under. Hands grab my ankles, pulling me into the darkness. Now I'm on the track, waiting for the race to start. But I'm alone and it's pitch-black night. The stands are filled with dark figures. All I can see are hollow eyes. Voices chant all around me.

Liar.

Traitor.

Thief.

Watch your back . . .

Watch your back . . .

Watch your back . . . !

The starting pistol fires. *Bang!* But I'm stuck on the block, legs frozen. I can't run.

I bolt straight up, heart pounding, disoriented and gulping for air.

It was just a dream. Just a dream.

I blow out a ragged breath, trying to calm my thrumming heart. I'm fine. I'm back in the real world, sun reflecting off the hot sand, glittering turquoise water stretched to the horizon, seagulls squawking. This is paradise. I've left hell behind.

Or have I?

Emi is coming up the beach, arms wrapped tightly around herself, eyes rough and red. She casts a quick glance in my direction, then hurries toward the suite. Giselle jogs up after her, shaking the water from her hair.

"Em!" she shouts. "Wait up!" For once, she doesn't seem to notice me sitting there.

Emi keeps going, ignoring her.

"Emi!"

I watch as Emi goes inside, quickly sliding the door shut behind her. Giselle walks onto the lanai and shrugs on the dress she'd left on the ground. There's a silver-domed tray on the table that must have arrived while I was sleeping.

"Viv, Maggie!" Giselle shouts, lifting the tray cover. "C'mere. Chocolate-covered strawberries and pineapple!"

Vivian and I join her at the patio table. Emi is nowhere to be seen. Vivian nibbles on a plain strawberry and tilts her head toward the suite. "What's up with Em?"

Giselle shrugs. "Oh, I wanted to go parasailing together. Emi said no, she wanted to chill."

"Meaning call Zane while we have a signal," Vivian says as she pops another strawberry in her mouth. "Mmmmm, these are sooooo delicious. They're organic, right?"

Giselle frowns, gazing past us to the beach. A couple is strolling along the water, holding hands, bronzed skin shimmering in the sunshine. Newlyweds, maybe. They have that look. Like two people who have yet to discover each other's flaws. The toilet seats left up. The milk cartons put back in the refrigerator empty. Two people who still have secrets.

Who haven't turned into a married couple like my parents; the only thing holding them together a sense of obligation.

And me and Soph.

The door slides open behind us, and Emi walks out. She's wearing a yellow sundress and fiddling with the lens cap on her Lumix. The dress's cotton skirt rustles in the breeze, and I'm reminded of Nana's sheets clothes-pinned to the line. The smell of Vermont summer and fabric softener and fresh-cut grass, and suddenly the coconut scent of Vivian's suntan oil seems cloying and overpowering.

"Hey, Em?" Giselle says. "Wanna look for shells? Like when we were little?"

"No thanks," Emi answers. "I'm all changed. Don't want to get sand in my shoes."

"Yeah, right. You and those shoes," Giselle says, voice cracking a bit. "I'm gonna change out of my suit, then, too."

She goes inside. Emi lifts the camera in front of her face and slowly moves it across the shoreline and tilts it skyward, trapping paradise in the viewfinder.

We spend the rest of our afternoon in a haze of fruit and cheese trays, flavored Sanpellegrinos, and beachside massages. As the sun begins to dip lower in the sky, Giselle unfolds the itinerary from her purse, declares it's time to go, and disappears into the bedroom.

When she emerges ten minutes later, her long, auburn waves have been replaced by a sleek shoulder-length black wig.

"Whoa," Vivian says. "Where'd you get that thing?"

"Sent Ivan into town," Giselle says with a grin. "I'd like to enjoy a night out with my besties without some rando trying to take my picture. What do you think?" She slips on a pair of oversized black sunglasses that practically swallow her entire face.

"I think you look just like your mom," Emi says softly.

"Thank you." Giselle's voice catches in her throat. She reaches a hand beneath her sunglasses and swipes at her eyes, then gives her head a little shake. "Okay! It really is five o'clock now. Let's get this party started!"

We pile back into the limo and travel a few short blocks to Duval Street, Key West's main drag.

Where the Casa was elegant and subdued, this part of town is vibrant and colorful—music pulsing from the open bar fronts, T-shirts with tacky slogans ("That's not a bald spot, it's a solar panel for a sex machine!") hanging in store windows, spicy jerk chicken scenting the air. We pass a bearded guy dressed as Hemingway offering himself up for selfies. Vivian presses five bucks into his hand and poses, immediately uploading the picture to her Instagram.

"Hashtag sexist dead writers!" she says.

She avoids a photo with the woman with a huge yellow snake coiled around her neck. Vivian does not condone animal exploitation. Plus, yellow sort of washes her out.

We make our way farther down the street. Men in studded leather stroll past, holding hands. A pregnant woman painted orange like a pumpkin and wearing a tiny green bikini—at least, I think it's a bikini, not more paint, but it's hard to tell—dances on a nearby lawn. Random cats dart down alleyways and tourists stumble along the sidewalks, drinks spilling from the tops of their tall hurricane glasses. It's anything goes, and nobody cares. The polar opposite of the manicured grounds and buttoned-up blazers of Prep. The inverse of home with its pickup trucks and gun racks and eternally gray skies. I think I could stay here forever.

"This way, mates!" Giselle says in a singsong voice like the queen of England as we weave through the crowd. On the limo ride over, she'd given us each British passports to use as our fake IDs for the evening. I'd flipped mine open and my skin prickled as I read the name—Beatrice Dickerson.

I can't stop thinking about Emi's words last night, the casino, wondering if this passport—this name—is Giselle's sly little way of telling me that she knows why I'm here.

And then, yesterday's message.

Watch your back . . .

What if this whole plan is about to go sideways?

Maybe it already has.

My eyes dart nervously across the other girls' smiling faces. I plaster a fake smile on my own as we tumble into a large, open-air bar called Sloppy Joe's. Dozens of colorful international flags hang from the ceiling, stripes and stars and country crests swaying in the breeze, and photos of Ernest Hemingway line the walls. It smells like musty wood, sweat, and rum.

"This isn't where Hemingway actually drank." Giselle offhandedly waves toward a black-and-white photo of the mustachioed author standing on a boat and hoisting a huge fish in the air. "The original Sloppy Joe's is a little hole-in-the-wall around the corner. This one is all for the tourists. A big show. Like most things, right, Maggie? All about the appearances. Like Hemingway and all that macho-man crap. Ha ha."

I don't have time to answer before Queen Giselle has bellied up to the bar, waving a slender hand for attention. The gold ring coiled around her thumb catches the light and shimmers like a snake in the sun.

"Cheerio!" she says brightly in an over-the-top British accent as a bartender in a white muscle shirt with Hemingway's head plastered on the front saunters over. I wonder how Hemingway, the macho man, would feel about his face covering the hairless chest of a guy with a man bun, ear gauges, and a rainbow triangle tattoo on his neck. On the other hand, perhaps that's what he liked about it here. I've read his description of F. Scott Fitzgerald's mouth, after all.

"We'll take four rum runners," Giselle says, scanning the menu board.

The bartender leans forward, elbows on the scuffed wood of the old bar. Or maybe it's just distressed to look old. Appearances, right?

"IDs, please," he says. It occurs to me that probably half his customers this time of year are underage spring breakers trying to score a drink.

I try to keep my cool as we slide our fake passports across the bar, even though the temperature in here seems to have shot up twenty degrees from hot and humid to hot and hellish. The bartender flips through the passports, staring at the pages for what feels like way too long. I begin to sweat. All I need is to get busted for something so stupid with graduation—freedom—right around the corner. Would that be a suspendible offense? My brain freezes. What is my full name again? *Beatrice Dickerson.* Born June—shit, I can't remember the date.

"Is something wrong, Bea?" Giselle says in her fake high-pitched voice. "You look a tad pale?"

I shake my head, eyes flicking back toward the bartender.

He grins.

"You're from Rye, then?" he says. "How 'bout that. Vacationed there back in college. Cool place. They still got that pub with the keg taps to flush the toilets, what was it called . . . ?" He snaps his fingers.

There's a moment of uncomfortable silence, and I'm pretty sure we're about to get busted over some far-off pub with wonky bathrooms.

The corners of Giselle's mouth quirk up. "Aye, the Waterworks, you mean," she says, still carrying on with her exaggerated accent. "Great spot, except for all the bloody tourists, am I right?" She laughs.

"Ha, I hear you," the bartender says with a wink. "This round is on me."

I blow out a loud breath as he leaves. Giselle—sorry, *Felicity*—spins to face me.

"Relax, Beatrice. Try not to be wound so tight. We're on vacation!"

Easy for her to say. The more I've gotten to know Giselle, the more I've come to understand that the rules are different for people like her. Money might not buy happiness, love, or even complete freedom. But it sure as hell can buy freedom from consequences. And some very real-looking fake IDs for you and your friends, I might add.

The bartender returns a few minutes later with four hopelessly tall hurricane glasses filled with sloshy frozen concoctions, red like blood. He pushes the huge drinks across the bar. Giselle tips him lavishly, ensuring we won't be paying for another drink again.

The rum runners are unnaturally sweet and go down surprisingly well. As does the round that follows. And the round after that. Even with the plates of conch fritters and coconut shrimp to soak up the alcohol, I begin to feel that giddy lighter-than-air drunk sensation—just on the verge of sloppy falling-down-sick drunk—and know I should stop. But it's like a valve has opened in my throat, and it's so easy to pour another drink down. Even though, of all people, I should know better. But I'm all warm and happy, and everyone here is so amazing, and, hold on, I really have to pee.

The bar is wall-to-wall people now, and I've kind of lost track of time. Vivian is chatting up some dude at the bar who's at least twice our age with a weathered, tan face and scraggly mustache. I have no clue what that's all about. Must have a Platinum Amex tucked away in his cutoffs. Her gaze drifts briefly across the room toward Giselle, who is dancing with Emi to a twangy song about being knee-deep in the water somewhere with not a worry in the world except the tide that's gonna hit their chair. Well, Giselle is dancing. Emi is sort of swaying from side to side, distracted and checking her phone, while Giselle grinds up against her with a devilish smirk. Giselle catches Vivian's eye, and a dark look crosses Vivian's face, until her attention is pulled back to the man next to her.

I get up and push my way between the sweaty bodies swarming around me, a singular focus on the restroom sign perched above an old wooden door. I stumble inside and into a stall, then close the door, latching it shut. The floor is sticky with spilled drinks and I don't really want to know what else. It smells like a disgusting combination of spoiled fruit, pee, and disinfectant.

A moment later, the bathroom door swings open. The sound of music billows in. Voices. And the door closes, muffling the noisy bar again.

"I told you before, I'm out, okay?" I recognize the voice. Emi. Something about her tone makes me feel like this is a conversation I shouldn't be hearing. Instinctively I sink back, tuck my feet onto the toilet seat, and crouch, holding very still.

"C'mon." It's Giselle answering. "You promised!"

"Yeah, well, I changed my mind."

"Right. You've been doing a lot of that these days, haven't you?"

"Omigod," Emi says. "Will you just drop it already!"

They move so now I can see them both through the gap in the stall door. I begin to regret tucking my feet. What if they spot me in here sneaking around behind their backs? Again. *Fool me once, shame on you. Fool me twice* . . . Well, I know how the saying goes. And all I know is Giselle is not one to play the fool.

"C'mon, Em," Giselle continues, her tone softening. She reaches out, gently gripping Emi's arm. "We used to be so close. I miss you." There's a fragility in Giselle's voice that I haven't heard since that day at the chalet. My heart clenches in my chest.

Giselle and Emi stay frozen for a beat, and it's all I can do not to take a noisy breath. The smell in here is suffocating enough already. And I still haven't peed. My thigh muscles burn.

Suddenly, Emi pulls her arm away and takes a step back. "Do you really miss me, though? Because it seems to me you were the one who shut me out first."

"What is that supposed to mean?"

"You're the one who took off all summer without a word, like you'd forgotten I even existed. Ignored all my texts. Didn't even answer that time I called. And then, whammo, you're back and expecting me to act like nothing's different."

The room goes silent.

"Right. That," Giselle says, her voice cold. "You know I didn't have a choice."

"Since when do you not have a choice?" Emi says. "That doesn't sound like the Giselle I know. The Giselle I know has always gotten her way."

"Well, then, why stop now, huh?" Giselle pulls out her phone and makes a big show of tapping the screen, then angles it in Emi's direction.

Emi audibly gasps.

"What the hell?" she says. "You told me you deleted that!"

"Guess I lied," Giselle says with a shrug.

"Oh. My. God. I can't even with you anymore!" Emi lifts her hand and swats at the phone. Giselle yelps as it falls and hits the floor with a cracking sound, then skitters to a stop just below my stall door. I stare at the edge of the pink case a mere foot away and wonder if I can flush myself down the toilet. My entire body vibrates. I've never seen Emi and Giselle fight like this before.

"Seriously, Em?" Giselle hisses. "What's the matter with you?"

She clomps across the bathroom and grabs the phone without looking in my direction.

I exhale silently.

"What's the matter with ME?" Emi says. "I'm done. I've got to go. I promised Zane I'd FaceTime before we left."

"Right. Of course you did," Giselle says.

Emi hurries out, fuming.

Giselle stays behind, back to me. She grips the sink and takes a deep breath. Then her shoulders begin to shake. She doesn't make a sound, but I can tell she's crying. For a brief moment, I wonder if I should go out and comfort her. Take her hand. But I can't without admitting that I've been hiding in here the whole time, listening. And maybe she doesn't want my comfort to begin with. Whatever bond I'd thought we shared feels fleeting and long gone, like maybe it was all just a figment of my imagination. Wishful thinking. A connection I'd dreamed up because I wanted it to be true, like so many things.

My foot slips, and the toilet seat creaks beneath me.

Giselle stands up straight, her red-rimmed eyes locking on the mirror and focusing on the stall doors reflected in it. My breath catches in my throat. I swear she's looking right at me. I can't let her find me here. I freeze, the seconds ticking past loudly in my ears as I count my heartbeats.

One, two, three, four . . .

Tha-thump, tha-thump, tha-thump . . .

Giselle sighs and grabs a paper towel. She wipes her face, crumples the towel into the trash, and walks out the door without looking back.

I exhale, trembling from head to toe. But I don't move for what feels like an eternity until I can be sure that this time, she's not coming back.

Dear Mom,

Ugh, I hate it when Emi's right.

I don't know what to think anymore. Or who to trust. I kind of feel like I'm losing my mind. Everything is falling apart around me, and I don't know how to stop it.

Homecoming weekend started out great. After the pep rally Friday night, we sent a bunch of juniors to drive around Chester as decoys in their sleek, unmistakably Prep, Audis and BMWs. While they were busy throwing the local sheriff's department off our trail, Maggie, Emi, and I piled into the front of Maggie's (very NON-Prep-like) truck. Zane (because of course we had to bring him *eye roll*) and his best friend, Max, hid in the flatbed with a screwdriver and large canvas bag. (Viv was back at school, covering just in case anyone came looking for us. She's perfect for the job—EVERYONE trusts Vivian. She could look you straight in the eye and swear the earth was flat. And you'd BELIEVE her. What a joke.)

It was dark, the roads were empty, and the moon was perfectly obscured by clouds as we drove the twisty road to downtown Chester. I was in the middle of the truck's bench seat, with Emi to my right, and Maggie driving. As I fiddled with the radio, searching for something to listen to, I noticed Maggie had an ACTUAL CD PLAYER.

Oh my God! I said. I didn't know they still put these things in cars!!

Yeah, I don't think they do, Maggie answered. This thing was my grandpa's. He loved to tinker with old cars and stuff. I think this one is like a thousand years old . . .

In response, the truck's engine groaned as we rounded a bend. I laughed. You have any CDs in here? I asked, reaching for the glove compartment. As soon as I touched the latch, Maggie's arm shot out and she leaned over and slammed it shut.

I jolted back, shocked.

Sorry! Maggie said, flushing. That thing is broken, and it'll come unhitched if you open it all the way. CDs are down there.

She pointed at an old canvas CD case on the passenger-side floor under Emi's feet. I grabbed the case, unzipped the side, and flipped it open. Emi peered at the selection, nose scrunched.

Country music big in Switzerland these days? she said, barely concealing her sneer. Or are these your grandpa's, too?

Uh . . . Maggie started.

No way! I said, interrupting and pulling out a shiny silver CD. I LOVE the Pistol Annies!

You do? Maggie said.

You DO?! Emi said. Since when? I didn't know that.

Maybe you don't know everything about me, I said, popping the CD into the player. Emi scowled and folded her arms across her chest, slouching in her seat.

I ignored her, pressed play, and cranked the volume.

By the time Maggie and I had finished shout-singing the lyrics to Hell on Heels and Bad Example (somebody had to set one, ha ha ha!), we had arrived at the Chester town square, voices raw, and doubled over with laughter. It took a minute to catch my breath.

And when I did, I felt something I'd hardly felt in months—a certain lightness, as though the heaviness of everything that had happened over the last year had been lifted. The way Viv betrayed me when I was at my lowest. Emi ditching me for Zane. Dad and his brand-new family. All of it just faded away in that instant.

I smiled at Maggie. A real, genuine smile. She smiled back. And for a brief, flickering moment, I felt a connection. Something I couldn't explain.

Something that was interrupted by the sound of Emi clearing her throat.

Helloooo, she said. Now that the concert is done, can we hurry up and get this over with?

I banged on the window dividing the cab from the bed, signaling Zane and Max. They sprang into action, faces smudged black to match their black hats and clothes, and ran into the square.

We watched as their dark outlines climbed into the fountain and started working the screws that held the statue down. Every second felt like an hour. The minutes ticked past. Emi pulled out her phone and sent a message. I watched the rectangular glow of Zane's phone as he answered. Emi looked up, frowning.

One of the bolts is rusted in place, she said. It won't come loose. We should just forget it and get out of here. We're going to get caught . . . (You know Emi, always throwing a wet blanket on EVERYTHING!)

We're not going to get caught, I said. Just tell your boyfriend to hurry up! He doesn't spend three hours a day in the gym for nothing, does he?

This is your worst plan ever, Emi muttered, typing a new message. *I don't know how I let you talk me into these things.*

It's FINE! I said.

Just then, headlights panned across the park. Emi squeaked. Zane and Max ducked down into the fountain, disappearing from sight. Maggie, Emi, and I slid down in our seats.

A long moment of silence passed.

Do you think they're gone? Maggie whispered.

Blue lights flashed across the truck's ceiling in response.

Emi started to squirm.

Stay down, I said, trying to keep calm. *They're probably doing a drive-by . . .*

A car door slammed. Another moment passed. Then knuckles rapped loudly on the driver's-side window.

Maggie, Emi, and I slowly sat up. My heart raced as Maggie lowered the window. A mustachioed deputy in a blue uniform stood on the other side, arms folded across his barrel chest. He was such a stereotypical small-town cop, with his hat perched high atop his head (and, I swear, doughnut crumbs in his mustache), that in any other circumstance I would have burst out laughing.

Evening, ladies, the deputy said. *Any particular reason you're hiding out here in this truck?*

We shook our heads.

Hmm, the deputy said. *Don't suppose it has anything to do with that fountain across the street, now, does it . . . ?*

I kept my eyes straight ahead and tried to become invisible. I did not need to be identified. Dad would KILL me if I got caught doing something stupid. Again. Though I set the bar so high on colossal mistakes last time, maybe he'd laugh this one off. Or not. A juvenile arrest record would not bode well for Dad's political career. Can you even imagine how much fun the gossip sites would have with my mugshot??

Before I could come up with an excuse (We were waiting for someone? Got lost and checking our GPS?)—Maggie sucked in a breath and put her hands in the air.

Busted, she said sheepishly.

Emi grabbed my hand in a viselike grip. I could feel her glaring at the side of my head, but I refused to make eye contact.

I tried to keep my breathing steady as Maggie kept talking. What was she doing?

I'm spending the weekend in town with my cousin—Maggie pointed at me—she goes to Chester High. We decided to watch and see if any of those Prep assholes showed up to mess with the statue.

Is that so? the deputy said.

Maggie nodded. Yeah, we saw one of their Beemers drive by a little while ago. But we flashed our headlights at them and they drove away.

I see. So you three cop wannabes thought you'd pull a little stakeout, huh? the deputy asked, smirking a little.

Guilty, Maggie said, a flush creeping across her cheeks.

And tell me, the deputy said, what was your plan if they didn't drive away when you flashed your lights?

Uh, call you? Maggie said with a shrug. *I'm sorry, sir. We didn't really have a plan. We're just tired of them getting away with stuff all the time. Entitled jerks. It's like they never have to answer for anything. It's irritating as hell, you know what I mean?* Maggie's voice took on a distinctly sharp tone as she said this, almost like she really believed what she was saying.

The deputy blew out a loud breath. I held mine.

Right, he said. *Took me three hours to scrub the paint off after last year's so-called prank. Tried to bill the school, but you know the old line about how they help the town with their tax dollars and all that.*

Maggie nodded sympathetically.

But listen, the deputy said. *I don't need a bunch of vigilantes roaming around here trying to exact their own brand of justice. Especially not you three girls. You leave the patrolling to the big boys, okay?*

I seethed a bit inside. Didn't he know that girls could be just as dangerous—maybe even more so—than a bunch of boys trying to deface a statue?

The deputy leaned down, elbow propped on the edge of the window, and inspected our faces.

Hey, he said. *Don't I know you?*

I froze and glanced ever so slightly in his direction, stomach churning. Just when I thought we'd gotten away with it. That I was Maggie's cousin from Chester. But to my surprise, he wasn't looking at me. His focus was directed at Emi on my other side.

Yeah, you're Maya, Tucker's little sister, aren't ya? he said. Almost didn't recognize ya!

Emi didn't answer.

I nudged her with my knee. Uh, right. She nodded. Tucker's sister, Maya. That's me!

Wow. Aren't you all grown up, then? the deputy said. Haven't seen you since Tuck and I played ball together, back before he took off for Texas. Man, what was the name of that ratty doll you used to drag around everywhere . . . ?

Emi tightened her grip on my hand, fingernails digging into my skin.

Just then, Maggie craned her neck and looked past the deputy. Oh no! she said, pointing.

What is it? the deputy said, and spun around.

I just saw a couple of guys, all dressed in black, Maggie said. Running away! They had a duffel bag or something. They came from behind the fountain!

You see which way they went? the deputy asked in a rush, facing us again and gripping the holster around his waist.

Down that alley. Over there. Maggie pointed across the street to a darkened area between a closed coffee shop and the CVS. They were running, fast!

The deputy nodded at us and tapped the truck's hood. You ladies get on home. And tell Tuck I said hey!

With that, he took off across the street and disappeared into the alley. Maggie twisted the key in the truck's ignition. It rumbled to a start. She backed carefully out of the parking space.

What is your problem? Emi burst out. Did you just send him after Zane and Max? You trying to get them arrested? Or shot?!

Nooooo, Maggie said, drawing out her words. I sent him AWAY from Zane and Max. So maybe text your boyfriend and tell him to hurry up because we're coming by to get him.

I had to stifle a laugh.

Maggie pulled onto the road and made a slow loop around the fountain, where she rolled to a stop.

Zane and Max jumped in the flatbed—with the pissing-boy statue stuffed inside their duffel bag.

The next day, the statue made its grand appearance in the bleachers, wearing a Prep uniform, and we were the heroes of homecoming. It was awesome. As I stood at the top of the pyramid during the halftime show, I felt INVINCIBLE! That's my favorite part of the routine. The moment when I'm poised to leap, suspended midair on the verge of falling, watching the eager eyes watch ME from the stands. Because I know they're hoping—just a little—that maybe I'll fall. Land hard. Twist my perfect ankle. Smash my perfect face. Shatter like a porcelain doll.

But I never do.

I land on my feet.

Every.

Single.

Time.

After the game, Emi, Viv, Maggie, and I hung out in my room. When it was time to get ready for the dance, Vivian headed to her room, and Maggie went to take a shower.

Emi just sat there on my beanbag chair, not saying much.

Are you okay? I asked.

Emi didn't answer, but her gaze drifted to Maggie's bag, slumped next to my desk.

What? I said. Seriously—Maggie? Don't tell me you STILL have a problem with her. She's cool. I mean, last night was epic! You have to give her props for getting us out of that jam.

I guess. Emi shrugged.

You GUESS? Would you rather be in jail?

No. Emi sighed. Of course not. But . . . doesn't it ever bother you?

Doesn't WHAT bother me? I asked.

How easily she lies? Emi's eyes held mine. She just made up that story last night, right on the spot, without even thinking about it. What else is she lying about? Nothing about her makes sense. She's even starting to look like you. It's weird. It's like . . . It's like she wants to BE you.

Oh, c'mon, Emi, I said. Half this school is trying to imitate me. Why do you care, anyway? Don't you need to get changed or text Zane something?

Emi glared at me.

Just then, Maggie returned from the shower, steamed pink and wrapped in a towel.

Emi pushed past her and left, slamming the door behind her.

What's up with her? Maggie asked, eyebrows furrowed with concern.

Nothing, I said. I'm gonna take a shower now, too. The dress is over there for you.

You sure you don't mind if I borrow it? Maggie asked.

I told her it was no big deal. She'd explained a few days ago that her formal dresses had been held up in transit from Switzerland, so I'd offered to lend her one of mine from last year. It was too big for me now anyway. She could have it, for all I cared.

I left the room to shower while Maggie got dressed.

When I returned, Maggie was sitting at my desk, all hunched over with her backpack by her feet. The minute she heard me come in, she slammed a drawer shut and sat up straight.

Are you looking for something? I asked.

Oh, she answered, turning sideways. *I wanted to see if you had some eyeliner I could borrow. I hope that's okay.*

Right, I said. *That's no problem.*

But Emi's words echoed in my mind: *Doesn't it bother you how easily she lies?* Because my eyeliner was right where I always kept it—in the makeup bag on my dresser. And Maggie knew it. I pointed it out.

Oh yeah, I forgot, Maggie answered. *Sorry!*

She began to stand, kicking over her backpack in the process. As it tipped sideways, I caught a glimpse inside and froze, heart pounding in my ears. Maggie zipped it up quickly and turned to face me, smiling.

As she rose to her full height, my skin prickled. Even though my dress hugged her curves tighter than they'd ever hugged mine, with her wild curls smoothed into soft waves and pink blush highlighting her cheekbones, I finally saw what Emi did:

Maggie looked like a mirror image of me. Albeit a distorted

one. Like looking into a fun-house mirror. I shivered.

What's wrong? Maggie asked. This dress is too tight, isn't it? I should change.

I shook my head, trying my best to regain my composure. No, I said, smiling a bit too brightly. You look great. Let's finish getting ready and get out of here.

Maggie seemed to relax, letting out a small sigh (of relief?).

But my entire body stayed tensed.

Because all I could picture was what I'd just glimpsed inside her backpack.

A creamy linen envelope with a broken red wax seal.

Just like one of your letters.

Subject: VIVIAN PAGE (VP)

Interviewer: Detective Rebecca Bennett, RCIPS

Date: 4/16

VP: You know, some tea does sound good. Do you have Numi?

RCIPS: Numi tea? I'm sorry, I am not familiar with that. We have Earl Grey.

VP: Oh, that's okay. Maybe just some water, then. Is your water bottled?

RCIPS: It comes from a faucet, Miss Page.

VP: Is your tap water safe to drink?

RCIPS: You are in George Town, Miss Page, not the middle of a jungle.

VP: I'm sorry, I didn't mean to imply . . . well, you know. I'm fine. I don't need anything.

RCIPS: Okay, then, so a few minutes ago you were mentioning how this vacation was supposed to be a celebration before you all graduate and head your separate ways. Where will you be going to college next year?

VP: Me? Oh, I've been planning to take

a year off before college. So I can work on growing my brand. I have a very popular Instagram; I guess you could even call me an influencer. Maybe you've seen it?

RCIPS: Not sure I have, but I will be certain to look. Anyway, it sounds like you girls were all close, having fun, and— What is it? Is that not a correct statement?

VP: I mean, sure, me, Emi, and Giselle were close. But like I said, we really didn't know Maggie that well. Giselle is the one who invited her on the trip.

RCIPS: Are you saying that Maggie was more Giselle's friend than yours?

[long silence]

RCIPS: Miss Page?

VP: Yeah, sorry. It's just, I hate to speak badly of anyone. It's bad karma, you know. And I really did like Maggie!

RCIPS: We are not here to pass judgment. We are simply trying to get to the truth.

VP: Okay.

RCIPS: So how would you describe Miss Mitchell and Miss Haverford's friendship?

VP: Well, see that's the thing—I don't

know if I would really describe it as
a friendship.

RCIPS: No? How would you describe it, then?

VP: More like [sound of fingernails
clicking on the table] an obsession?

RCIPS: Interesting. So you're saying that
Miss Mitchell was obsessed with Miss
Haverford?

VP: Uh, no. Yes.

RCIPS: Which is it?

VP: Well, maybe in the beginning Maggie
was sort of obsessed with Giselle. We
all noticed it. Like, she even started
wearing her hair like Giselle's and
talking like her and stuff. But
then . . .

RCIPS: Then?

VP: Then, well, at times it almost seemed
like it was the other way around.

RCIPS: Wait, so you are saying it was Miss
Haverford who was obsessed with Miss
Mitchell?

VP: [inaudible] You know, I think I will
have that water now, if you don't
mind.

Dear Mom,

After homecoming, I went through all your letters to try to figure out which one was missing. But I couldn't tell. And I don't know what's bothering me more—that I can't remember every word you wrote or that Maggie might have taken one. And if she did, WHY?

All I know is that I'm not going to get burned. Again. I learned my lesson with Beatrice.

So if Maggie thinks she's going to sell one of your letters to some gossip site for a little payout, she's SADLY mistaken.

I thought about asking Emi what to do. But I'm not in the mood for one of her I-told-you-so's. She's too busy with Zane anyway. And I'm definitely not going to Viv for advice. I guess I'm on my own. Again.

I need to figure out Maggie's real story.

But my efforts have been going nowhere. I tried searching online and couldn't find anything about her, either. Of course, without knowing where to search, everything I did was a shot in the dark. And Maggie is totally sticking to her story about the boarding school in Switzerland. She was even going on yesterday about how much she missed the chocolate. (As if you can't just walk into a gourmet store and BUY Swiss chocolate, sheesh.) The more she talked, tucking her hair behind her ears exactly like mine, the more I began to doubt EVERYTHING about her. What was she doing here? Why was she hanging out with ME and all my friends?

Then I had an idea:

Maggie's student transcripts.

Surely they held info about Maggie's last school and why she left.

There was just one problem.

I couldn't get my hands on her records without help. Even the Haverford name only goes so far around here. Pretty sure Headmaster Unterman wasn't going to hand over Maggie's file just because I asked nicely.

I could only think of one person who could help me—but it wouldn't be without consequences. Dangerous ones.

Despite myself, I went ahead and messaged him right before dinner.

I was on edge the rest of the evening. It was Taco Tuesday, but everything tasted bland. (Maybe it always does, though. These are New Hampshire tacos, after all.)

My ears wouldn't stop ringing, like there was an alarm bell going off inside my head that I couldn't stop. Even though I did my best to hide it, Emi and Vivian could tell something was up. They kept glancing at me, then each other, then back at me. Finally, I gathered my things and stood.

Hey! Emi said. Where are you going?

Need to work on my chem lab analysis, I said.

Want help? Viv offered.

I shook my head, dumped my uneaten food in the trash, and left. I knew Viv didn't really want to help me, anyway. It's not in her best interest for me to get an A, is it? There can be only one valedictorian.

When I got back to my room, I flopped onto my bed, slipped my ear buds in, and cranked my music as loud as I could stand. I left my chem homework on the desk and bobbed my head along to the sound of Olivia Rodrigo scream-singing in my ears. I'm so sick of seventeen, too, Olivia. Where IS my fucking teenage dream?

I knew I should be doing homework. Or finishing my Dartmouth application. But honestly, what was the point? They were going to let me in, regardless, like every other Haverford before me. Besides, does some admissions officer really want to read my essay on a moment in my life that defined me? Maybe one about how losing you made me . . . what, more aware of my own mortality? Appreciative of everything I have? How it reminded me to be good and gracious and kind because life is short?

The thing is, I don't feel grateful. I feel angry. Angry because what did you ever do to deserve being gone from this world? And I'm angry that the world JUST KEEPS GOING without you in it. Even Dad didn't wait five seconds to marry the next Haverford wife he had lined up. Britney, who was not-so-patiently waiting in her Soho loft (courtesy of Dad) for her chance to slide into the empty space in your bed, before it even had a chance to go cold.

Doubt Dartmouth wants to hear about that.

But the worst part is, I'm angry with you.

For leaving me alone.

And what am I supposed to do with that?

My phone buzzed.

I read the message: Ok, fine. 11 p.m. The usual spot.

It's 10:52 as I write this, and I'm still on my bed. If I sit here for another minute, I won't make it in time.

Maybe I should just stay here. Forget this whole stupid idea.

Leave the past dead and buried, where it belongs.

But there's no escaping the past, is there, Mom?

It follows you straight to the grave.

DAY 4

APRIL 15—EARLY MORNING

Latitude, longitude: 25.607555, -78.949680

168 nautical miles off the coast of Key West

A crack of thunder jolts me awake, and I bolt upright as my stateroom illuminates in a flash of lightning, casting eerie shadows against the walls. Outside, the wind howls and rain streaks down the balcony door. I peek at the digital clock next to my bed and see it's 1:42 a.m. A little more than five hours until we dock in Key West. It feels like an eternity.

There's another crack, and this time something deep within the bowels of the yacht creaks and groans like a beast in pain. I can't help but picture my mom hugging me before I left on this trip. She worried about me out here. The untamed seas frightened her. But then, everything frightens her now. If she could, she'd keep us all—me, Sophie, Dad . . . especially Dad—in a bubble, where she could watch over our every move and keep us safe. As if that could work. No bubble can contain us. She should know that by now.

Mom worried about me attending Prep, too, after everything I'd been through at my old school. *Will the kids at Prep be any better?* she'd asked. *You're not like them, Maggie. You don't know how they see people like us.*

Oh, I knew, I thought, but didn't have the heart to tell her. Probably the same way people at my old school saw me. A Mitchell. Nothing more than a weed, rooted deep in the loamy soil. Destined to go nowhere, like every other Mitchell that came before me. Like Dad. Like *her*. The woman he'd married straight out of boot camp. A rebound relationship that resulted in yours truly, then proceeded to spiral down the drain.

But I couldn't say that, now could I?

At least at Prep I'd have a chance. A fresh start. Maybe they'd see the real me. The loyal friend. The good daughter and sister. The hopeful flower blooming in the sun.

I *needed* to go to Prep in ways I could never explain to Mom. Not without tearing her heart out and stomping it to bits.

I drag myself from bed, unable to sleep with the boat lurching and my thoughts swirling. I can't shake this need to *do* something. Anything feels better than sitting around, waiting for the right moment to make my move. Waiting for the other shoe to drop. I open my stateroom door, peer outside, then slip into the hallway.

There's a small light coming from the library. I creep toward it, wondering who else is awake. Maybe it's Giselle. Maybe I can finally get her alone for ten seconds. End this thing for good.

But as I get closer, I spot Vivian. She's hunched over her cell phone, typing rapidly, blond hair loose around her face. She mutters something to herself that sounds like, *I'm so done with this.* Or did she say *her*?

Her head snaps up, and she turns in my direction, startled.

"Maggie!" she says, blinking. "You scared me! I didn't hear you coming."

"Sorry," I say, leaning on the doorframe. "Couldn't sleep."

"Me neither," Vivian says, quickly shoving her phone away.

"Storm?"

"No, Emi."

My eyebrows furrow. "Emi?"

"She's asleep on my couch," Vivian says with a sigh. "Came into my room like an hour ago. Said Giselle's snoring was keeping her up."

I can't help but snort out a little laugh. The thought of perfect Giselle snoring like a grandpa is kind of hilarious. But confusing, too. Because I never heard her snore once at the chalet.

Vivian seems to read my mind.

"Yeah, I don't think that's the whole reason, either," she says, shrugging.

"You don't?"

"Nah. I mean, I'm sure you've noticed Em and Giselle are sort of like sisters," Vivian says, and I stiffen. "Super close, but also super in each other's business all the time. Every now and then they just need a break, you know? Don't get me wrong, I understand. It can be . . . exhausting at times, being Giselle's friend."

A moment of silence, layered with tension, hangs in the air.

"You mean with all the snoring," I say, breaking it.

Vivian tosses her head back and laughs. "Maggie, you crack me up!"

"I do my best." I grin.

"I'm glad you came to Prep," Vivian says, suddenly serious. "It's been nice, you know, not being the third wheel to Giselle and Em all the time. Not that I'm complaining! They're awesome and I love them. Really, I do!" She catches my eye, and there's something in her look. Like there's more that she wants to say, but has to stop herself.

"I get it," I say, thinking about everything she told me on the second day of this trip. For a moment, I almost feel like I could confide in Vivian. She might even understand if I explained.

A bolt of lightning illuminates the room, interrupting my thoughts. Vivian starts to count out loud. "One Mississippi, two Mississippi . . ."

When she's hit five Mississippis, thunder sounds. "Storm is moving away," she says. "Think I'll see if I can get to sleep now."

Vivian stands and a scrap of paper falls from her lap onto the floor. She quickly scoops it up, but not before I see some letters and numbers scribbled on the front. Her eyes flick to mine as she stuffs the paper in her pocket.

"See you later," she says with a shaky smile.

"Yeah, see you."

Vivian squeezes past me, then disappears around the corner in the direction of the spiral staircase that leads upstairs.

I wait a beat, thinking. And then, before I can talk myself out of it, I follow the path Vivian just took. I'm acutely aware of the sound of my footsteps, echoing as I climb the stairs and walk down the hallway toward the pair of suites at the front.

I come to a dead stop in front of Giselle's door.

She's in there.

Alone.

I grab the door handle, cool beneath my fingers, and begin to turn it slowly. Then I quickly drop my hand and jump back, breath catching in my throat.

What am I doing?

This is absurd. It's nearly two in the morning. I can't just barge into Giselle's room, unannounced, wake her up, and . . . do what, exactly? I need to get a grip. Go to bed. Get some rest before I do something stupid. I haven't waited this long just to mess everything up by being rash.

I turn and run all the way back to my own stateroom, flinging myself inside and locking the door behind me. But instead of climbing back into bed, I find myself drawn to the safe hidden inside my closet.

I punch in the code. Everything is right where I left it. Letter. Journal. *Money.* I stare in disbelief at the thick stack of bills I stuffed in there earlier tonight, my mouth dry. So. Much. Money.

Money that could change my life in so many ways.

Except it's not enough.

And that's the problem, isn't it?

Because what is *enough*? I glance around my luxurious suite, reminded once again that this stack of cash is merely a drop in the bucket for Giselle. The equivalent of some loose coins rattling around the bottom of a purse. I understand what Vivian meant when she said it was exhausting being friends with Giselle. Because deep in my gut I know this is a race I can't win.

Once upon a time, I told myself that all I wanted was to meet her. That was it. Get to know Giselle Haverford. Become her friend. Live a bit of her life just by being close.

But those were lies, weren't they? Little lies I told myself.

Because the truth is, I want *more*.

I've always wanted more. Running, running, running. Never satisfied with crossing the finish line. Always striving for the next thing. For whatever lies just out of my reach.

Or locked away on the other side of a closed door.

BREAKING NEWS ALERT—4/16, 11:25 A.M.

ANCHOR: More from the investigation into the disappearance at sea of eighteen-year-old heiress Giselle Haverford. While the Coast Guard triangulates the last known location of Miss Haverford's cell phone, believed to be in her pocket when she went overboard, we are hearing from a source inside the investigation. Our source tells us crew found traces of blood on a dented lower railing consistent with Miss Haverford hitting her head or body while falling from the upper deck, along with a broken necklace belonging to the teen. Retired Coast Guard Captain Peter Bergeron is here with us to give us some insight into the search. Hello, Captain Bergeron.

CAPTAIN BERGERON: Thank you for having me, Miss Joiner.

ANCHOR: As I understand it, this latest discovery of blood on the railing brings a new urgency to the search. Can you elaborate?

CAPTAIN BERGERON: Yes, obviously if an injury is severe enough, it can impact a victim's ability to stay afloat. Not to mention blood will draw predators like sharks. And if it was, in fact, a head injury—

ANCHOR: Yes?

CAPTAIN BERGERON: Well, if Miss Haverford suffered a head injury in the fall that was severe enough to knock her out, her odds of survival in the open water drop exponentially.

ANCHOR: Meaning?

CAPTAIN BERGERON: Meaning this quickly becomes a recovery mission, not a rescue.

Dear Mom,

I did it.

I went.

At 10:53, I snuck down the hall past our house mother's room and made my way outside.

It was quiet and still, and as I headed down the path toward "our" spot in the woods, I was struck by the memory of the first time we'd met here. It was last year, just after you'd died. He'd asked me to meet him. Late.

I'd had no idea what he'd wanted. After all, we'd never talked before. Why would we? It wasn't like we had a thing in common.

Not that I knew of, at least.

When I'd arrived, he was already there, standing beneath an old oak tree. I hadn't spent much time studying him up close before, but that night I saw he was actually kinda hot in a quiet sort of way. Not in the loud look-at-me way of the sleek, suntanned Hamptons boys with their bright white smiles and chiseled cheek bones, or the alpha-boy way of the legacy Preppers with their perfectly mussed hair and uniform ties ironically askew.

Instead, he was long and lanky and awkward, as though his body hadn't quite finished catching up with the sudden growth of his arms and legs. His dark hair was messy and in need of a proper cut. There was a zit on his chin he'd clearly picked at. But, oh, those warm brown eyes and full lips . . .

I'd blushed.

Hey, he'd said, blushing, too. I'm glad you came.

You said you wanted to give me something? I'd answered, then mentally kicked myself for being so weirdly blunt. Like the only reason I'd shown up was for a gift. Was it?

He'd held out a plastic grocery bag. Something blue and fuzzy poked from the top.

I'd taken it from him, eyebrows raised.

It's a blanket, he'd explained in a rush. *When my dad died a few years ago, people kept bringing me and Mom flowers and casseroles and then they'd hurry away, like they could catch death just by standing near us. When all I really wanted was a hug, you know? Not another card or tray of lasagna that Mom would leave in the fridge until it molded. So that blanket, it's like a hug you can wrap around your shoulders when you need it.* He'd cleared his throat. *I know we don't really know each other well. You just . . . I saw you looking out the window in class the other day and thought you could use a hug. So I made that blanket for you. I mean, don't get too impressed, it's not that great, just a hand-loop thing. I watched a video on YouTube how to make it . . . And I'm talking way too much. I'm going to stop now.*

His face had flared bright red. Probably because I was standing there, blinking rapidly while I'd stared at him, speechless. All that time he'd sat across from me in creative writing, head down and quietly focused on his laptop, hair covering his eyes, I hadn't been aware he was actually paying attention. Even more than my so-called friends had, it seemed.

And he'd MADE me something. Nobody had ever done that before.

Anyway, that's it. I'll go now, he'd mumbled.

Wait, no! I'd said as he'd turned to leave. Don't. Please, stay.

And before I'd realized what was happening, tears had streamed from my eyes. It was the first time I'd really cried since you'd died. I hadn't realized how much I'd been holding in, trying to be strong for Dad, my friends, because that's what they'd expected from me. No, because that's what they'd WANTED from me. Because he was right—sadness was contagious, and once I'd been infected, nobody really wanted to stand too close.

Except for him.

But tonight, here in the clearing where we used to meet late at night and talk and hold each other close and share our dreams, he didn't have a gift.

There was no nervous smile.

His hands were stuffed in the pockets of his jeans, his cheeks pink from the brisk walk through the woods from town not embarrassment. They'd filled in a little, I noticed, along with those arms and legs that looked more muscular than awkward now. I'd spent so much time attempting to ignore him I'd failed to see how he'd changed. Became stronger. Maybe even more hardened around the edges. Not fragile like that first night. Not open and giving.

Had I done that to him?

Hey, I said, trying to sound calm when I was anything but. How are you?

How am I? he said. There was an unfamiliar sharpness to his voice. Are you serious? You could have asked me that at school.

Oh, wait. I guess then you'd have to acknowledge me in public, wouldn't you?

Wyatt . . . I began, my stomach churning like a pit of snakes.

He shook his head. Don't bother, Giselle. His hands were out of his pockets now, fists curling and uncurling. Maybe just tell me what you want. Because you want something, right? I can't think of any other reason you'd ask to meet me. Here of all places.

My bottom lip began to shake. I bit down on it so hard I tasted blood. A bitter reminder that I was human. Because I knew, deep in my gut, that what I was about to do to Wyatt was not.

Well, what do you want? he pressed. Or are you afraid to tell me? I mean, it's got to be scary being out here in the dark with me alone, right? What is it your buddy likes to call me? The stalker? Yeah, that's right. I've heard her talking. My mom might clean your rooms, but that doesn't mean I don't know what you all say about me.

I'm sorry, I said. Please don't let Emi get to you. She doesn't know what she's talking about.

Really? Wyatt huffed. And why's that, huh? Maybe you could explain it to her, then. Except that would mean telling her the truth about us, and you're not going to do that, are you?

No, I wasn't. But not for the reasons Wyatt thought. Not for any reasons I could explain. Not to anyone. And especially not to him.

I stood up straight, throwing my shoulders back and lifting my chin like the good little Haverford I am. (Wouldn't Dad be proud? Stare the thing that can destroy you right in the face—and destroy it first!)

You're right, I said. I do want something, and you're the only person who can help me.

What?

I need to get into Unterman's office, I said.

You've got to be kidding, he said. Forget it, Giselle. You can't ask me to do this. I can't believe I actually came here to meet you.

He began to stomp away.

I ran to catch up with him and grabbed him by the shoulder. He spun around, glaring at me.

What? he hissed.

I'm not asking, I said slowly.

What is that supposed to mean? he asked.

It means I. Am. Not. Asking. I know you can get in. I know your mom has a key. My spine stiffened as the words fell from my lips. Little grenades that exploded the minute they hit the ground. Boom, bang, boom!

I know you've used that key before, I said. And I know why. It sure would suck if anyone found out how you passed that trigonometry midterm last year, wouldn't it?

Jesus, Giselle. Are you fucking BLACKMAILING me? he said, shaking. I was going to lose my scholarship if I failed. And unlike YOU, I don't have a daddy who can pay someone to clean up my messes. My mom is all I have.

It was everything I could do not to crumble. There'd only been one other moment in my life that I'd hated myself this completely. When my heart had been ripped from my body. But I didn't break down then, and I wouldn't now.

So you'll do it, then, I said flatly.

You're unbelievable, Wyatt said through clenched teeth. I can't believe there was a fleeting moment that I thought . . . you . . . this . . . He waved his hand around. That you wanted to meet me here because . . .

Tears filled his eyes, and he pinched them shut and open again.

Fuck it, he said, swiping a hand across his face. I was stupid to think you actually cared about me. That you EVER did.

His words were like tiny knives, stabbing at me. I stared at him, keeping my face blank and holding back my own tears.

I'll text you when I have the key, he said. And then I don't ever want to speak to you again. His voice cracked.

He turned and walked away. This time, I didn't chase after him. Instead, I watched him disappear down the path until he was just a shadow in the trees.

A ghost.

Something I couldn't touch or hold.

Like everything I've ever really loved.

DAY 3

APRIL 14—NIGHT

Nassau, Bahamas

The noise and flashing lights of the casino recede behind us as we walk outside into the mild Bahamian night and down a long set of stairs to a beachfront boardwalk. It's beautiful and serene, the air salty and warm, filled with the soothing sound of waves lapping against the shore. But I can't stop looking over my shoulder, waiting for a security guard to burst through the casino doors and cuff me. Could that happen? Or am I safe now that I'm outside?

Watch your back . . .

The purse full of cash weighs heavily on my side, like it's loaded with dynamite. I alternate between exhilaration at what this money means for me and terror that I'll be caught red-handed with it.

All I want right now is to hop in the limo and get the hell out of here, but the parking lot—freedom—is in the other direction.

"We still have half an hour till departure," Giselle says, stopping to do a random pirouette in the middle of the boardwalk. I'm reminded of the spinning ballerina in the jewelry box I bought for Sophie at the church rummage sale last Christmas, the prettiest thing I could afford, that she uses to store her shiny rock collection. "What do you guys want to do?"

"Go for a swim?" Vivian says with a little grin as she tilts her head toward the beach.

"What about our dresses? And shoes?" Emi frowns. "These flats are lambskin. They'll get totally destroyed in the water."

"We could skinny-dip." Giselle's green eyes flash with mischief.

Vivian giggles, and then her eyebrows knit together as she stares past us and back at the casino. Security? Adrenaline courses through my veins and I contemplate running. My calf muscles twitch in anticipation. It's almost like I'm back on the starting line, waiting for the sound of the starter pistol. My last race feels like a lifetime ago.

How was I to know that once I started running, I'd never stop?

"Weird," Vivian murmurs.

"What?" Giselle asks.

"I thought I just saw Rita," Vivian answers. "Up there, on the walkway to the casino. But when I tried to get a better look, she slipped behind that row of palm trees. I can't see her anymore."

"Rita? Are you sure?" Emi says. "What would she be doing here?"

"Yeah, I'm pretty sure," Vivian says. "She wasn't in uniform, but she was wearing those navy Top-Siders she always has on."

A nervous laugh slips past my lips, partly out of relief that security isn't headed this way. And partly because of course Vivian identified Rita by her shoes, right down to color and brand.

"You find stalkerish yacht staff funny?" Emi says.

"No," I say, straightening. "Of course not. Maybe she had the night off and wanted to gamble a little."

Giselle clears her throat and frowns. "Maybe," she says. "Not likely. The staff don't usually hang out here. For obvious reasons." She rolls her head from side to side, cracking her neck. "I bet my dad hired her to spy on us. Make sure I don't do anything 'stupid'"—she makes air quotes with her fingers—"to tarnish his image."

"That's crappy," Vivian says. "Where do you think she went?"

"Who cares?" Giselle says with a smirk. "If Dad's going to have me followed, might as well give her something to report."

She yanks off her heels and starts down the beach. It's nearly empty, save for a few couples strolling hand in hand. Emi pulls off her flats as we walk and holds them so far above her head, she'd have to be hit by a tidal wave to get them wet.

"Sheesh, Em," Giselle says, looking back over her shoulder. "I don't think you need to worry about water all the way back here."

"These flats are new," Emi says. "I don't want to wreck them. They're not even for sale to the general public yet. Mom got them straight from Christian Louboutin himself."

She gives me and the borrowed dress I'm wearing a sideways glance. I'm acutely aware of the delicate fabric against my skin. I wonder which designer hand-presented this to Emi's mom. Perhaps it was custom-made for Emi herself.

Giselle and Vivian drop their shoes in the sand and run to the water. I stay put next to Emi. The last thing I need to do is ruin her dress on top of everything else I've done. I feel like I've been walking a tightrope this entire trip. One that keeps getting narrower and narrower, higher and higher off the ground, with every step I take. One misstep, and I'll plummet to my death.

"I think maybe I'll go back up to the boardwalk, where it's dry and sand-free," I say.

"Yeah, okay," Emi says. "You do that." But she's not really paying attention to me. Her eyes are fixed on the shoreline. Giselle looks almost otherworldly, her gold dress sparkling in the moonlight, auburn hair tumbling in waves down her back as she wades into the surf, deeper and deeper. She's almost up to her waist now, far ahead of Vivian, who is just getting her toes wet and snapping selfies. For a moment, I think Giselle's going to keep right on going. Disappear into the ocean like some kind of sea nymph.

But then she stops and tilts her face toward the moonlight. She spins around, laughing, and runs back to the shoreline by Vivian, water splashing around her feet. Vivian jumps back, lifts her phone in the air, and scowls at Giselle.

Emi stiffens next to me.

I feel like I should say something to break the tension

between us. She's barely spoken to me since the mini makeover back in her room.

"She's pretty amazing," I say. "I wish I could be that comfortable with myself."

"What, who?" Emi says.

"Giselle," I say. "I've never met anyone like her."

"I'm sure you haven't."

"Listen." I suck in a breath. "I get that you and Giselle have been besties forever, and I want you to know I'm not trying to come between the two of you or anything."

There's a long pause. Then Emi turns to me.

"Come between us?" she says with a little snort. "I don't think you could, no matter how hard you tried. So maybe you should stop trying, huh?"

With that, she walks back up to the boardwalk, flats held high above her head. She sits on a bench and looks past me.

Fine, then. I was only trying to be nice.

Ten minutes later, Giselle and Vivian come running up the beach, sand sticking to their wet feet and legs. The bottom half of Giselle's dress is damp with salt water. She shakes a clump of seaweed from her toes and laughs.

"Any sign of the stalker?" Giselle says.

I haven't been paying attention, but I shake my head.

"Let's get out of here, then," she says.

The limo picks us up in the parking lot, and relief washes over me as we put more distance between ourselves and the casino. We navigate the narrow streets, passing Bahamians riding old bicycles, brightly colored houses with peeling paint stacked tightly together, locals sitting on their sagging front porches. It's a completely different world from the one we just left. A world that time and casino dollars haven't touched. I'm reminded of home, and the multimillion-dollar ski chalets in the mountains—like Giselle's—that look down from their lofty perches on the modest homes in the valley.

The limo skirts the water near the main cruise terminal, where three hulking ships are berthed, their dark silhouettes squatting against the night sky. Beyond the main tourist area, the streets are dotted with TAKE BACK OUR PORT signs. I shift uncomfortably in my seat. Here I am, just another sightseer passing through, staring at the weathered faces of the people sitting under the dim lights of their front porches from behind the shelter of the limo's tinted glass. When not that long ago, I was the one on the outside, looking in.

We reach the private marina and board *The Escape*. Suddenly, I'm overwhelmed with exhaustion. All I want is to slip into a pair of sweatpants and a T-shirt and go to bed. This dress feels like a costume. An ill-fitting second skin that I need to be free of.

After we enter the yacht's main lounge area, the other girls split off to head to their rooms and I turn in the other direction toward mine. I'm almost to the hallway when a hand catches my shoulder. I spin around to see Emi regarding me, lips pursed.

"Yeah?" I say. I'm really not in the mood for her and whatever she's got to say to me now.

"You should give it back."

"I'm going to change right now," I answer. "And I'll bring the dress right to your room, okay?"

"Not that," Emi says. "I couldn't care less about the dress."

Of course not. She probably has a hundred more like it at home.

"I meant the money," she hisses. "It's not yours."

The heat rises in my cheeks. "It wasn't my idea, okay? And I tried. To give it back."

"Yeah, I'm sure you tried really hard."

"What is your point? I don't see why it ma-aa-aa-atters to you?" I breathe loudly through my nose, irritated with myself. I've gone years without a stutter, and all of that's gone to shit on this trip.

"My p-p-p-point," she says, mocking me, "is that Giselle is not your piggy bank, okay?"

I'm tired and I've had enough. "What is your deal, anyway?"

"Excuse me?" Emi says.

"Why do you care so much what I do?"

"Maybe because I care about Giselle," she answers. "And I don't know what *your* deal is with her or why you're always hanging around, trying to take stuff that doesn't belong to you. But I'm watching you."

"Is that right?" I say, straightening my back. "Whatever. You don't scare me."

"Well, Mitchell, maybe I should."

"Or—" I hold her gaze. "Maybe I'm the one who should scare you."

Emi's eyes widen, then her gaze drifts past my shoulders. A dark look crosses her face. I turn. Giselle is standing on the spiral staircase leading to the next level, leaning casually on the railing. She's watching us with a half smile and twirling her thumb ring.

"Hey Emi, Maggie," she says. "Sorry to interrupt your . . . little chat." She waves her delicate hand around. I wait for her to comment on our conversation. But she just gives me a sly little grin. "Anyway, wanted to let you guys know the captain said there's a storm moving in from the southeast. If we leave now and move quickly, we should be able to get ahead of it. But we might have a bumpy ride ahead."

"How bumpy?" Emi asks.

"Nothing that'll kill us. At least, I don't think so, ha ha. We'll be fine. Captain Hjelkrem is the best at his job. And I know Maggie won't go down without a fight, will you?" Giselle says with a mischievous—no, terrifying—glint in her eyes that's aimed straight at me.

My skin prickles. I don't know what this dance that Giselle and I are caught up in is about anymore. Maybe it's more like a game of musical chairs. The kind we used to play in PE class when I was little. But now the music is speeding up. Faster, faster, faster . . .

And there's only one chair left.

Dear Mom,

It took Wyatt an entire week and a half to text me back. The wait was driving me crazy. I did my best to focus on other things: cheer routines, writing up some boring story for the school paper about the renovations underway in the boys' dorm (thank you, alumni donors, gag!), working on that pointless college essay. I feigned excitement when Vivian landed the lead role in Mamma Mia. I pretended to be interested in every stupid detail of Zane and Emi's dates. All the while, Maggie had practically glued herself to my side. I couldn't turn around without running into her, my new self-appointed BFF.

I was a bundle of nerves by the time Wyatt and I finally met in the woods after lights-out. Wyatt stared at me, keeping his hands jammed in his pockets. I stared back. Two could play that game.

Do you have the key or not? I finally said.

I have it, he answered.

Well? I held my hand out.

Sorry, nope, he said.

What do you mean NOPE? I thought we'd been through this already. I need that key.

Yeah, message received, Giselle, he said. You can have the key. But I come with it.

I looked at him in disbelief. I don't need a chaperone, I grumbled.

Well, I don't care, he answered. This is my MOM'S card, so

you're getting one. Unterman's office, in and out, and nothing else. That's the deal. Got it?

Got it, I said with a groan.

We walked in silence to the main hall, keeping away from the security lights out front. Wyatt swiped the key card at the side door. Time seemed to stop while we waited for the light to flash green. When it did, we quickly pushed the door open and slipped inside. The automatic lights flicked on in the hallway, illuminating the Prep banners and glass cases filled with silver and gold trophies. An ode to excellence at every turn.

Wyatt quickly switched the lights off, cursing under his breath.

We crept silently to the headmaster's office. Wyatt swiped the key card again. The door clicked open. I bypassed the reception area, headed straight to Unterman's huge mahogany desk, and sat in his cushy leather chair. Wyatt stood lookout.

I powered up the computer only to be greeted by a screensaver photo of Unterman all decked out in his golfing gear—standing next to the esteemed Senator Robert Haverford and the vice president. I groaned inwardly. There's no escape from Dad's ever-present influence, is there? Can you imagine how much worse it'll be if he actually becomes president? Secret Service lurking around every corner? Ugh, kill me now.

Can you hurry up? Wyatt hissed from the doorway.

I rolled my eyes and began combing through Unterman's files. Thankfully his computer wasn't password protected (as I'd suspected—old school Unterman probably thinks the lock on his office door is security enough, ha!). But it still took a few long minutes to even locate the student records on the shared drive. Finally, I found Maggie's file. There wasn't much to it. Current class schedule. Grades. Financials. Transferring school transcript.

I clicked on that.

The file loaded, filling the screen, and I had to read it three times before reality sunk in.

How was this possible?

Suddenly, lights flicked on and footsteps tapped down the hall outside.

Wyatt rushed into the office, grabbed my arm, and before I could power down the computer, he pulled me beneath the desk. We squished together, so close I could feel the heat radiating off his body. I tried to ignore it, but my heart thumped wildly against my rib cage. I don't know what scared me more—getting caught or being this close to Wyatt again.

The footsteps got closer. The clank of the maintenance cart rolling toward us grew louder. The night janitor whistled to himself. The illuminated computer screen on the desk above our heads felt like a spotlight shining right at our hiding space.

A pair of worn work boots appeared on the other side of the desk and came to a halt. The computer screen dimmed. The whistling stopped.

Huh, the janitor mumbled to himself. He shuffled around a moment, and I was sure we were about to get busted.

I let out a small gasp. Wyatt placed his fingers gently across my lips. Electricity coursed through my veins like I'd been touched by a live wire. My eyes locked with Wyatt's, and for a moment, time stopped completely.

After what felt like a lifetime, the janitor grabbed the trash can, emptied it, and rolled his cart away, whistling again.

I exhaled. That was close, I said.

Too close, Wyatt answered.

Neither of us moved.

I became acutely aware of just how easy it would be to close the gap between us. Bury my head against his chest, the only place I've ever felt safe. Loved. And before I could think better of it, I leaned forward. My eyelids fluttered closed. I felt the warmth of Wyatt's lips as they brushed gently across mine—like the very first time, out beneath the oak tree, wrapped in velvet night.

It felt like coming home.

But then Wyatt pulled abruptly away, banging his head against the desk. The screen above us flicked back to life.

No, Wyatt said, voice wobbling. NO, Giselle. Not here. Not like this. Not hiding under a desk. If you want to kiss me, it happens out there, in front of everyone. It happens in the light of day. I'm not going to be your dirty little secret. Not anymore.

I . . . I started to speak, but Wyatt had already disentangled himself from me and scrambled to his feet. I caught my breath and stood next to him. The glow of the computer screen cast a soft light over his face.

His expression had turned to stone.

What is this? he asked, not looking at me. *What are you doing here?*

Nothing, I said. *It doesn't matter.*

Doesn't matter? I thought you wanted to come in here to switch a grade or something, not go poking around someone else's stuff. What are you mixing me up in, Giselle? I thought she was your friend.

It's NOTHING, really. I just wanted . . . I just needed to look at something, okay? Honest.

Honest? Wyatt scoffed. *Like you know the meaning of the word.*

I let out a bitter laugh, closed Maggie's file, then pushed the computer's power button and held it until the screen went black.

But the image of Maggie's transcript stayed burned into my brain:

Margot Mitchell, transfer student from Westville High School in Westville, Vermont.

Yes, *that* Westville. The town where we've owned a ski chalet for more than twenty years.

No wonder she'd looked familiar. I'd probably seen her around the village.

I googled "Margot Mitchell Westville" the minute I got back to my room.

Finally, some hits. There weren't many. Mostly results from WHS track meets. Maggie was a pretty good runner, it seemed. She'd placed second and third in several races and was part of a first-place relay team that actually broke a state record last year. There was even a picture of that record-breaking team. Maggie stood in the center, her arm draped around the team co-captain next to her, wearing a huge smile.

Why hadn't Maggie ever mentioned she was a runner?

Why make up the whole Switzerland thing in the first place?

Then I read a headline from the local television station a bit farther down in the results, and I knew exactly why Maggie had conveniently left that piece of her history out:

Doping scandal rocks Westville High School girls track team: coach steps down, team banned from state finals, further races. Investigation ongoing.

DAY 3

APRIL 14—EVENING

The Purple Orchid Resort and Casino
Nassau, Bahamas

The noise of the casino overwhelms my senses as we step inside, all flashing lights and coins pouring down into metal trays and raucous laughs and shouts. We're in the main carpeted foyer, slot machines to our right, a huge bar area to our left, and game tables straight ahead. A massive chandelier made of glittering purple crystals hangs from the center of the high ceiling. The spacious room is filled with men in tuxedos, women in slinky dresses, and servers gliding past with trays full of drinks. There's a hum in the air that's hard to define, an intoxicating combination of booze and bucks that's somehow louder than the jazz music being piped in from unseen speakers.

Dad would hate it here. But I like the noise, the commotion. Even if it can't completely drown out my own nonstop thoughts.

I think back to when I was little, when we'd hold family casino night every Friday after dinner in the cozy kitchen of our bungalow. It wasn't huge, but I loved that house and its dormer windows stacked with pillows where I'd sit and draw. The building block wallpaper that lined my bedroom and my toy box full of Legos tucked under the bed. The kitchen always smelled like chocolate chip cookies and fresh bread and sunshine.

Or at least, that's how I remember it. *Warm.*

Safe.

We'd sit at the butcher block table Dad had built in his shop. He would don a cheesy green visor and dole out plastic betting chips, cool and rough around the edges. They made the best sound, clinking together when we placed our bets. Our game of choice was blackjack. Dad taught me how to figure out when to draw more cards, when to split, and when to hold. We annihilated Mom every time. And it wasn't long before I was beating the pants off Dad, too.

That was before.

Before we traded our warm home for a borrowed trailer at Nana's farm. Before the chips were packed into a box and the deck of cards got shoved in a drawer, beneath the pot holders and random screwdrivers no one ever uses. Before the deployments took their toll on Dad and the hands of an expert craftsman that could once turn a simple piece of wood into something beautiful shook too hard to hold a saw.

No more sneaking up behind Dad for tackle-hugs. No more loud squeals or boisterous games. No more shouting "Hit me!" and slapping the table while Dad flicked a playing card in my direction with a grin.

Tiptoe, whisper, and try not to trigger the flashbacks.

Count out the pills, hope they work.

When they stop working, smile and pray it gets better.

Giselle tugs my arm, snapping me out of my thoughts. "Maggie, what do you want to play?"

"I'm not really sure I should play," I answer in a whisper. "I'm not eighteen. It isn't legal."

"Oh, come on. I gave that bouncer at the door enough to make sure nobody cares!" Giselle says, opening my purse and shoving a huge handful of chips inside. She laughs, and I will myself to relax and laugh along. It comes out more like a nervous bark. What does someone like Giselle really know about consequences, anyway? I've seen her vacation home. Life is so much easier when you have gates to keep the bad things out.

"Well?" Giselle taps her foot, waiting. Why does this feel like some sort of test?

I glance around the huge room full of tables surrounded by glamorous people holding drinks and rolling dice, placing bets, tapping cards. A little itch tickles the back of my brain, daring me to scratch it. Daring me to play. I haven't felt this way since our relay last spring when we broke the state record. I like the weight of the chips in my purse.

I like to win.

"Blackjack," I finally say. "Blackjack is my thing."

"Really?" Giselle says, holding my gaze. "I always took you for a poker player."

"Nope," I say slowly, not sure what that was supposed to mean. "Just blackjack. I don't know how to play poker."

"Spoken like a true poker player," Giselle says with a smirk.

"Blackjack it is, then!" She claps her hands together and begins walking.

But when we reach the blackjack tables, I stop short. It's not the game I remember from our kitchen. Everyone—except the dealer—has their cards face up. We always played that each player started with one card down, one card up. I frown, confused. How can you bet against each other when everyone knows what cards you hold? What's the point in that?

"What's the matter, Mitchell?" Emi says. "Having trouble adding to twenty-one?"

"No, I just . . ." Ugh, why is Emi so annoying? "Why are all the cards face up?"

"That's how the game is played." Emi rolls her eyes. "It's you against the dealer, not the rest of the table. Why do you think they say the house always wins?"

"Always?" I say. "We'll see about that, won't we?"

We sit. The mood in the casino is lively, but the air around us has shifted, thick with tension. Emi casts a sideways glance in my direction as we place our bets. It's a fifty-dollar minimum just to play. *Fifty dollars.* That's more than three times what Mom earns an hour. To get one hand of cards.

This can't be real.

I immediately go bust on the first round, and I swear I hear Emi snicker.

But after a few more rounds of play (and a few infusions of chips from Giselle), I begin to get the hang of the game again. And then the wins start outnumbering the losses. By a lot. I'm laser focused, watching my stack of chips grow larger in front of me. Before I know it, I've completely lost track of time. I check my phone, shocked to see we've been playing for more than an hour and a half.

I place a new bet. Sweat trickles down the back of my neck as the dealer hands out the cards. I really need to get up and stretch, but I want another win. One more. That's it. And then I'm quitting (says every gambler ever, I know). But this is just as fun as I remember. Maybe even more, because now it's real money. There are actual stakes.

But then, I think with a shudder, aren't there always?

I look down at my cards. A seven of clubs and a ten of spades sit in front of me. Not bad. The dealer shows a five of hearts, which means he'll have to hit. Maybe even go bust. I shift in my seat, and the skintight dress I'm wearing inches up my thighs, dangerously close to giving the entire casino an unintended show. I tug it down as a server breezes past, holding a tray of champagne. The other girls grab glasses, but I wave him away. I need to stay focused.

I'm not legal to drink here anyway.

Or gamble, I remind myself, stomach tightening. I'm the only one of us who hasn't turned eighteen yet thanks to my late September birthday. It's one thing always being the youngest in my class. Underage gambling is a whole different story. I have no idea what the penalty is for that. I don't really want to find out.

There's a uniformed security guard hovering near the table

next to ours, watching the play with a critical eye. Small black domes in the ceiling overhead are a not-so-subtle reminder that there are security cameras hidden everywhere. I rub the back of my neck and take a slow breath. If I was going to get kicked out—or worse—it would have happened by now, right?

I'm up. The dealer nods in my direction. I glance at my cards again. Seventeen. It's a solid hand. And odds are, I'll go bust if I draw. But I'm feeling kind of risky tonight. I'm taking a card anyway. I double down on my bet and tap my cards.

The dealer raises an eyebrow questioningly. I hold my breath as he flips me a card, afraid to look. And . . . it's a four. Ha! Twenty-one. I smile to myself.

Giselle's up next. A queen and a four sit in front of her. She could stand, but that's a tough call. She motions to the dealer to hit. He slides a queen across the green felt table. Twenty-four. Bust.

"Oh man," Giselle says. "Guess I should've stood."

Emi huffs on her other side. "No, that four should have been yours," she says, referring to the card I was just dealt. "If your friend there was playing fair. Who draws a card on a seventeen?" she says pointedly.

"Eh, what is it they say? All's fair in love and war, right, Maggie?" Giselle asks, flashing me a wicked grin. "Besides, it's only money." Another bead of sweat rolls down the back of my neck. I force myself to smile back. *Only money*. Of course Giselle would say that.

The rest of the table plays and now it's down to the dealer.

He flips his hidden card. A king of clubs. He draws a two. Seventeen.

The pile of chips in front of me doubles in size. So do Vivian's eyes.

"Where did you learn to play like that?" she asks.

"What do you mean, like an asshole?" Emi says.

I ignore her. "My dad taught me."

"Wow," Vivian says. "Only thing my dad ever taught me was how to say no to boys."

"And how'd that work out for ya?" Giselle says with a laugh. Vivian mock punches her arm and grins.

"Yeah, well, it's always easier to take chances with someone else's money, isn't it?" Emi says, glaring at me.

The tips of my ears burn. Emi's dress wasn't the only thing I had to borrow tonight.

I'm reminded again of the uniformed security guard one table over. I glance in his direction. He takes a step closer, eyebrows raised. I immediately push the mound of chips in front of Giselle. She can have them. This has been fun and all, but I don't want to spend the night in a Bahamian jail cell.

"I think that's it for me," I say. "I need to hit the bathroom. See you guys in a few."

I take my time using the bathroom and wandering around the casino, wanting to put as much distance as possible between me, my illegal winnings, and that security guard. I watch a poker game, then window-shop in the boutiques that run alongside the casino's edge. High-end items like Chanel perfume and

Hermès scarves and Colombian emeralds, all for sale, "duty-free!" How thoughtful of them to help you part with your newfound winnings, right?

I meander a bit more until I find the girls again, sitting at the bar and sipping champagne from tall flutes. There's a full glass in front of an empty stool, clearly waiting for me.

"There you are!" Giselle says. "About time. Your drink was about to go flat."

"Sorry," I say, taking a seat and ignoring the champagne. "Doing a little sightseeing. This place is wild. I watched a lady win at slots and then lose it all again in the next five minutes."

"Did you know that the odds of winning at slots are actually a fraction of a percent?" Vivian says. "There are thousands of combinations. For example, twelve thousand one hundred and sixty-seven on that machine over there," she adds, reminding me that while Vivian might look like a Barbie doll, she can calculate complex math problems (and who knows what else) in her head. If Vivian has a secret weapon, it's that she's a hell of a lot smarter—and more cunning—than she appears. I wouldn't want to cross her.

"Show-off," Giselle snorts. Viv flips her hair around and pouts, then giggles.

Emi raises her hand, flagging down the bartender.

A tall Bahamian with her hair in a tight bun and a friendly smile places fresh white cocktail napkins in front of us. "Another round?"

"Actually, I'd like to buy a case of the Cristal," Emi says.

"Delivered to our limo out front. Would that be okay?"

"Of course," the bartender says. She prints out a receipt and slides it in front of Emi. "Sign here, please, and write down your vehicle information."

Emi takes the pen and paper, angling it in my direction so I can see the total.

Two thousand and fifty dollars.

Plus tip.

Emi glances quickly at me and my cheeks flush because I'm gawking. And I know that's exactly what she wanted. A little reminder that Giselle isn't the only one around here with money to throw around. That no matter what I do or how I dress, I'll never have the looks or cash to be one of them.

Giselle tugs at my arm.

"Come with me, Mags," she says. "I need to cash in my chips. Let's see how much you made me tonight!"

My stomach bottoms out. "I don't think you need me for that, do you? It's your money."

"Don't be silly," Giselle says. "You won it. Now, come with me!"

I really don't want to go anywhere near the cashier's booth, but Giselle drags me along anyway. We get in a short line in front of a caged window. As we reach the front, my heart is thudding in my chest so loudly, I think everyone around me can hear it.

Including the two uniformed security guards standing on either side of the cashier windows, walkie-talkies clipped to one side of their belts. Guns clipped on the other. I stare straight ahead, willing myself to breathe like a normal, nonguilty human being.

Giselle thumps her bag full of chips onto the counter.

"My friend here is a pro at blackjack!" she announces loudly. "She'd like to cash out."

Seriously? Why on earth did she have to go and say that? Does she want me to get caught or something?

The cashier takes the chips with a nod and counts out the winnings. I'm vaguely aware of the word "thousand" being repeated over and over. When she finally finishes, she glances at Giselle, then me.

"How would you like that, miss?" she asks. "Bank deposit or cash?"

I pretend not to hear and turn my attention to the action at a nearby craps table. A tuxedoed man holds a pair of dice under the lips of a woman in a slinky dress, who blows a sultry kiss on them. It's like a freaking Bond movie in here. I wonder what that makes me? Bond girl? Or villain?

Or neither. Just a farm girl playing an extra on the set.

The man throws the dice and the crowd surrounding him cheers. My ears ring.

"Bank deposit or cash?" the cashier repeats.

"Oh," Giselle says. "I'm sorry. My friend doesn't speak English. I'll ask her."

She flips her hair over her shoulder and turns to me, eyes wide.

"Argent comptant ou dépôt?"

I have no idea what she just said or how to answer.

Giselle focuses her attention back on the clerk. "I'm sorry again," she says. "My friend also has trouble with speech. She'll take cash. *Merci.*"

The cashier slides two bundles of hundred-dollar bills across the counter, along with a printed form and pen. Giselle fills out the form and slides it in my direction, tapping the bottom with her pen.

"Signez ici." She holds out the pen. I hesitate, and Giselle stabs the pen in my direction. "Signez ici!" she says urgently, then leans over and whispers in my ear. "You don't have a problem faking things, now, do you?"

I take the pen and look at the form, feeling like I might faint as I read the total cash amount in the winnings column: $20,125.00. Giselle has written *Beatrice Dickerson* beneath it, with an address in England. Beatrice. Wasn't that the name Emi said earlier? And why do I speak French if I'm from England? Trying not to pass out, I scribble an illegible signature on the bottom of the form, drop the pen, and take a quick step back.

Giselle hands the paperwork to the clerk with a smile, along with a passport she's dug from her bag. The clerk looks back and forth between me, the paperwork, and the passport for what feels like an entire lifetime. Once I've sweated enough to completely ruin Emi's dress, the clerk stamps the paperwork, files it away, and shoves the passport and money across the counter.

Giselle scoops it up and we turn to leave. Not fast enough, if you ask me.

"That was fun!" Giselle says brightly as we head back toward the bar.

Fun? For who? I wonder. Definitely not me.

"What?" Giselle says, coming to a complete stop. "Don't you enjoy seeing what you can get away with?" She grabs my purse, opens it up, and shoves both bundles of cash inside.

I stiffen. "What are you talking about?" I say in a low whisper. "I don't want that." What I want is to get out of here. This can't be legal, taking this cash under a *fake name*. I begin to panic. If they're going to bust me, will they do it now—or wait until I walk out the doors with the evidence, like a shoplifter?

"Don't you, though?" Giselle says.

The thing is, Giselle is right. I do want the money. And so much more.

"Go on! You won it, fair and square," Giselle continues. "Well, mostly fair and square, *Beatrice*. So you should keep it." She flashes a huge smile.

I feel eyes on me. The security guards, who seem to have grown in number around the casino. The hidden cameras in the ceiling, trailing my every move.

Emiene.

She's sitting at the bar ahead, long legs crossed and champagne glass in hand, *watching*. Waiting for me to slip up. She's like a gun aimed right at me.

And Giselle keeps handing her bullets, one by one.

151

Dear Mom,

I'm back at the penthouse for Thanksgiving right now, and yeah, it sucks. Britney made a Tofurky (yes, a tofu turkey) last night for dinner. And Dad (you know, Mr. Steak-and-Potatoes, ketchup on the side) actually pretended to LIKE it! (It tasted like a poorly seasoned sponge.) If that wasn't bad enough, Britney made us go around the table to share what we were thankful for (you should have heard Dad gush about HER, and then her big thankful speech for her family, gag!), and all I have to say is that she should be thankful I didn't accidentally stick a fork in her eye.

Today, the two of them went to some function. Josie was out running some errands while Knox napped, and I was bored just sitting around by myself. So I printed out a bunch of maniacally grinning Willem Dafoe faces. Then I snuck into Dad's office and taped them over the faces of the various heads of state and Very Important People that Dad has all those handshake pictures with (and as you know, there are a LOT—I actually had to print a second batch of Dafoe heads, ha ha!). Let's see how long it takes Dad to notice he's spent the last twenty years rubbing elbows with the Green Goblin and not the Windsors. Snort!

After that, I texted Emi to see if she wanted to hang. But, big shocker, she's not in the city this weekend. Instead, she's with Zane and his family in Philadelphia.

Josie was still out when Knox woke up early from his nap and started to cry. I panicked. I was all by myself and had no idea what to do with a crying baby! But I couldn't just leave him there, howling, could I? So I crept into his nursery, feeling like an intruder, and carefully lifted him from his crib. Mom, he was so small and I was so scared I might break him (seriously, how did you know what to do with me??). But the weird thing was, as soon as I cradled him in my arms, his cries stopped.

I gently rocked him, singing that lullaby you used to sing to me (remember the one about the boy who lost his apple . . . Señora Santana, por qué llora el niño?). And then you know what happened? Knox smiled at me, the purest little smile, and this awful feeling of guilt washed over me. I'd been so wrong about him. Blaming him for coming along and upending my world. When it's not his fault, is it? He's just a baby. An innocent bystander in this entire mess. He never asked to be born. He sure didn't ask for crappy parents like Britney and Dad. Right then, I resolved to always look out for him and be his protector, to act like the good big sister I'm supposed to be.

Anyway, I head back to Prep tomorrow morning, and I'm sort of dreading it. Emi will be talking about her weekend with Zane. Viv will be stressing about her early decision app to Dartmouth while giving me the side-eye the entire time.

As for Wyatt, ever since that night in Unterman's office, he won't even look at me anymore. It's like I've ceased to exist. I thought I could handle it. But it hurts, Mom. So much more than I expected. I can't stop replaying that moment with him beneath Unterman's desk, over and over in my head. The soft brush of his lips as they touched mine. The woodsy scent of his skin, like pine needles and fresh air. The way my heart swelled, just to be near him again.

The horrible ache in my chest when he pulled away, hurt and angry.

I'll never forget the look on his face. Like I'd morphed from the Giselle he'd loved into something terrible. Someone he didn't recognize. I'm not a horrible person, though, am I?

Don't I deserve love? Happiness?

Ugh, and then there's Maggie.

What am I supposed to do about her?

I thought about confronting her. But what would I say? Oh, hey, I broke into your student file—no biggie!—and it turns out you're a liar! A liar who clearly has some sort of fixation on me, and by the way, can I have the letter back that you swiped during homecoming?

That wouldn't work, though.

Besides, as Dad always says, keep your friends close . . . and your enemies closer.

I can do that.

So, I've kinda been . . . watching. And testing her. Whenever I can, I work Switzerland into the conversation and ask her questions. Just to watch her squirm a little. And a couple of days ago, I asked if she played any sports because I was thinking of doing track in the spring and maybe she'd like to do it with me. (Emi nearly fell out of her chair—I know, first country music and now running. Oh well, it's kinda fun to watch her squirm a little, too.)

Maggie, though, she looked at me with a straight face and said she was too much of a klutz to run. Would probably trip over her own feet and face-plant.

And so the lies continue.

But that's okay. I know how to play the long game. We'll be at the chalet in a few weeks for winter break, and I'm going to do a little digging around town.

So for now, I'll wait and watch. Watch and wait.

And when the time is right, I'll strike.

DAY 3

Latitude, longitude: 25.095549, -77.400134
Just off the coast of Nassau, Bahamas

The Escape's engines grind down as the yacht slows, preparing to dock in Nassau, Bahamas. I can hear the deckhands shouting to each other just outside the lounge area, where the girls and I have gathered to disembark for our night at the casino.

One look at their cocktail dresses and it's immediately clear I've misjudged the dress code for tonight. Vivian is decked out in her favorite pale blue that perfectly matches her liquid-blue eyes and the coordinating streak in her hair. Emi and Giselle have both gone for strapless sequined numbers, one silver, one gold, that make them look like a pair of twin glittering disco balls.

I'm wearing a pair of denim shorts, a T-shirt, and a Prep sweatshirt tied around my waist in case the AC in the casino is cranked too high.

"Hmm, you're not planning to wear that, are you?" Giselle asks in an overly sweet voice, eyebrows raised.

I'm immediately taken back to the fourth-grade playground, standing in front of Allison as she looked me up and down with a smirk on her face.

"Hey, Maggie," Allison had said that day. "Did you forget to brush your hair this morning? I think there are twigs stuck in it!"

I'd reached up and touched my head. For all I knew, there *was* a twig stuck in there somewhere. Mom didn't have the time—or energy after working all night—to help untangle the knot that was my hair. My stomach began to ache. Allison giggled, twirling a perfect blond pigtail around her finger. A pack of curious playground onlookers inched closer to see what was going on.

"M-m-m-m," I began, feeling the burn of eyes watching me.

"What did you say?" Allison asked, cupping her hand over her ear. "I can't understand you. Are you trying to talk? You sound funny."

My face flamed red. "M-m-m-m . . ." I stammered out.

"Oh!" Allison said, eyes wide with fake innocence. "You want your *mommy*! Is that what you said?"

I wanted nothing more in that moment than to run off that playground, down the street, and far, far away. Keep running until dumb Allison and the dumber town of Westville were little more than a tiny dot in the distant horizon.

I tried again to answer, but I couldn't. The words sat on my tongue like a herd of cows that refused to get out of the road. I'd been practicing with the school's speech language pathologist, but the more stressed I got, the harder it got to speak.

"M-m-m-m . . ."

"Hey!" Allison shouted. "Has anyone seen M-M-M-Maggie's

m-m-m-mommy?" She cracked up. "Oh, M-M-M-Mommy! Where are you? M-M-M-Maggie needs you!"

I sucked on my cheeks so I wouldn't cry.

Allison cackled.

And then something happened. I started to get mad.

What was Allison's problem, anyway? Out of all the kids in our class, why was *I* the one she'd always single out for ridicule? My pants were too short. Or my jacket smelled like the barn. Or why did I bring those no-name cookies in my lunch and, eww, didn't they taste *gross*?

It made no sense. Because the truth was, very little separated me from Allison (even if she did wear a brand-new—nonsmelly—North Face jacket and packed golden Oreos in her lunch every day). We were still just varying degrees of small-town nobodies. It wouldn't be until much later that I'd understand. Allison lashed out in my direction—not because she hated me—but because she saw in me the one thing that scared her most about herself.

Back then, though, I'd had enough. All I'd wanted was for her to STOP.

So I walked over to the swings and picked up a clump of mud. Then I walked back to Allison and smooshed it on top of her head. I watched, wordlessly, as it dribbled slowly down the side of her face, leaving streaks of wet dirt behind.

Allison's eyes went wide in shock.

The rest of the playground went silent.

I breathed in through my nose, screwed up my courage, and

looked her right in the green-blue eyes. Speaking slowly and carefully, I said, "Hey. Allison. I think you've got sssssssome-thing in *your* hair."

Another moment of dead silence passed.

And then the rest of the kids began to laugh. Nervously at first, then louder and louder. Nobody had ever stood up to Allison before. Nobody knew what to make of it. But something changed that day. She never bothered me—or anyone else—again. Then, two years later, when we started middle school, she was suddenly gone. Transferred by her parents with no explanation to the local Catholic school. By the time she rejoined our class in high school, she was completely different. Quiet. Kind. A little withdrawn. We never spoke about that day in fourth grade.

She became my best friend. My ride-or-die. My everything.

Until I blew it all to bits.

And now here I am. Alone. *Again.*

But then again, maybe I always have been.

Maybe it's just taken me seventeen years to fully realize it.

I stand up straight and look Giselle right in the eyes, not letting myself stutter, sorry there isn't a ball of mud nearby to heave in her direction. Then I return Giselle's fake sweet smile. My chance will come to balance the scales later.

"At least my sandals are sort of cute?" I say.

Giselle laughs. "True. There's plenty of time to run back to your room and change the rest of it. We'll wait."

"Yeah, about that . . . I didn't exactly pack any dresses."

"What, still waiting on your luggage from Switzerland?" Emi says.

I tug at the hoodie around my waist, annoyed. Because I can't help but feel like I've been set up. That everything about this trip has been designed to push my buttons.

"I'd let you borrow something," Viv offers. She hesitates, because clearly none of her dresses will fit me and we both know it. "But, um, my undertones are more yellow-gold and yours are definitely a pink, so I don't think my stuff would really complement your coloring."

"Emi, maybe you have something she can borrow? You two are about the same size," Giselle says with an Allison-on-the-playground look of wide-eyed innocence.

"What?" Emi says. She looks back and forth between me and Giselle.

"You must have something she can borrow, right, Em?" Giselle says again, with a bit more force in her voice. "You packed at least a half dozen dresses. I'm sure you won't be wearing them all in the next two days, right?"

Emi exhales loudly. "Yeah, sure. I probably have something."

I follow Emi to the suite at the front of the yacht that she and Giselle are sharing. I have to stop myself from gasping out loud when we walk inside. Earlier today, I was too worried about getting caught and didn't take much time to look around. Now I do. The suite is even more massive than I'd realized. Nearly twice the size of the one I'm staying in, with an enormous bedroom, separate sitting area, wet bar, and night-sky mural painted across the high ceiling. When Emi flicks on the lights, the constellations overhead twinkle.

I stand with my arms folded across my chest while Emi opens the door to the walk-in closet. *A walk-in closet.* On a boat. Just when I think I've seen it all, I get a gander at something else.

Emi drags a bunch of padded hangers across the rod, flicking through more clothes than I've probably owned in a lifetime. The start of a headache claws at the base of my skull. I consider calling it a night and going to bed early. Let the girls casino it up without me. I'm honestly not sure how much more pretending I can take before I crack.

Then Emi grabs a dress. The most beautiful dress I've ever seen. Vibrant red, cut above the knee, with a single shoulder strap of sewn-together delicate fabric flowers.

"How about this one? Matches your hair perfectly, yeah?"

Nana always said redheads shouldn't wear red. But when I dodge into the bathroom and try the dress on, I realize how wrong she was about that. One hundred percent, totally *wrong.* I inspect myself in the full-length mirror by the door, in awe of how the bright color contrasts perfectly with my fair skin and makes my blue eyes pop. My legs look a mile long, not at all like the pair of tree trunks I usually see. Is this really me? I feel like Julia Roberts in that old movie Mom loves so much.

"Big mistake," I say with a grin as I push the bathroom door open. *"Big. Huge!"*

"Huh?" Emi says, nose scrunched. "You don't like the dress?"

"Sorry, just quoting a movie," I say, blushing. *"Pretty Woman?*

The scene in the boutique?"

"Yeah, right," Emi says. "Never saw it. Misogynistic crap."

Sort of an ironic statement coming from someone who as far as I can tell lets her boyfriend call the shots, but whatever.

She cocks her head to the side.

"What is it?" I say, hit with a sudden wave of self-consciousness. "Is it too short?" Although we have similar builds, I'm a couple of inches taller than Emi. I yank on the hem, wondering if I'm showing just a bit too much thigh, long legs be damned.

"No, no. It's perfect. You look incredible. Better than I do in that thing, really. *Bitch*," she says with a forced laugh.

The heat rises in my cheeks.

"Kidding," Emi says. Except, of course, I know she's not.

"Listen, I'll change. You don't have to let me borrow your dress," I say. "It looks really expensive. I can just hang here while you guys go to the casino. This has been fun anyway. Like playing dress-up. Haven't done that since I was little. And your dress-up selection is a lot better than that trunk full of mothballed clothes in my nana's basement."

"Ha," Emi says. "It's fine. You can wear it. Giselle's right. I have more dresses than I need. I was just thinking you should put your hair up. Do something a little different. I can do your makeup, too."

I feel the yacht connect with the docks. "I don't know if I really have time for that."

"Sure you do. Sit down. I'll help." Emi motions to a chair in front of a dressing table and disappears into the bedroom. Why is she suddenly being nice to me?

Watch your back . . .

I slowly lower myself into the chair, still tense from that message this morning, and face the mirror. There are a bunch of photographs and Polaroids stuck around the edge: Emi and Giselle building sandcastles on the beach; Giselle, Emi, and Vivian posing on the Prep green in formal dresses, arms wrapped tightly around each other. My gaze flicks to a time-faded snapshot of Giselle's mom, holding baby Giselle and gazing lovingly at her. I can't tear my eyes from it. I pluck it from the mirror, closely inspecting the image, immediately recognizing the hand-hewn beams of the art studio in the background.

"What are you doing with that?" Emi says, startling me. She's coming out of the bedroom, clutching a giant Caboodle and scowling.

"Nothing. Just looking." I force a casual smile, trying to calm my trembling hand. "Giselle's mom was really pretty."

"She was," Emi says flatly, staring at the picture. "You should put that back. It doesn't belong to you. It's not cool to take things that aren't yours, you know."

"Yes, I know." I jam the picture into its spot, biting back the urge to tell Emi off once and for all. I don't need her to distrust me any more than she already does.

Emi plunks the Caboodle onto the dressing table and silently begins twisting my hair into a loose bun, securing it with a handful of gold bobby pins. A few tendrils escape next to my face. Emi twirls them around her fingers and spritzes them with hair spray, leaving behind soft ringlets.

"You've known Giselle forever, huh?" I ask, hoping to steer the discussion to something more useful.

"Since we were babies." Emi catches my eye in the mirror. "We pretty much grew up together. But you knew that already, didn't you?"

"Just trying to make conversation."

"Is that what you're doing?"

I give her a little shrug in response.

"Yeah, I thought so. That's enough talking. Hold still." Emi spins my chair around, then grabs black liner and carefully rims my eyes. Her minty breath is hot on my face. I don't say anything else as she dusts powder over my cheeks and chest and dabs mascara onto my eyelashes.

"Okay. Ready to have a look?" she says.

I nod. She turns me back toward the mirror. "Voilà!"

It's almost hard to believe that it's me in the reflection. I look glamorous, like a movie star. One of the beautiful people. Not a trace of that knotty-haired girl from the fourth-grade playground to be found on my glistening lips or the delicate curve of my neck.

"Wow, thanks," I say, lightly touching a hand to my updo. "You're really good at this."

"Eh, I spent half my childhood stuck backstage at fashion shows with my mom. Picked up a few tricks. It's no big deal. The thing is, you need to cultivate your own look. You know, instead of copying someone else's." My stomach twists. Emi's mouth opens again, but she doesn't say anything.

"What?" I ask, not sure I even want to know.

Emi pauses briefly. "Well, probably I shouldn't say this, but—"

"But?" I don't like the feeling working its way up my spine.

"Giselle does this sort of thing," she says with a sigh. She packs up her Caboodle, clicking brushes and compacts into place.

"Does what?" I ask. "Doesn't tell people to pack dresses?"

"No. Gets fascinated with someone new," Emi says. "She collects people. She's been like this forever, always getting enamored with the new and different. Random summer people in the Hamptons, some barista at the corner coffee shop who's suddenly the most fascinating person she's ever met. A couple of years ago it was this girl Beatrice from England she couldn't get enough of."

"Beatrice?" I ask. I can't think of anyone at school with that name.

"Yeah, it was right around the time Giselle's mom got sick, so I don't know. Maybe she was a distraction. Something new and shiny to take Giselle's mind off her mom. She even started talking with an accent and drinking tea. Every day they were off on their own little planet, swapping clothes and giggling at their own private jokes. And then one day, Giselle was just . . . done with her. Bored, I guess. The thrill wore off and she dropped her without a word. Next thing you know, Beatrice gets expelled and we never saw her again."

"Why are you telling me this?" I can barely squeak the words out. Emi's dress suddenly feels too small, too fancy, too ill-fitting on me.

"So you won't be surprised," Emi says matter-of-factly.

"Surprised?"

"When she does it to you," Emi says. "Because Giselle always comes back in the end. To me."

Dear Mom,

We're at the chalet for winter break. Got here yesterday. I haven't had a chance to leave once because this place has been crawling with reporters who are doing feature stories on Dad as he gears up for his big campaign announcement. It's been torture. Plus, everywhere I look, I see reminders of you. Your painting of the mountains that hangs over the fireplace. The antique washbasin you found at that farmer's market and refinished that now holds fresh-cut flowers in the foyer. I keep expecting to see you come around the corner wearing a paint-splattered smock, laughing and chasing me with a paintbrush.

Instead, I'm treated to Britney prancing about in her designer ski outfits (even though I'm pretty sure she doesn't ski—just sits in the lodge taking selfies for her blog).

I've been spending most of my time playing with Knox, and hiding out from Dad and his handlers in your art studio. The one that you had built the summer before I was born, separate from the main house, with the floor-to-ceiling windows overlooking the mountains. Sometimes I feel like the hand-hewn wood beams that crisscross the ceiling have absorbed your spirit or something, like your essence has been captured in the dappled sunshine that filters through the skylight.

Everything is like you left it (mainly because I won't let them change anything!). Your paintbrushes and jars line the window-sill; your last painting still sits on its easel, missing half the sky. Dad wanted to clean out your stuff so Britney could turn the space into a meditation studio. A MEDITATION STUDIO!!!

Over my dead body is all I have to say.

A reporter from the Times was here this afternoon, doing a day-in-the-life story on Senator Haverford and his young family. Dad put on his flannel shirt and jeans and did his best impression of a man of the people (Health care for all! Let's not forget the small-businessperson is the backbone of our great nation! Blah, blah, blah.). Then he propped me and Knox in front of the Christmas tree for a family photo shoot with him and Britney (gag).

Of course, the minute the reporter left, he forked Knox over to Josie, because heaven forbid Dad actually play with him or change his dirty diaper.

It's pathetic. I can't even imagine how Josie feels. Every day she misses tucking her kids into bed back in Guatemala—all so Dad can ignore his own.

You know what else sucks? I actually thought Dad might be different when it came to Knox. That maybe Dad kept his distance when I was growing up because he couldn't get into all the "girl" stuff you and I did together—the tea parties and dress-up and spa days. I thought maybe having that son he always wanted might change him.

Yeah, right.

Knox is another prop.

Just like me.

I tried to talk to him tonight at dinner about something other than school, grades, Dartmouth, blah, blah, blah. Something meaningful, you know, that didn't have to do with his image (or mine). Then I tried to make him laugh by asking if he'd run into Willem Dafoe lately, and all he did was admonish me for my immaturity and say it took the housekeeper an hour to clean up his Very Important Photographs.

Sometimes I really hate him.

Even worse, I swear it's like he hates me back. Like tonight, I caught him giving me this look that I couldn't quite read. Like he was analyzing me. Maybe I look too much like you. Maybe I'm a constant reminder that he couldn't completely erase his old life.

Not without erasing me, too.

DAY 3

APRIL 14—MIDDAY

Latitude, longitude: 31.240985, -77.838093
200 nautical miles from the Bahamas

The sun loungers have been perfectly spaced around the infinity pool, a carefully rolled white towel placed on each. I drag my chair into the shade beneath the upper deck's overhang, away from the other girls. Emi shoots me a questioning look.

"What, do we smell or something?" she asks.

I shake my head. "Too much sun over there. Only way I'll ever get a tan is if my freckles suddenly decide to spontaneously merge." I try to feign a casual smile, but my heart is thumping against my rib cage, refusing to let me relax. I lower myself into the lounger and close my eyes, trying to pretend I'm not trapped here with someone who wants to torment me.

The Escape glides up and over the waves, and my stomach bottoms out each time the ship drops back down. On the deck above, I can hear the crew moving chairs, mopping, and undoubtedly shining every surface until it sparkles. There's an occasional request from one of the girls to another to pass the sunscreen, but it's mostly quiet otherwise.

The sun blazes in the cloudless sky above, and I can feel its intense heat beating down, even here in the shade. I turn to my side, then my back, then my front. But I can't get comfortable. And it's not the nonstop motion of the boat making me queasy or the sun's heat that's making me sweat. Every time I open my eyes, I check for someone. Watching me. Coiled like a snake in the grass, ready to strike. I search their perfect faces for clues. Which one of them sent the message?

Watch your back . . .

I edge my chair even closer to the wall. I'd drag it straight off this boat if I could.

Vivian laughs at some joke I didn't hear, and the other girls join in.

We're only halfway through this trip, and already I want to get away.

But we're in the middle of the Atlantic Ocean, miles from shore. There are two decks below me, one above, and then nothing but endless, churning water. I fight back the nausea creeping up the back of my throat like a slimy hand, reaching its fingers into my nose, behind my eyes. If I let it grab hold, I might go under. And then what? Everything falls apart, and I'm back where I started.

"You okay over there?" Vivian says, squinting in my direction with her hand cupped over her eyes. "You don't look so hot."

"A little seasick," I say.

"Want me to get you some of my herbal tea?" she asks. "It really helps."

I shake my head. "I'll be fine, thanks."

"Okay, let me know if you change your mind."

"I have a better idea." Emi swings her legs off her lounger and walks to the small bar next to the pool. There are three bars on the yacht: one on this deck, one on the top deck by the hot tub, and one in the dining lounge on the second deck. Emi riffles through the bottles and sighs.

"Ugh," she says. "Who drinks this much gin?"

Giselle laughs and flips from her back to her stomach, bronze skin shimmering in the sunshine, and unhitches her silver bikini top. I'm reminded of a chameleon basking in the hot sun, changing colors with its surroundings. Dad's classic rock music from the barn suddenly plays in my head. *All things to everyone . . . run, runaway.*

"You'll have to take that up with Senator Haverford," Giselle says. "Or go upstairs and get something else."

"Nah, don't feel like it," Emi says. "We'll make do. Who wants a Long Island iced tea, heavy on the gin?"

She doesn't wait for an answer, mixing four drinks and passing them around. A glass clunks on the table next to me. I take a tentative sip, just to be polite, and have to stop myself from spitting. Apparently, Emi's idea of a Long Island iced tea is dumping a bit of everything over ice.

Giselle sips hers and gags. "Yuck, Em. What is this?"

"A quick way to loosen things up?"

"Reminds me of sophomore year," Vivian says. "What did you call that concoction, Em? The garbage pail? Which is about right because I barfed into one for an entire weekend after drinking it!"

172

Emi laughs.

As the day gets longer, the sun inches around the overhang I'm sitting beneath. The tops of my feet begin to burn. I climb from the lounger. "Be right back," I say. "Need to grab some more sunscreen."

"Oh!" Vivian says. "You can use some of mine. It's organic."

Of course it is. I glance at the bottle in her hand. "Thanks. That won't work. I need SPF one thousand. Just going to run to my room real quick."

Giselle sits up, clutching her loosened bikini top to her chest. "Hey, Mags? I left my phone in my room to charge. You mind grabbing it for me on your way? It's on the nightstand next to the bed."

"Yeah, sure. Of course."

I slip my cover-up over my head and walk down the hall to Giselle's suite. It's all of twenty steps from the pool, which makes me wonder why she'd bother sending me to get it.

I walk into the room and hurry through the massive sitting area to the bedroom in the back. I'm tempted to look around, but there isn't time. I have a few minutes alone with Giselle's phone, and I'm going to take full advantage of it.

I find the phone sitting facedown on the nightstand and unplug it. The screen lights up with a picture of Giselle in a pair of red-and-green-checkered pajamas, holding baby Knox in front of the Christmas tree at the chalet. Her hair is pulled back off her makeup-free face and her smile is genuine and warm, crinkling the corners of her eyes. It's a smile I haven't seen since before we returned to school from winter break.

I palm the phone and glance over my shoulder, stomach clenching with guilt.

This may be wrong, but I need to know if Giselle is You-CantRun. Heart thudding, I tap the screen and a password prompt appears. I blow out a breath and try a few number combinations—Giselle's birthday, her mom's, the date her mom died. None of them work, and I'm three attempts away from getting locked out completely. On a whim, I suck in my cheeks and raise my eyebrows slightly to see if I can fool the facial recognition. It doesn't work, of course. I drop the phone in my pocket, frustrated.

I'm about to leave when the corner of something pink and sparkly wedged under the mattress catches my eye. Kneeling, I yank the thing out. It's a journal, hot pink and covered in sequins, complete with a heart-shaped lock. It doesn't look at all like something Giselle would own. Way too cheap and tacky. I wonder if it's even hers. Maybe it's Emi's. Or maybe it's been stuffed under this mattress since Giselle was ten. I lick my lips and pull at the lock. It doesn't budge. I squeeze the sides of the journal and try to peek in at the pages. Definitely Giselle's handwriting. And I think I saw my name. A shiver snakes up my spine.

"Maggie?"

I jolt upright, nearly jumping out of my skin. Heart racing, I shove the journal into my pocket and turn around, feeling the heat creep up my neck. I do not need to get caught snooping.

Again. What is the matter with me? Curiosity kills the cat, as Nana always says. And at this rate, I should be dead several times over.

"Why were you on the floor?" Emi asks from the doorway.

"Dropped Giselle's phone," I answer. "Thank God it didn't break. Anyway, gonna pop to my room for the sunscreen and I'll see you back on deck."

I hurry past her, the journal burning a hole in my pocket. I hardly breathe until I've made it back to my room. I try a few times to spring the lock, twisting it and prying it with a pen. But all I manage to do is break the pen. This is ridiculous. The smart thing to do would be to slip into Giselle's room and put this journal back where I found it.

But I don't do the smart thing.

I open my room safe and lock it inside, where I've been keeping all my secrets.

Then I grab my sunscreen, catch my breath, and head back upstairs. I hand Giselle her phone, palms still slick with sweat from fiddling with the journal's lock.

"Thanks," Giselle says with a smile that doesn't quite reach her eyes. "I was beginning to wonder if you were coming back. Was getting ready to send out a search party, ha ha."

Emi is back on her lounger, stretched out in the sun. Her eyes flick suspiciously in my direction. "Find what you were looking for?"

I hold up the bottle of sunscreen and quickly retreat to my own chair. I close my eyes and try to tune out the other girls.

But my mind races; the hole I've decided to dig myself getting deeper by the minute.

The afternoon melts away, and Christopher shows up in his perfectly pressed white uniform, carrying trays of mini sandwiches and fresh fruit. "Afternoon tea is served, as you requested, Miss Haverford." He sets the trays on a round table, staring straight ahead. "Do you require anything else?"

"Yes!" Vivian says, sitting up. "You could hang with us a little! Emi will make you a drink. She's excellent at it!"

Giselle shoots her a look, and I'm not sure if it's in reference to inviting Christopher to stay or Emi's terrible bartending abilities.

"I am sorry, Miss Page," Christopher answers, sounding way more formal than anyone just out of college should. Even a yacht steward. "That would be against the rules. I need to get back to work. Will that be all?" His eyes dart nervously toward Giselle and then he stares at his feet, cheeks flushed.

"Yes, thank you. You can go, Christopher," Giselle says dismissively. I can't help but think of Mom, hauling linens and answering midnight buzzers at Nightingale Eldercare. The stiffness in her neck and aching in her knees that seem to get a little bit worse after every shift. The paychecks that are never quite enough, even when she pulls back-to-back shifts. Resentment bubbles just beneath the surface of my skin.

"Yes, Miss Haverford." Christopher hurries off, and I swear I can hear him exhale a sigh of relief the minute he turns the corner and practically runs down the stairs.

Emi whistles and shakes her head. "Aw, look at poor love-struck Christopher. What happened between you two after we left last night, anyway?"

A look of irritation crosses Vivian's face. "I thought you said *nothing* happened."

"Nothing did," Giselle answers, and I know she's lying through her teeth. "He's nobody. Forget about it. Let's eat."

Nobody.

Who does Giselle think she is, anyway? Maybe she's nobody, too.

I try not to let my irritation with her take over my brain as we sit at the table and nosh on miniature tuna and lobster sandwiches, mangos, and strawberries. Everything tastes like it was just plucked from the vine or fished from the ocean. I nurse my Long Island iced tea until it's basically melted ice, and then grab a Sanpellegrino from behind the bar. We still have a night at the casino ahead, and I need to pace myself. I can't let myself get too wasted around Giselle—or any of them, really. I need to keep a clear head.

When we finish our food, Vivian pushes the plates aside, then rubs her hands together and grins.

"Stay right here," she says. "I've got something fun for us!"

She grabs her beach bag and pulls out a deck of cards.

"What are those? Getting ready for tonight?" Giselle asks, eyebrows quirked.

"Even better!" Vivian says. She sits back down and spreads the deck in front of her. The cards are oversized, deep blue with an eye in the center, surrounded by multicolored shards of light. They don't look like a regular deck of playing cards.

"Are those tarot cards?" Emi asks, nose scrunched.

"Yes! I'm learning how to do readings. Who wants to go first?"

"Not me," Emi answers, scooting back in her chair. "Those things creep me out."

"How about you, then, Maggie?" Vivian says, eyes wide and imploring. "You're not afraid, are you? They're just *cards*. They can be very useful, you know."

I clear my throat. "Okay, sure. What's there to be afraid of? I'll do it."

Vivian hands me the cards.

"Okay, first you need to shuffle them." She pauses. "Ooh! Emi, can you record this? My followers would love it." Vivian hands Emi her phone and turns her focus back to me. "So, while you're shuffling, you should focus on a question or intention you have. That's super important. Make sure to really concentrate. Otherwise, you won't get a good reading."

"An intention?" I ask. "What do you mean?"

"You know, like 'Someday I will be a great architect and design beautiful buildings around the world!'" she says. "Or you can ask a simple question, like 'What does the next month hold in store?' But don't say it out loud!"

"Okay."

My thoughts are a mash-up of questions and intentions, continually circling back to: *Which one of you is YouCantRun?*

I don't think a deck of cards can answer that.

I finish shuffling.

"Good!" Vivian says. "Now divide the cards into three piles and place them in front of you."

I do as she says, setting the cards on the smooth surface of the table. Vivian waves her hand across the cards like a magician, making sure to smile at the phone in Emi's hand.

"Now," Vivian says, "flip the top card of each pile."

"Okay."

Vivian's face twists to the side. I look at my cards. There's a man hanging upside down by one ankle on the first one, a tower engulfed in flames being hit by lightning on the second, and a naked man and woman standing in what looks like a pair of tombs on the last. Yikes.

Vivian lets out a shuddering breath.

"What's the matter? What do those cards mean?" I'm not sure I even want to know, because they all look pretty terrible. As far as I can tell, I'm going to get hung, hit by lightning, and then put in my grave. Maybe Emi was right about these things.

"So this first card, the Hanged Man, is your past," Vivian says. "It represents some sort of pause in your life, surrendering something. Letting go. Does that make any sense to you?"

I shrug, even though Allison's tear-streaked face slides to the front of my mind.

"That could mean coming to Prep," Vivian volunteers brightly. "Leaving your old school. Something like that. What do you think?"

179

"Yeah, maybe," I say, shifting uncomfortably in my chair, ready to move on. "Could be. What about the rest of them?"

Emi and Giselle lean in closer to inspect the cards, suddenly interested.

"The next card represents the present," Vivian says with authority, one finger in the air. "That's the Tower card. It signals a sudden upheaval, broken pride." She clears her throat. "Disaster."

Nobody says anything. Finally, Giselle breaks the silence.

"Jeez, glad we're docking in a few hours, then," she says with a laugh. "I don't need a disaster at sea!"

"Ha, yeah," Vivian says. "It doesn't necessarily mean *literal* disaster, though. The upheaval could be more like an insight. You know, that you have about yourself? You've been hit by a proverbial bolt of lightning, like on the card." She taps it with her manicured finger.

"Sure, got it," I say, but my eyes have already roved to the last card.

The tombs.

That can't possibly be good.

"That one," Vivian says, swallowing hard. "Is the Judgment card."

"And?" Giselle asks.

"Hold on," Vivian says. "I need to check my book."

She pulls a small paperback, *Guide to the Tarot*, from her bag and flips to a page in the middle. Her lips move as she reads. Then she slams the book shut and stuffs it away.

"Okay," she says, clearing her throat. "The Judgment card represents your future. Judgment Day. Some sort of reckoning."

"Like when I'm dead?" I say, a shudder coursing its way through my body. "Standing in my own grave? Like that?"

"Only metaphorically speaking," Vivian says. "The card represents reflection. You could even say an awakening, if you choose. Standing before the ultimate judge. The cards are open to interpretation."

I sure hope they are. This is one time I'm kind of in agreement with Emi. These things are creepy as hell.

Giselle grabs the deck, shuffles, and sets them down. "Do me."

"Okay. First you need to divide them into three piles," Vivian says.

"I don't want to," Giselle says. "I'm only interested in one card. My future."

Vivian shrugs. "It doesn't work like that, but suit yourself."

Giselle reaches over and flips the top card. She stares at it, but her face is a neutral mask, revealing nothing. Emi lets out a little gasp and the hair on the back of my neck pricks up. Nobody says anything as we wait for Vivian to speak up.

It's at that moment Christopher appears out of nowhere to clear our dirty dishes, breaking the silence and making us jump.

He quickly stacks the dishes on a silver tray and scurries away, as though the floor around us is made of hot lava.

All that's left on the table now is the pile of cards.

And the one sitting on top: a skeletal grim reaper, cloaked in a black shroud and wielding a scythe.

Death.

Emi stops recording and grabs the entire stack. She shoves them at Vivian.

"Put these freaky things away, Viv," she says. "Seriously!"

"Fine." Vivian sighs. She jams the cards back in her bag with a little huff. "You didn't even give me a chance to explain. Death isn't always a bad card. It doesn't just mean actual death. It can mean a new beginning. The death of one thing and the start of another."

"Whatever," Emi says. "I don't like them."

I don't like them, either. Even though they're gone, I can't shake the image of the last two cards from my head. Giselle's, the Death card, the hand reaching out with bony fingers.

And me, a desperate figure standing in an open grave with eyes cast skyward, awaiting final judgment.

LIVE REPORT FROM KEY WEST, FLORIDA
APRIL 16, 1:45 P.M.

ANCHOR: Good afternoon. More breaking news at this hour in the tropical island town of Key West, Florida, as the frantic search continues in the Gulf of Mexico for Senator Robert Haverford's teenage daughter, Giselle. We are joined live by Marilyn Macy with new developments that might shed some light on this evolving situation. Over to you, Marilyn.

MARILYN: Thank you, Cameron. I am here on Duval Street at the famous Sloppy Joe's Bar, where Giselle Haverford and three friends were reportedly seen partying last evening by Key West resident Kenny Harris. Thank you for joining us, Mr. Harris.

KENNY HARRIS: Call me Kenny! And call Handy Kenny's Repairs Service for all your handyman needs!

MARILYN: Okay, thank you, Kenny. Now, about last night. Can you tell us what you witnessed?

KENNY: Yeah, so I was sitting right here, same spot I always sit. Can see where my elbows have rubbed the finish off the bar right there, he-he. Right, sorry . . . so anyway, these four girls come in 'round happy hour time. Couldn't miss 'em. Young. Beautiful. Definitely tourists. They're easy to pick out. The tourists, I mean. Always staring at the pictures and flags and ordering those awful frozen drinks. Couldn't pay me to drink one of those things. I reckon I've spent half my life at this very spot, and I've never seen 'em open up one of those drink machines and clean it out.

MARILYN: And how did you know these four girls were Giselle Haverford and her friends?

KENNY: I didn't at first. But then I saw their pictures all over the news. Recognized the blonde. She was a damn looker. Took me a minute to figure out which one was the Giselle girl. Then I realized she was in a disguise.

MARILYN: A disguise?

KENNY: Yep. Had on a black wig. Looks better without it, if you ask me.

MARILYN: A wig, okay. Interesting. So did you notice anything else?

KENNY: Mostly just the usual stuff. They sat here drinkin' a bunch, making noise. Talkin' in these funny accents.

MARILYN: Funny accents?

KENNY: Yep, like they were Australian or from England or something. And then they kinda split off. The Giselle girl and the other dark-haired girl went off on their own. They were in the middle of the dance floor talking about something all intense-like. The redheaded one was sitting alone at the bar.

MARILYN: Interesting. And where was the fourth girl?

KENNY: Yeah, that's the funny part. Had to do a double take.

MARILYN: Why's that?

KENNY: She was sitting at the other side of the bar, talking to Buddy.

MARILYN: Buddy? Is he a local?

KENNY: Yep. Works a shrimp boat in the Tortugas, some odd jobs, you know. Surprised he ain't here right now.

MARILYN: And this was significant why?

KENNY: Well, you know. Girls like that blonde don't talk to guys like Buddy.

MARILYN: So this wasn't some random bar flirtation?

KENNY: He-he, no. Buddy wishes. Some cute blonde ain't chatting up Buddy, unless . . .

MARILYN: Unless?

KENNY: Unless they want something, you know what I mean?

MARILYN: Like?

KENNY: Some of the *good stuff.*

MARILYN: I see. What kind of good stuff are we talking about here? Prescription or illicit?

KENNY: Ah, crap, you figure what you want, I ain't saying more. Probably shouldn't be sayin' nothin' at all. Buddy ain't gonna be happy.

MARILYN: Very interesting insights . . . Thank you for speaking with us today, Kenny. Well, Cameron, as you've heard, it seems there was some underage drinking, possible drugs, and disagreements going on here among the spring breakers. Whether that contributed to what happened on board the Haverford yacht, we do not know. But we will continue to ask the tough questions and have more to you as the story develops. And, as always, our thoughts and prayers are with the Haverford family at this difficult time.

Dear Mom,

The reporter visits have let up and Dad and Britney went skiing, so I was finally able to get out of the house today. My first stop was for a huge cup of coffee from the cute little general store near the base lodge with the wooden bear out front. I haven't been sleeping much. That's not exactly new, though. I haven't really slept a full night in the last year. How could I?

And if you can believe it, last night I actually thought about swiping some of Britney's sleeping pills (that's right, the woman who preaches on her blog that all you need for a good night's rest are daily meditations and a positive attitude takes SLEEP-ING PILLS. She's such a phony!). But I couldn't bring myself to do it. Because the problem is, I don't WANT to sleep. If I sleep too long, too deeply, I might start to forget. Already, the memory of you is beginning to blur around the edges, like a photograph going out of focus.

After I got myself a giant coffee, I plugged Maggie's address from her file into my GPS and started driving.

I made my way into the valley, past a sad looking dollar store missing the R in dollar, a service station with a collection of wrecked cars parked alongside, a diner, and a small firehouse. There were no cute little candle shops or artisan cheese places or cozy brew pubs like in the village near the ski resort. No shiny Range Rovers or BMWs. Just a massive box of a store, Couture Hardware, with bags of salt and sand stacked alongside, and a bunch of pickup trucks with gun racks idling in the parking lot.

I followed the GPS down a long dirt road that snaked between the tall trees, their leafless branches clawing the gray sky like bony fingers. The road arched up and over a hill and the landscape opened to rolling fields covered in a layer of fresh white snow. The road forked in two different directions.

And that's where the GPS came to a dead stop.

I looked around. There wasn't a house in sight. Or a single road sign. Which way was I supposed to go? I was literally in the middle of nowhere.

I turned around, drove back into town, and parked at the hardware store. Maybe someone in there could give me directions. I tucked my hair into a hat and zipped my coat up to my chin, hoping nobody would recognize me. I walked into the store and a little bell jangled. The register to the right was empty. A bunch of dusty grills and lawn equipment sat to the left with "marked down" signs taped to the sides. The old wood floors creaked beneath my feet as I made my way across the narrow aisles stuffed with fishing poles and drawer pulls and nails and hoses and other random stuff.

I finally found someone standing on top of a ladder, rummaging through fishing supplies. She was about my age, with blond hair that hung halfway down her back.

Excuse me? I said.

The girl turned around. Oh, sorry! she said. I didn't hear you come in. She climbed down the ladder. Can I help you?

I read the name tag pinned to her blue apron: Allison.

Thanks, Allison, I said. I'm just trying to find a friend of mine who lives near here, but my GPS completely stopped while I was driving down Poor Farm Road.

Ha, Allison said with a smile. Sounds about right. Whose place are you looking for?

Maggie Mitchell's, I said. We go to school together.

The girl stopped smiling. Turn left out of the parking lot, she said flatly. Then go right onto Poor Farm, follow it to the fork, and bear right. Her place is about two miles down. Can't miss it. It's the one with the barn that looks like it's about to collapse, if it hasn't already.

Thanks, I said.

Yeah, well, don't thank me, Allison said. It's your funeral.

What do you mean by that? I asked.

I mean, you'd be better off going in the OPPOSITE direction of Maggie Mitchell, she said, and clomped up the ladder.

Wait, why? I said.

Allison took a deep breath and looked over her shoulder. Because . . .

Allison! a man called out from the next aisle, interrupting her. I don't pay you to hang around chatting with your friends!

You don't pay me at all, Dad, Allison mumbled under her breath, then glanced back at me. Sorry, I've got to work.

Then she turned around and started slamming tackle boxes into place, pointedly ignoring me.

I got back in the car.

And drove to Maggie's.

Her house was exactly where Allison described. And it was

189

exactly how Allison described it, only worse. I slowed to a stop in front of a battered sign that read "Mitchell Farms Est. 1807."

Maggie's truck was parked in the gravel driveway in front of an old farmhouse. White paint flaked from the sides like dead skin. Beyond that sat a barn so close to collapse it looked like all that held it together were a few rotten beams and a whole lot of wishful thinking. A cattle auction sign with a date from last June hung crookedly on the barn's faded red side. Behind the barn I could make out a small, dented blue trailer perched on cinder blocks.

Just then, the front door to the house swung open and a woman stepped out. She ran a wrinkled hand through her white hair, squinted at me, and waved. She said something I couldn't hear so I rolled down the window.

You lost? the woman asked.

It would have been easy to lie, say yes, and drive away.

But, well, I was here. Time to go ahead and confront this thing head-on.

No, I said, back with a smile. I'm Giselle. I'm a friend of Maggie's. From school. I was in town and thought I'd stop by and say hi.

Oh, the woman said. Come on in, why don't you? Get out of the cold!

I parked next to Maggie's truck and got out. The woman introduced herself as Gwen, Maggie's nana. I followed her inside.

The farmhouse floors were weathered, wide-planked oak that groaned as I walked across them. We passed through a small living area, where a black woodstove cranked out smoky heat. Plastic sheeting stretched across the windows, but the house still felt drafty and cold the farther we moved from the stove.

In the kitchen, a little girl who looked like a miniature version of Maggie—wild red hair and all—sat at a butcher-block table, stuffing her face with pancakes.

Who's that, Nana? she asked, mouth full.

Manners, the woman said to her. This is Maggie's friend Giselle. This is Maggie's sister, Sophia.

Nice to meet you, Sophia, I said, trying to remember if Maggie had mentioned having a sister. I don't think she ever did. But then, she never mentioned living just down the road from our chalet either, did she?

Sophia's eyes darted from me to her grandmother. I thought Maggie didn't have any friends, she said.

Oh dear, Maggie's grandmother said, shaking her head. Five-year-olds have no filter. Please, have a seat, Giselle. And have some pancakes! Won't hurt you to put a little meat on those bones. She winked and slid a plate full of steaming pancakes in front of me.

I had to grin, considering I'd spent the second half of junior year fending off faux "concern" from my friends about the fact I was drowning my sorrows in pints of Ben & Jerry's. Viv must have offered me a thousand different types of teas to help me "relax," which of course was her way of trying to nicely say "Fit in your jeans" again. Lord forbid any of us not be Insta perfect, right? I tucked in and took a big bite, thanking Gwen.

191

She smiled and dabbed away a little blob of syrup from Sophia's round cheek, and I suddenly felt so alone. What I wouldn't give for a kitchen that smelled like fresh pancakes and an aproned grandmother all soft in the middle who I could already tell gives amazing hugs. Like you did, Mom.

Still, there was something sad about this place. It wasn't the peeling paint or the old scuffed floors or the icy air creeping in around the windowsills. It was the circles under Gwen's eyes. The silence that even the small television in the corner playing cable news didn't seem to fill. The way everything felt stale and stagnant, like the inside of a tomb. I shuddered.

Maggie should be in from morning chores any minute, Gwen said. Nice of you to come by. Between us, I think Maggie's been a bit lonely. Been a tough year for her, as you know.

I nodded like I knew.

This is a beautiful table, I said, running my hand over the thick wood of the butcher block.

Why, thank you! Gwen's eyes lit up. My son, Maggie's dad, handcrafted this. He was, I mean is, quite the artisan. A hint of sadness flashed across her weathered face.

Just then, the back kitchen door swung open and Maggie stepped inside, shaking snow from her boots and carrying a basket of eggs. Her cheeks were pink from the cold and her red curls were gathered loosely on top of her head in a scrunchie, not smoothed out like she'd been wearing it at school. Maggie stopped short, nearly dropping the basket when she spotted me at the table.

Giselle? Her voice stuttered as she tried to compose herself. Um, what are you doing here?

I had to bite back the smirk that was trying to sneak out. *Gotcha!*

She's having breakfast with me and Nana! Sophia shouted around a mouthful of pancake. *Why did you lie, Maggie?*

Maggie blinked wordlessly at her sister.

You do have friends. See! Sophia pointed at me and jammed a piece of pancake in her already stuffed mouth. *She's sitting RIGHT THERE!!!*

I—I—I . . . Maggie choked out.

I let her squirm a minute, then I apologized. *Sorry to just pop in,* I said. *We're spending break at the chalet. I was bored and decided to take a drive and I couldn't believe it when I saw your truck! Why didn't you tell me you lived close by?*

We didn't always, Maggie said softly, not quite looking me in the eye.

Her grandmother must have sensed something was off because she quickly jumped in and explained Maggie's family had moved in to help on the farm after Maggie's grandfather died. She motioned for Maggie to sit. Maggie slumped into a chair while her grandmother loaded a plate of pancakes for her. Tension hung thick in the air.

Maybe you'd like to show Giselle around the farm? her grandmother said. *Take her snowshoeing on the trails out back?*

Maggie looked like she'd rather walk barefoot across hot coals.

Actually, I said impulsively, *I was just thinking—Maggie, do you want to come to the chalet for the weekend? We can hang out in the spa. Have s'mores by the firepit. Would be fun, yeah?*

What's a chalet? Sophia piped up. *I want to make s'mores! Can I come, too?*

Her nana shushed her.

Maggie pushed a piece of pancake around her plate, dragging it through the maple syrup until it fell apart. She hadn't taken a single bite. *I don't know*, she said. *I have a lot of chores around here. And there's Soph . . .*

Don't you worry, Gwen said. *I'll keep an eye on Sophia, and the chores can wait. We're going to have to manage when you go off to college next year, you know. Can't be spending all your time worrying about us. Go. It's an order!*

Maggie dropped her fork and mumbled, *Okay, thanks, Nana.*

She left to pack a few things. I hung back with her sister and grandmother, watching through the kitchen window as Maggie trudged, shoulders drawn, to the small, blue trailer behind the main house, and went inside.

That's where we live, Sophia said. *I don't like it in there. We have to be extra quiet all the time so we don't bother Daddy or wake up Mommy. That's why I come here. Nana says she loves my exorbitance.*

Exuberance, her grandmother said with a tired sigh. *Yes, I love your exuberance, Soph. Keeps me on my toes.* She rubbed the little girl's head, and that hint of sadness crossed her face again as she looked back toward the beat-up trailer. I could make out the profile of what looked like a man, sitting motionless in a chair by the front window. He was so still, for a moment I thought he might not be real. But as Maggie came out the front door he flinched, then went still again. My skin prickled, wondering if that was Maggie's dad, and what his story really was.

Maggie and I loaded her stuff into my car and headed to the chalet.

I let the quiet hang there like a curtain between us. Did you know that most people can't resist speaking to fill the silence? It's one of the best interrogation techniques. Learned that in AP Psych last semester. No, I take that back. I learned that from you, didn't I, Mom? How else would you have gotten me to admit I was the one who drew all over my face with markers during a playdate with Emi? (Especially since I'd already convinced Emi to take the blame in return for letting her play with my limited-edition Elsa doll for an extra half hour!)

After a few minutes of just the sound of my tires crunching over the snow-packed road, Maggie began to speak softly.

Listen, she said. Obviously, I lied. About Europe. And the boarding school. I didn't mean to, it just popped out when I met you all. I wanted to fit in. And, well, you saw where I live . . .

She angled herself away from me and stared out the passenger-side window.

So, your dad wasn't posted overseas as a diplomat? I asked, thinking of that man in the window.

Not as a diplomat, she said. But he was overseas. National Guard. Five deployments. So far. He just got home from his last one two weeks ago. And he doesn't really handle the transitions well anymore. Nightmares. That sort of thing. And then there were the pills. PTSD sucks . . . Maggie's voice cracked. I'm sorry, she said quietly. It was stupid to lie. Hanging out with you has been, like, amazing. What Sophie said before was true. I don't really have a lot of friends around here. Well, not anymore. Not since the lawsuit.

What? I looked at her and the car jerked to the right. I wasn't expecting THAT. I quickly turned the wheel back to the left.

Yeah, my family sued my old school, Maggie said. For failing to protect me from bullying. I'm not supposed to talk about the details. We signed an agreement. But it got pretty bad. It's why I'm not allowed on social media. It's also why the school district agreed to pay my tuition to Prep. If we agreed to drop the suit.

Oh, I answered as I quickly tried to rearrange this new information in my mind. I wanted to ask more, like whether the bullying had anything to do with that doping scandal I'd read about. Or that girl in the hardware store. But I had the distinct feeling Maggie wasn't going to tell me. Not without some type of extra nudge.

Do you hate me? Maggie said. I would totally understand if you do.

No, I said. I don't hate you. I wish you had told me. I don't care where you live. Or that your dad isn't an international man of mystery like Vivian thinks. Or that you didn't pay your own way into Prep. Really. It doesn't matter. Consider it our little secret.

Really?

REALLY, I said.

And it was true. I didn't care. In fact, I could have told her right then about Grandfather Haverford, the big H of Haverford & Sons Brokerage, and how he blew most of the family's fortune on junk bonds in the eighties. How the Haverfords are basically broke and have been trading on their name for years. How Dad wouldn't have any of his *stuff* without your family's money, Mom. It might be "new" money from *gasp* selling cans of beans, but it works just the same when it comes to loading up with houses, yachts, penthouses, and luxury cars, doesn't it?

Instead, I kept my mouth shut.

We spent the rest of the weekend doing everything I'd promised: hanging in the spa, making s'mores, playing with Knox. Maggie's a natural with little kids. Knox adored her, and giggled until his face was bright pink when she tickled his toes. I began to wonder if I'd just imagined that letter in her backpack.

Then I showed her your studio. Something about her changed when she walked into the room, I guess because she's planning to study architecture. She stood in the middle, silently admiring the interlocking beams across the ceiling, the dappled sunlight filtering through the arched windows. She ran her fingers across the custom-built shelving on the back wall and picked up a jar of paintbrushes.

What was she like? she asked.

I swallowed hard. How do I put you in words, Mom?

She was amazing, I finally said. Like, you know how people say that someone lights up a room? Well, she actually did. It's *impossible to explain. But she just had this . . .*

Magnetism? Maggie asked. Everyone fell in love with her?

I nodded. Yeah, like that.

Like you, Maggie said.

My eyes teared up. I really miss her, I said softly.

And then, out of nowhere, Maggie hugged me.

It was so unexpected, I was caught totally off guard.

I hugged her back. And in that moment, I felt safe. Like I could tell Maggie my darkest secrets. The ones that were chipping away at me from the inside, threatening to crack me wide open. And maybe if I did, she would see the real me hiding underneath, instead of the dolled-up Giselle puppet dancing across the stage with a fake smile plastered across her face. It was freeing somehow being with Maggie, away from Prep and our uniforms and every expectation ever placed on me. Perfect Giselle. Happy Giselle. Top-of-the-pyramid Giselle.

I opened my mouth to speak.

But I was interrupted by the sound of someone turning the door handle.

Maggie and I jumped apart as Nelson, one of our security guards, walked inside.

He jumped back, too, startled.

I'm sorry, Miss Haverford, he said. Just doing the evening rounds. I didn't realize you were doing another interview in here.

Interview? I said. No, this is Maggie. She's my friend from school.

My mistake, Nelson said with a quick headshake. He looked

Maggie up and down. Usually, I'm great at faces, he said. Could've sworn you were that reporter I found parked outside the gate last spring in a beat-up old truck, looking for an interview.

Maggie's face went completely white.

A lot of people drive old trucks around here, she said, voice wobbling slightly. But it wasn't me. I'm a high school student, like Giselle said.

And just like that, whatever I'd felt moments ago evaporated. Gone. Poof.

It was clear Maggie was lying through her teeth.

Once again, I've gone and let the wrong person get too close. You'd think I'd have learned by now, wouldn't you?

So what is Maggie after, then? Access? Money? A secret she can sell?

Unless . . . Oh, crap, Mom.

What if your letter isn't the only thing she's found?

Anon1407: I'm ready to make a deal.

HFord25: Excellent, when?

Anon1407: Tomorrow.

HFord25: Okay, before I agree to pay up, I need some proof. Do you have proof?

Anon1407: Of course I do. But first, how about a little good faith deposit so I know you're serious? Then you can have your proof.

HFord25: What do you have in mind?

Anon1407: $1,000 crypto, deposited into [redacted] by 7 p.m. or the deal is off.

DAY 3
APRIL 14—MORNING

Latitude, longitude: 32.472695, -77.090524

240 nautical miles from the Bahamas

I towel off and slip into my bathing suit and cover-up, not really sure why I've bothered showering since we'll be spending the day poolside. But I can't get enough of this shower. Eight jets. Eight! I could stand in it for hours, letting the water massage my neck and back.

My phone buzzes on the nightstand.

Probably some SeaChat message from one of the girls about outfits for the day or where to sit for maximum sun exposure by the pool.

I pick up the phone, swipe it open, and immediately drop it onto the bed, horrified. I take a step back, staring at my phone like it's a rabid animal preparing to bite me. The warmth of the steamy shower evaporates and my body erupts in goose bumps.

This can't be real.

The memories of junior year crash over me like a tidal wave, threatening to drag me under. The taunts and sideways looks. The whispers beneath cupped hands. The chair swiped from my desk in homeroom and put in the hall, my books knocked to the floor when I briefly looked the other way. One by one, my friends drifted away.

Until no one was left.

I was alone.

In retrospect, I guess that's when my fixation on her began to grow. The princess in her castle on the hill, living the upside-down image of my life in the valley.

Giselle.

I'd seen her in town that winter, shopping for cold-weather gear. Just dumping hats and gloves and whatever she fancied at the register, never once checking the prices. Never once putting something back because she couldn't afford it. Never once having to choose whether to buy a warm wool cap for herself or for her little sister, who was always cold.

She'd breezed past me, arms loaded with merchandise, and slapped a metal credit card down at the register that was so heavy it actually thunked against the old wood counter.

She never noticed me standing by the glove display, watching her.

But why would she?

I was nobody. A local. Some redneck in a flannel shirt with unruly hair and chewed-down nails. On impulse, I'd left the store and followed her shiny BMW, keeping my truck at a safe distance, and watched her disappear behind the tall gates of her estate. What was it like on the other side? I wondered. What was it like to be *her*?

As the months went on and everything went to shit, the space Giselle occupied in my mind grew. I found myself driving to the chalet, again and again, stopping outside the gates and watching for a glimpse of her, despite the fact she only vacationed there. Until a security guard caught me. I made up a stupid on-the-spot story about being a local reporter looking for an interview, and he shooed me away. Like a cow swinging its tail at a persistent fly.

I didn't think I'd ever find a way to get close.

Until last June, when everything finally blew up.

As I walked into school that morning, I knew my day was about to go to hell. The whole place was silent. Too silent. Just the squeak of my shoes on the linoleum floor as I made my way down the junior hallway, a single florescent light popping overhead like in a horror movie. And the sound of my heart, pounding out a warning in my ears as I approached my locker.

Boom! Boom! Boom!

Run! Run! Run!

But my feet carried me forward, on autopilot, straight toward my fate. I passed Allison and the team, huddled in a cluster outside the girls' bathroom, holding their phones and watching me go.

I reached my locker. The entire hall stilled. Hands shaking and eyes watering, I spun the combination. It didn't matter, because my locker was already unlocked, like I knew it would be. I could feel eyes on my back, waiting in breathless anticipation as I lifted the latch, pulling it open.

And there it was. My picture—copied dozens of times and crudely stuck to every surface—staring back at me. A single image. Over. And over. And over. Me, at Kyle Parker's party, passed out facedown in the flatbed of my truck, a line of drool on my cheek. Which would be bad enough, really.

Except a target had been drawn on my back, with a message scrawled beneath:

WATCH YOUR BACK, BITCH. SNITCHES GET STICHES, DON'T YOU KNOW? ☠

It was the same photo and message that an anonymous Instagram account had posted right before school started, tagging me and the entire track team. The same photo that by then had already been shared dozens of times among my classmates.

I swallowed hard and took the risk of glancing at Allison to see what she would do. She stared back at me, eyes a mixture of hurt and defiance. She didn't say anything, just shook her head, turned her back to me, and walked away. Like I knew in my heart she would. Why had I hoped for anything different? Anger bubbled up and I slammed the locker shut with more force than I intended. My finger caught in the latch, slicing the skin. I jolted back, staring as blood oozed from the cut and dripped onto the floor.

All at once my world turned blurry, tilting sideways in a burst of black ink and exploding stars.

I came to a half hour later on a cot in the nurse's office, my finger wrapped in bloodstained gauze and an ice pack on my forehead.

Mrs. LaPan, the school nurse, hurried to my side.

"You took quite a fall there, dear," she said gently. "Your grandmother is on her way to pick you up. I don't think you should be driving yourself home."

I tried to stand anyway. My knees buckled. Mrs. LaPan shook her head, gently guiding me back onto the cot. "Not a good idea," she said. "But if you're up for it, Mr. Brennan is waiting in the hall and would like to speak with you."

I nodded. What difference did it make? I knew exactly what Principal Brennan would do. The exact same thing he had done for the last month:

Nothing.

No. That wasn't true. Now he would *have* to do something. There was no denying what had happened anymore. Not with pages of proof hanging from my locker. Not with that photo pinging its way around my classmates' phones.

The next five minutes were spent listening to Principal Brennan expound on how he "wouldn't tolerate bullying" and reassuring me I was safe at WHS (I was not). Could I tell him who was responsible for the picture?

I lied and said I didn't know.

As he droned on, I tuned him out and focused instead on the muffled sound of voices in the hallway—laughing, talking, gossiping. Lockers banging open and closed. The walls of the nurse's office closed in around me like a sterile, white-painted prison.

One that I was determined to break free from.

I turned my tear-stained eyes to Mr. Brennan and explained I would never be safe at WHS. My parents would be contacting him, requesting a transfer to a new school.

What I didn't say, not yet, was that I already had a school in mind. One far enough away from my tormenters. Someplace no one could reach me. But a place where I could reach *her*.

Andover Preparatory.

A soft rap on my stateroom door jolts me from my thoughts.

"Miss Maggie?" a voice says outside. "It's Marina. I have your laundry and coffee. May I come in?"

"Sure," I answer, trying to regain my composure.

The lock clicks and my cabin steward, Marina, walks in. She's rolling a cart with a silver carafe of coffee and pastries on top, my folded laundry tucked on the bottom shelf. Marina is in her early twenties, like most of *The Escape*'s staff, with dark brown hair, bronze skin, and a friendly smile.

"It looks to be a beautiful day," she says, placing the tray of coffee and pastries on my table. Then she stacks my laundry on the luggage valet by the closet.

"Yes, it does," I say. "Thank you, Marina."

She turns to leave. I glance at the folded clothes she just delivered.

"Oh!" I say, hurrying over and grabbing a cover-up, still warm from the dryer. "This one isn't mine." I give it back to Marina.

"I'm sorry, Miss Maggie," she says. "These all look the same! Your laundry must have been mixed up with Miss Emi's or

Miss Vivian's. It won't happen again."

"It's no problem, really." I smile. "It's just a cover-up. Thanks, Marina. Hope you have a nice day."

"You're welcome, Miss Maggie," she answers. "Have a lovely day, too. Perfect weather. Sunny skies and calm seas." She rolls her cart back into the corridor and the door clicks shut.

I stand there a moment, wishing Marina was still in here to distract me, because I feel anything but calm. I grab the phone from my bed and swipe it open. The message taunts me:

Watch your back . . .

It's from an anonymous account, YouCantRun. Like before, there's no profile picture or name. Nothing to identify the sender. Except this time, my phone is on airplane mode. The only messages we can receive and send here on *The Escape* are via SeaChat, the app Giselle had us download before we left New York so we could communicate with each other on board.

Just the four of us—me, Giselle, Emi, and Vivian.

That's it.

Which means this message couldn't have come from anyone in Westville.

It came from someone on this boat.

Somebody knows.

George Town, Royal Cayman Islands
Police Service (RCIPS)
interview transcript (cont'd)

Subject: EMIENE KAROUSOS (EK)
Interviewer: Detective Rebecca Bennett, RCIPS
Date: 4/16

RCIPS: Sorry for the interruption and delay, Miss Karousos. I hope you are feeling better and the coffee helped.

EK: Yes, thank you. [speaking rapidly] What's going on? Have you found Giselle? What about Maggie? Have you—

RCIPS: I'm sorry, I don't have any news about Miss Haverford to share, and I can't discuss the investigation with you.

EK: Right, yeah. Of course not.

RCIPS: I did hope you could help us identify some items we found during the search of the yacht, since you knew it and Miss Haverford so well.

EK: Oh! Did you find Giselle's journal?

RCIPS: Miss Haverford had a journal?

EK: Yes! I couldn't find it anywhere and I know she had one. [under her breath] I bet Maggie swiped it. She was always sneaking around, trying to take stuff.

RCIPS: I will make a note to check for it, thank you. What I wanted to ask you about are these. [sound of plastic evidence bag crinkling]

EK: Where did those come from?

RCIPS: Interesting story, actually. Investigators found them stuffed in the bottom of the trash can in the stateroom you shared with Miss Haverford. Which is surprising, no? I mean, I'm just a police officer and no shoe expert, but they appear to be quite expensive. A very fine leather, it seems.

EK: Lambskin.

RCIPS: Excuse me?

EK: They're lambskin.

RCIPS: Oh, I see. Thank you for clarifying. Did they belong to you or Miss Haverford?

EK: [mumbles something]

RCIPS: I'm sorry, I didn't understand you.

EK: I said they're mine. And yeah, I didn't want to throw them out. But they got wrecked on the beach in

Nassau. I must've stepped on broken shells or something.

RCIPS: Broken shells?

EK: That's what I said.

RCIPS: [bag crinkles again] Ah, yes, I see what you're talking about. The soles are all torn up, aren't they? Well, that's a shame, then. Looks like they were beautiful shoes. But thank you for helping me clear that little mystery up.

[long silence]

EK: Is that all?

RCIPS: Almost. I do have a couple more things I'd like to show you, if you don't mind.

EK: I don't mind. Like I told you before, I'd do anything for Giselle. Anything.

Dear Mom,

I spent the entire drive back to Prep turning over the situation with Maggie in my mind. I'd managed to fake my way through the rest of my time with her at the chalet, pretending nothing was wrong. But I didn't take my eyes off her. Not once.

When I walked into the dorm, my day only got worse. The whole place was buzzing. But nobody was talking about what they got for Christmas or Hanukkah, or how wasted they were on New Year's Eve, or showing off their diamond studs or the keys to their shiny new cars.

Whisper, whisper, darting eyes.

I dropped my bag in my room and rushed to find Emi.

What's going on around here? I asked.

You didn't get my messages?

Reception sucks between here and the chalet, I said. Then my phone died anyway. So what's happening?

Well, it may be GOOD news for you, actually, Emi said.

What do you mean?

No more stalker is what I mean, she said.

All I could do was shake my head in confusion. Was she talking about Maggie?

Wyatt Garcia, Emi said, emphasizing each syllable of his name. He got kicked out. Some big investigation over break. They fired his mom, too.

WHAT? I said. Why?

Emi shrugged. I heard he was using his mother's key card

to sneak around the school. Stealing tests and selling them to people, maybe. I feel bad for his mom, though. But how could she not know what was happening . . . ?

Emi kept talking but I'd tuned her out. I said I had to go and numbly went back to my room.

What had I done?

I texted Wyatt, but he didn't answer. I called. I texted again. And again. All week. Nothing.

I could hardly concentrate. The scandal was all anyone could talk about. And the more people talked, the wilder the theories got. Wyatt was running an entire cheating ring. No, he was changing grades. No, he was selling tests, grades, AND drugs, too. Everyone had a theory. Except me.

And Maggie.

She was still hanging around but acting totally bizarre. Like today at lunch when Emi started talking about Wyatt, Maggie excused herself from our table, saying she'd forgotten to get a book at the library.

Her aura is very dark, Vivian said, watching Maggie disappear into the hall. Like she's channeling storm clouds.

Emi gave Vivian the side-eye. Seriously, she said, you don't need a bag of crystals to pick up on that.

I'm an empath, Vivian said. We intuit all sorts of things, you know.

Oh, please . . . Emi said and went back to texting Zane.

You could really stand to lose some of your negative energy, Vivian answered. It's not healthy. That's not all, though. I'm not sure if I should even say anything because it's probably nothing . . .

Vivian's eyes flitted toward mine.

Okay, I said, still half-distracted thinking about Wyatt and totally not interested in whatever New Age nonsense Viv was getting ready to spout.

I saw them hanging out, Vivian said. Wyatt and Maggie. Right before winter break.

Wait, what? I asked, caught off guard. Viv had my full attention now.

I mean, I'm sure it doesn't mean anything, Vivian said, talking faster. They have art together, right? But it was sort of weird. I was coming out of the student lounge and they were kinda huddled up in the portico outside. They jumped apart when they saw me, like I'd caught them doing something wrong. Then Maggie just kind of thanked him, waved to me, and hurried inside with her head down. You don't think she was one of the people buying tests from him, do you?

Wouldn't surprise me, Emi said, without even looking up from her phone.

My mind was racing. I didn't know what to think.

The minute I got back to my room, I texted Wyatt for like the hundredth time.

Finally, he answered.

Just STOP, Giselle. Why do you keep bothering me? It wasn't enough to break my heart, blackmail me, AND get my mom fired?? Now you want me to forgive you, too? I'm sorry, but it doesn't work like that. This time, you've gone too far. You destroyed the one person who has always been there for me, who took that job at your school so I could get the education she never had. She didn't deserve ANY of this! Please, just leave me the fuck alone. I DON'T WANT TO TALK TO YOU!!!

I wrote back, apologizing again, begging Wyatt not to shut me out. I watched for five long minutes as the dots in his text bubble appeared and disappeared, over and over, until his reply came through and shattered my heart into a thousand pieces.

Shut YOU out? HA! You mean like how you came back to school after summer break and pretended I didn't exist? Or refused to tell your friends about me? I seriously can't believe I ever loved you. That I thought you meant it when you told me I was your everything—your safe space, your center, your heart of hearts. I'm such a fucking fool. So no, I don't forgive you. I can't even forgive myself! You're nothing but an empty promise wrapped in a lie, and I don't want to see your face or hear from you EVER AGAIN. Got it? I'm blocking you now. You can keep texting all you want, but it won't matter because you're dead to me now. DEAD, do you understand???

BREAKING NEWS ALERT
BODY FOUND—4/16, 2:32 P.M.

In an exclusive report—a source close to the search for missing American heiress Giselle Haverford tells us that the shark-ravaged remains of what appears to be a young woman have been found washed up along the Guanahacabibes Peninsula in Cuba. As seen on this map, the Haverford yacht would have passed by this area during the early morning hours, roughly around the time when Miss Haverford is believed to have gone overboard. According to marine experts, the remains could have easily washed ashore due to prevailing winds and tides. We'll have more on this rapidly evolving situation as it develops.

DAY 2

APRIL 13—EVENING

Latitude, longitude: 34.741612, -73.993167
320 nautical miles from the Bahamas

Dinner this evening is served in the lounge, a glassed-in room on the second deck with panoramic views of the ocean and the setting sun. I pull out my phone and snap a picture of the pink clouds streaking across the sky. I can't wait to show Sophie. She loves sunsets—or as she says, the way the sky melts at the end of the day.

She hates bedtime, but that's another story.

I try not to worry about her, home without me right now, probably defying bedtime with demands for another story or a fresh glass of water. Nana is taking good care of her, I reassure myself. She promised she would. But how long can I expect her to keep that up? As she's quick to point out, she's not getting any younger. Dad's not getting any better. And Mom's not getting any rest. I don't know what they'll do next year when I leave for college. Who will tuck Sophie in at night? Braid her hair in the morning for school?

My whole family is on the brink of falling apart, and here I am at this elegant table set with more forks, knives, and spoons than I know what to do with. Two bottles of wine are propped in ice buckets on either end of the table, white linen napkins wrapped around their necks.

It's all so elegant and mature. I feel totally out of place, like a plastic spork among the gleaming silverware.

A few years ago, I would have considered dinner at the Colonnade up the road in Granfield to be the fanciest meal ever, with their white tablecloths and sticky buns covered in maple syrup with a little walnut stuck on top and the candles stuffed in old wine bottles layered in wax. Of course, back then, my only other frame of reference for dining out was the blue plate special from the diner downstreet and a Happy Meal from McDonald's.

Needless to say, Giselle's private chefs and ocean view dining room blow all of that completely out of the water.

Despite my nerves, my stomach grumbles. Hunger is a funny thing, isn't it? Always there beneath the surface, demanding to be fed.

And I want to devour life. I don't want to be the girl with the stutter from the rundown farm who never leaves. I want polish on my nails, not dirt underneath them. I want to break free and *be* somebody.

Is that really so wrong? What makes me any different from Giselle, other than the bad luck of being born on the wrong side of the mountain?

Why should *I* be the one who has nothing?

Our deck steward, Christopher, arrives carrying a tray full of tofu, shrimp, and crab cakes. He places individual appetizers on our silver plates, then wordlessly fills our glasses with sauvignon blanc, a linen napkin draped over his sleeve. Tonight his dark hair is combed back off his forehead with gel, and his golden tan has already deepened since we set sail yesterday. Vivian's eyes follow as he retreats down the stairs, while I take a bite of flaky crab cake.

"He's really hot," she says under her breath.

"I guess." Giselle shrugs. "If you're into that type."

"Reminds me of Raphael," Vivian says with a sigh.

"Except he's not French," Emi points out. "Or fake."

Vivian ignores her.

We raise our glasses for a toast and everyone digs in. I decide, for now, to just live in the moment. Leave my worries onshore. Savor each delicious bite that's placed in front of me. I polish off the shrimp and crab cakes and practically lick my plate, eager to find out what's being served next.

Christopher returns to clear our appetizer plates. More courses follow—crisp salads, tender filet mignon (grilled mushroom steak for Vivian), sorbet to cleanse the palate, and perfectly paired wines. I'm positively stuffed by the time dessert rolls around: delicate puff pastries filled with fruit and chocolate mousse, and a vegan blueberry tart for Vivian.

Aw hell, I'll make room.

Christopher places a dessert in front of me. It looks nearly too beautiful to eat—layers of chocolate, pastry, luscious berries, with a dollop of fresh whipped cream and a twist of shaved chocolate on top. Christopher bows with one arm behind his back and turns to depart.

"Wait!" Giselle says, stopping him in his tracks. He backs up, tray tucked neatly beneath his arm, eyebrows raised.

"May I get you something else?"

"Yes," she says, a mischievous gleam in her eyes. "*You.*"

"Excuse me?" Christopher says, eyes widening just a bit. A hint of red creeps above the white collar of his uniform shirt and I'm actually embarrassed for him. That comment was wildly inappropriate, to say the least.

Giselle laughs. "I mean, I want you to join us. You've been working really hard and deserve a break. Have a seat!"

"I'm not sure—"

"How old are you, anyway?" Giselle queries.

"Twenty-two," he answers. "But—"

"So you're practically the same age as us," she says, cutting him off. "Pull up a chair and grab a glass of wine."

"I'm not sure that's a good idea. What would your father say? I don't need to piss off the future president of the United States." His face flushes completely. "Sorry, I shouldn't have said 'piss.'"

Giselle cracks up. "Well, Daddy Future President's not here, is he? Come on. I'm not going to tell him, if you promise not to tell him we *pissed* away all his Opus One." She laughs again and after a moment, Christopher does, too. He drags an extra chair to an empty space between Giselle and Vivian and folds himself into it.

"It's only for a couple of minutes, though. I could catch a lot of grief from Rita for this," he says.

"Eh, don't worry. I'll deal with Rita," Giselle answers with a wink. "So, tell us all about Christopher. For starters, how did you end up here, working on this boat?"

"I'm taking a year off before graduate school," he says, leaning back and threading his hands behind his head. "I've always loved to sail. This seemed like a fun way to see the world and help pay my tuition."

"And is it?"

"Yes, Miss Haverford."

Giselle rolls her eyes. "Stop calling me that. It's Giselle, okay?" she says.

"Giselle," he says with a small grin. "Got it."

Already, I can see he's under her spell. And who can blame him? If you were to look up "bewitching" in the dictionary, you'd probably find a picture of Giselle right next to it. A siren whose beautiful song lulls sailors off course and sends them crashing into the rocks.

Christopher's "few minutes" turn into a couple of hours. The sky darkens, the wine keeps flowing, and the conversation gets raunchier. I can't decide who is flirting harder with Christopher—Giselle or Vivian. They've both inched their chairs closer to his, and he's already been treated to a scroll through all of Vivian's best bikini shots on her IG feed. Giselle has managed to find a way to casually drape her bare legs across his lap and make it seem totally normal.

Christopher doesn't look like he minds one bit.

Emi, on the other hand, is more interested in keeping her wine glass full and complaining that she can't text Zane with no cell signal, and why can't she have the Wi-Fi password, anyway? Giselle responds with a disinterested shrug. "Not my rules," she says.

I'm, as usual, the proverbial fly on the wall. The truth is, I've never been entirely comfortable around guys like Christopher. Even though he works on this yacht from dawn until dusk, he still gives off a certain sleek tennis club vibe, like a lot of the guys at Prep. A farm boy he is not.

After we've successfully emptied another bottle of wine (so long, Opus One!), Christopher stretches and slides Giselle's legs to the floor with a lopsided grin.

"I really need to get back to work and clear these dishes," he says. "Unless you're actually trying to get me fired."

"Wouldn't dream of it," Giselle purrs, giving his nose a friendly poke with her index finger and leaning in close. "Stay. I'm the boss and that's an order."

Christopher blushes. Vivian bites back a scowl and stands.

"Au revoir," she says with a little wave. "I'm going to write a letter to Raphael. An actual letter, handwritten with a real stamp on the corner of the envelope! I'll mail it from Nassau. Doesn't that sound old-fashioned and romantic?"

"Completely," Giselle says. "He's going to love it. So will your followers. I sure love a good letter. Don't you, Maggie?" Giselle's eyes catch mine, and goose bumps attack my arms. Has she been poking around my room?

Vivian nods and disappears around the corner. Emi follows suit. I head out immediately after with a quick goodbye, eager to check my safe and make sure the letter is still exactly where I put it. I hear a cork pop on another bottle of wine as I walk away, followed by Giselle's throaty laughter.

I'm about to open the door to my room when I realize that in my rush I've left my phone on the dinner table. With a sigh, I turn around and head back. I can't afford to lose it. There are still fourteen months until it's paid off. Mom would kill me.

Halfway down the hall, the sound of heavy breathing stops me short. I peer around the corner. Giselle and Christopher are kissing furiously. Wow, that didn't take long. Giselle's back is pushed up against the wall, her leg curled around Christopher's, bare foot massaging his calf. He lets out a low moan as she grips the fabric of his uniform shirt, clutching it tightly in her hand. He moves closer, running his hand through her hair.

I see my phone, sitting there on the table, and inch my way forward. Maybe if I'm extra quiet, I can slip past them, grab it, and go to bed. I take a cautious step, breath held.

Suddenly, Giselle pushes Christopher away and slaps him across the face.

Hard.

I freeze where I stand, shocked, then back up slowly.

"How dare you?" Giselle shouts at Christopher.

"Wh-What?" he stammers, clearly stunned.

"I was only trying to be nice, including you tonight!" Giselle says. "You think that's license to get me drunk and take advantage of me? Do you have any idea who I am?"

Christopher backs away. Even from here, I can tell his body is shaking.

"I guess I misunderstood," he says, both hands raised. "I'm sorry."

"Well, you'd better be," Giselle answers. "Because if my dad found out about this, he'd make sure you never worked on another yacht again. And you could kiss grad school good-bye, too. I'm pretty sure no admissions board would approve of that!" She gestures angrily at something before stalking away.

I follow Christopher's line of sight as he stands there trembling in Giselle's wake, tilting his gaze up to the wall above his head.

To the security camera fastened on top, green light blinking ominously.

"Shit," he says. "Shit, shit, shit."

Then he punches the wall, shakes out his hand, and begins clearing the dinner dishes, his face bloodred.

Subject: VIVIAN PAGE (VP)

Interviewer: Detective Rebecca Bennett, RCIPS

Date: 4/16

RCIPS: How was the water, Miss Page? Are you feeling better now with a little break?

VP: Yes, thank you. Just what I needed. It's important to stay hydrated.

RCIPS: Good, I'm glad. Now, if you don't mind, I'd like to backtrack a bit to something we were discussing earlier.

VP: Okay.

RCIPS: You mentioned your Instagram feed. I did get a chance to check it out while we were taking a break. You weren't kidding—you are very popular.

VP: Thanks!

RCIPS: That must be a lot of work.

VP: Yes, it is. You have no idea. Most people think being an influencer

is super easy. Just take a few pictures and pile up the likes, right?
But I plan everything, and I mean
EVERYTHING, in advance to maximize
engagement and cultivate sponsor-
ships. I actually have an LLC set up.
That's a limited liability company.

RCIPS: I'm sure your relationship with Britney Haverford hasn't hurt, either,
right? She is quite well known as a
lifestyle guru, too.

VP: Well, sure . . . but I have worked
very hard on my own to grow my brand.

RCIPS: Yes, I see that. You do work very
hard, don't you? Straight As all
through high school. AP classes. Lead
role in the school musical. I am very
impressed.

VP: Thanks. I do try to be my very best
self.

RCIPS: That must make it hard to be such
good friends with someone like
Giselle Haverford, no?

VP: Huh? I'm not sure what you mean.

RCIPS: Oh, you know—you're both very bright,
beautiful, talented. I'm sure things
get competitive sometimes.

VP: Competitive? With Giselle? No. [laughs awkwardly] I don't believe in competition. We're all on our own journeys.

RCIPS: Interesting. Still, as someone who works so hard to be your "best self," as you put it, it must have been very disappointing when you weren't accepted into the college of your choice.

VP: Wait, what? No, I'm taking a gap year, remember?

RCIPS: Interesting. [papers shuffling] Because earlier last fall, you posted a screenshot of your application to Dartmouth with the hashtags "dream school" and "please say yes." So it must have been upsetting not to get in, especially with your stellar grades, SAT scores, and activities. Oh, and your LLC. I don't think many high school students can boast about having one of those.

VP: I wasn't rejected. I was waitlisted. There's a difference. That means they think I'm qualified. They just won't know if they have space until they see how many of the accepted students actually enroll.

RCIPS: Ah, I see. Thank you for clarifying that. I also understand that given your small class size Dartmouth usually only accepts one—possibly two, tops—students from Andover Preparatory each year. Is that correct?

VP: Well, sure. That's what people say. But really, you'd have to talk to their admissions office about that. Not me.

RCIPS: Of course. But I assume you do know who Dartmouth accepted from your class this year?

VP: [mumbles]

RCIPS: Can you repeat that? Who did Dartmouth accept?

VP: [deep breath] I said Giselle Haverford.

DAY 2

APRIL 13—MORNING

Latitude, longitude: 36.809285, -74.614607

450 nautical miles from the Bahamas

The bright sun streaming through my balcony doors awakened me early this morning, so I decided to come up here, to the top deck, and watch it rise. Now I'm relaxing in a lounger with my sketchbook, scraping my pencil across a new sheet of paper, tracing the horizon in front of me. It's beautiful but at the same time so blank. No mountains to mark the end of the landscape. No trees or buildings. Just blue water merging into blue sky at some distant point it feels like I'll never reach.

The breeze cuts a chill across my neck, and I zip my sweatshirt up tighter. It's a bit colder than I'd expected, but I'm hoping that once the sun has been out for a few hours it will warm up as we continue to head south.

It's also a bit more disorienting being at sea than I'd anticipated, and there's not much I can do about that. I get why people once thought the earth was flat. Horizon in all directions. Endless but trapped at the same time. There's no place to go if something goes wrong. Just into the deep, churning water.

Vivian comes up the stairs and plunks down in the lounger across from me. She's wearing a coordinated—and undoubtedly very expensive—workout getup, complete with matching hair scrunchie to pull her shimmery blond hair into a high pony.

"Good morning," she says, a sharpness in her usually chipper tone. "You're up early."

"Yeah, hard habit to break," I say. Our first milking used to be at 3:00 a.m., and I always got up to help Dad. Even now, with the herd auctioned off for pennies on the dollar, my eyes always open at 2:59, ready to go. It was early, but there was something special about that time with Dad. Leading the cows into the milking parlor. The earthy smell of hay and animals. That coffee we'd share afterward, before Sophie woke up and Mom came home from work. The barn was the one place Dad seemed at ease. Where the nightmares didn't chase him. Where the sound of a door banging shut didn't send him diving for cover beneath the nearest table.

I flip my sketchbook closed and struggle for something to say. I haven't seen Vivian since last night and I can only imagine how she feels about me right now. I take a deep breath. Probably, it's best to confront the whole thing head-on. Clear the air. That's what an honest person would do, right? And I'm trying to be honest.

"Listen, I want to apologize," I say, chewing my bottom lip. "What I did was wrong and I feel terrible. I barely slept. I know that probably doesn't mean much to you, and I don't expect you to forgive me, but I really do feel like a jerk. I think I got all caught up with imagining what it must be like to be . . . Oh, never mind. I'm sorry. It won't happen again."

Vivian sighs, and her face softens. "It's okay."

"No," I answer. "It's really not."

"Yeah, it is. I get it, all right?"

"You do?"

"Yeah, all of this." She waves her hand around. "It can be pretty overwhelming. I can see why you'd want to, I don't know, try it all on for size. I don't think we're all that different, you know."

Before I can stop myself, I've barked out a laugh. I can't even begin to imagine anyone I'm *more* different from than Vivian Page.

She cocks her head.

"You do know I'm not a legacy like Em and Giselle, right? I'm at Prep on scholarship. My parents are both elementary school teachers in Staten Island."

"Wait, what?" No, I did not know this. "What about the . . ." I stop myself, feeling foolish. How about I just close my mouth now?

"It's okay," Vivian says. "You want to know about Paris? And all my expensive makeup and lotion?"

I shrug.

"Paris was with the French Club. We fundraised for like an entire semester. You have no idea how many rolls of wrapping paper I sold to go on that trip," Vivian says. "And all the nice stuff? I get that from my sponsors, for promoting products on my Instagram. It's a lot of work. More than people realize."

"I'm such an asshole," I say.

230

"No," Vivian says. "You're not. At least, I don't think you are. You just make assumptions. Like most people do. Guess you can't judge someone by looking at them, can you?"

I, of all people, should know that.

"I mean, it's like Britney," Vivian continues, now that she's on a roll. "People think she's this gold digger because she's young and she married Senator Haverford. But she's not like that at all! She's kind and super generous. I should know. My Insta never would've taken off so quickly without her."

"Wait, what?"

Vivian blinks a few times, staring at me. "Wow, you really don't do social media, do you?"

I shake my head. Clearly I haven't been paying as much attention as I'd thought.

Or maybe I've been paying too much attention to all the wrong things.

"Britney's parents and mine went to college together," Vivian says. "I've known her since I was a little kid, and she's always been like this cool big sister to me. When I started my Instagram, she gave me a huge boost on her blog, and things really took off from there. I owe her. Everything."

"I had no idea," I say. But suddenly things make so much more sense. "That's got to be awkward. With Giselle, yeah?"

"God, don't you know it. Giselle totally blames me for Britney and her dad getting together, because I brought Britney with me to this party at Giselle's place in the Hamptons a couple of summers ago. That's where she met Giselle's dad," Vivian says, pausing when she sees the look on my face. "It wasn't like that," she adds quickly. "They didn't get together until after Mrs. Haverford died. I swear. But then there was the whole wedding thing."

"Wedding thing?"

"I was Britney's maid of honor," Vivian says with a grimace. "I mean, she asked Giselle first! But Giselle said no. And I guess she expected me to also. But how could I, after everything Britney had done for me?"

"That's rough."

"It was!" Vivian says. "And the thing is, Britney's not this monster Giselle makes her out to be. I mean, she's super successful on her own! All Britney's ever cared about, as long as I've known her, was having a family. That's why I was so happy for her when she found out she was pregnant with Knox, because she wasn't even sure Giselle's dad could have kids anymore. Something about a sports injury when he was younger. Don't say anything about that, though. Britney told me all that in confidence. I'm not even sure Giselle knows."

"Giselle knows what?"

Vivian pales. Giselle is standing at the top of the stairs, yoga mat tucked under her arm. I didn't even hear her coming. I swear, she's stealthier than a barn cat.

"You two aren't up here whispering about me, are you?" she asks, eyebrows raised.

"No," I say. "We were just talking about what we were going to do when we got to Grand Cayman. That's the only day you don't seem to have planned out on your itinerary."

"Mmm," Giselle says, still looking at us quizzically and I'm pretty sure seeing straight through my lie. "Guess we'll have to play it by ear!" She smiles broadly and unfurls her yoga mat. "Viv and I are going to do some yoga. Want to join us, Maggie?" Giselle asks.

"No, I'm good," I say, standing. "Last time I attempted a downward dog I landed on my head."

"Ah, right," Giselle says. "I'd forgotten all about your legendary klutziness."

"Huh?" I say.

"Remember?" she says. "The reason you didn't want to try out for the track team with me? Something about how you can't run?"

"Oh yeah, that," I answer.

Giselle smiles. "See you poolside later, then!"

"See ya." I wave goodbye and make my way downstairs to my room.

I drop my sketchbook on the bed and pour myself a cup of coffee from the pot that Marina delivered on a silver tray while I was out. I take the steaming mug and sit on a blue padded chair on the balcony. The coffee is rich and warm and nutty, just how I like it, and goes perfectly with the flaky croissant that was delivered alongside it.

The yacht rocks gently as it slices through the water. Sitting out here with the sun on my face, the ocean breeze brushing against my cheeks, and a coffee in my hand, I can almost forget all my problems. The vacant stare in Dad's eyes. The lines of worry around my mother's. The friends I've lost and the life I torpedoed.

Out here, I'm far enough away that I can hardly smell the smoke anymore from all the bridges I've burned. I can almost imagine sailing away, into the horizon, and never coming back.

The only problem is that the horizon keeps moving farther away the closer you get.

And the past keeps following, no matter how far you go.

RECOVERED WHATSAPP MESSAGE, 4/15, 6:55 P.M.

Anon1407: How's this for proof? [unrecoverable image attachment] I told you I could deliver. See?

HFord25: I see.

Anon1407: But you know what? I could lose everything if I get caught. My price has gone up.

HFord25: To?

Anon1407: You tell me. How much is it worth to you?

Dear Mom,

Right before you died, you told me that you had no regrets in life.
Except maybe one. And that is letting other people's expectations
define your path. If you could give me one bit of advice, you said,
it would be to follow my heart. My passion. Be good, be honest,
but be true to myself.

I've been thinking a lot about that lately.

Because in the end, we all wind up in the same place, don't we?

And sometimes the journey is too short.

Better to travel it with the people who truly matter.

I don't want to wind up like you and Dad. Separate rooms.
Separate worlds. Separate lives. Everything a big lie for the camera and the polls. I've tried so hard to remember a time when you
were happy together. That time I found you laughing about the
little brother who never happened?

I still don't know why you stayed with him.

No, I do.

Because of me, right?

I don't want to make the same mistake.

So today I decided to tell Wyatt the truth. All of it. Why I'd
dumped him so abruptly. How I never stopped loving him. I'd kiss
him right in the middle of the town square if that's what it took.
I'd post it on Insta and shout it from the rooftops.

Because the thing Wyatt never understood—that maybe I
didn't even understand at first—is that I wasn't keeping what
we had secret because I was ashamed of him. Okay, that's not

entirely true. I did worry about what my friends would think, especially Emi, because she's always been so protective of me. But as time went on, I kept us secret because I loved the little bubble we'd created. That bubble was the one pure and good thing in my life that no one else could touch. Not Dad and his handlers. Not some gossip blog.

With Wyatt, I was just me. Giselle. I didn't have to pretend.

And yet . . . I did.

I went ahead and behaved like I always did. One person for the cameras, one behind closed doors.

I needed to make things right.

And if he wasn't going to answer my calls, I'd have to go directly to him. So I drove to his neighborhood, nerves jangling, and pulled to a stop a little ways down the street from his house to collect myself. As I sat there, I began to feel even worse. The flowers that had once bloomed in ceramic containers on his front porch were dead and wilted. The grass in the yard was overgrown. Paint peeled from the window frames.

How was I going to make him understand?

That's when I noticed the truck.

A very familiar truck, parked a little farther up, on the other side of the street.

My stomach bottomed out.

Wyatt's front door swung open.

And then SHE stepped outside, red waves—the ones she'd smoothed to look like mine—sparkling in the sun as she stopped and turned to face Wyatt.

My drumming heartbeat became a crash, boom, gunshots firing. I wanted to rush from the car and scream. How could this be happening? What was she doing AT HIS HOUSE?!?

I got my answer soon enough.

Wyatt's arms wrapped around Maggie in a hug, drawing her toward his chest—toward MY spot. MINE! I wanted to vomit. I put my car in reverse, shaking, then backed into the nearest driveway and drove away in the opposite direction.

I looked back, just once, and saw them in my rearview mirror, lips pressed together. ~~Something~~ Something inside me snapped. It wasn't enough for Maggie to steal my hair, my clothes, the way I talked. YOUR LETTER! She had to steal Wyatt, too? How did she even know about him?

I thought back to the weekend at the chalet. When we were toasting s'mores, I'd asked Maggie if she'd ever been in love. Maybe. Sort of. Ahh, so it's a secret, I'd teased. She'd shrugged and turned away, face red.

Me too, I'd said softly. And I'd almost told her EVERYTHING!

But she already knew, didn't she?

That's why she didn't answer.

Wyatt must have told her. About us. Maybe he even told her about my snooping. Maybe she's known all along, and she's been the one trying to play ME. Like fucking Beatrice. Digging up as much dirt as she could about me so she could sell it to the Daily Mail.

Well, I took care of that bitch, didn't I?

It was so easy to get Beatrice to buy some weed and smuggle

it back into her room—just a suggestion, really, about how fun it would be to get high together. I bet she thought she'd get a great photo! Not my fault she went ahead and did it. Or that I let something slip about her stash to our house mother. For Beatrice's own good, of course. Drugs are dangerous!

Oh well. Hope she's having fun back in England with that pissy little brother of hers who's always wrecking her stuff.

I started to drive back to school, still fuming.

But then I had a different idea.

I got on the interstate and headed straight toward Westville instead. There's more to Maggie's story than what she told me, I'm sure of it. There's a reason that girl in the hardware store hates her.

And I'm going to find out every last sordid detail, and then I'll blow her world to bits.

Payback's a bitch, baby.

DAY 1

APRIL 12—NIGHT

Latitude, longitude: 39.673370, -73.625177

95 nautical miles off the coast of New York

I've never seen anything like the night sky at sea.

We finished dinner a couple hours ago—our choice of fresh Maine lobster with a delicate cream sauce or lentil Bolognese, followed by a warm apple crisp—and now we're seated at the bar on the top deck. I lean back and tilt my face skyward, where millions of stars explode across an infinite black velvet canvas. It's breathtaking. Even brighter than the stars back home, something I didn't think possible. I imagine the days of the explorers, using the night sky to chart their course, tiny points of light guiding them to distant shores.

Vivian glances up. "That's Orion, Taurus, and Pisces," she says, tracing constellations with her index finger. "Over there are Leo, Sagittarius, and Virgo."

"Wow," Giselle says. "I only know how to find the Big Dipper." She's following the path of Vivian's finger. I try to follow, too, but combined with the motion of the yacht, I'm hit with a touch of vertigo. I lower my eyes and focus on something more fixed, like the scowl on Emi's face as she listens to Vivian talk about astrology.

"I've been studying how to read the stars," Vivian says. "It's very illuminating. My astrologer gave me a detailed reading a couple months ago. Did you know that I can expect some monumental life changes this year?"

"Duh," Emi says with an eye roll. "We're all expecting monumental life changes this year. We're graduating from high school! Hardly takes a map of the universe to figure that out."

"Well, my followers appreciate my astrological insights," Vivian says. "The universe is a mysterious and beautiful place. We're all connected. Did you know that human beings are made of the same elements as stardust?"

"Except half the stars we see up there are probably dead and gone already. Burned out. Swallowed by a black hole before the light reaches our eyes," Emi says. "So I'm not sure how they're supposed to tell us our future."

"I prefer to think stars never truly die," Giselle says wistfully. "Maybe they are always there, as long as we can see their light. Maybe the light is all that matters in the end."

Nobody says anything after that. We all know what Giselle is thinking about. Her mom. I picture the studio at her chalet, jammed with paintbrushes and unfinished canvases. The heart dangling from Giselle's neck. My thoughts wander to my dad, a star who is still here but empty of light. My own heart feels heavy.

After a few minutes, Giselle stands and stretches.

"Who wants a night cap?" she says.

Vivian giggles. "You sound like my grandfather."

"Well, then, your grandfather sounds like a smart man," Emi says. "I'll take one. What do you have?"

Emi never turns down a drink. But from what I've seen, she never actually gets drunk, either. Just keeps her glass full enough to seem like she's down to party all the time. Like she thinks that's what is expected of her—to be the stylish, whip-smart, and snarky party girl of the group. Fiercely loyal, on guard against any outsiders.

Giselle steps behind the bar, clinking through bottles. "Grand Marnier, Drambuie, Sambuca . . ."

"Vivian, did your grandfather also stock this bar?" Emi says with a smirk.

"Ha!" Vivian grins.

"Do you have a little schnapps, maybe?" Emi asks. "I can't stand the bitter stuff."

"Schnapps? Who's the grandpa now?" Giselle says with a laugh. She clunks a green bottle on the bar and lines up a bunch of snifters. "Maggie, you in?"

The heaviness in my heart is working its way down my arms and legs, and tugging at my eyelids. I suddenly feel very sleepy. I hold back a yawn.

"Are we boring you?" Emi says.

"No, I'm just tired. It's been a long day." (Week, month, year.) "I think I might call it a night."

"Really?" Giselle says.

"Yeah, it was an early drive this morning." I picture the farmhouse receding in my truck's rearview mirror, Sophie on the porch, tiny arms wrapped around Nana's legs. *My sister.* The reason I'm here. I hold back the tears I feel pricking the corners of my eyes and rub them instead like I'm exhausted. This time, I do yawn.

"Okay," Giselle says. "I'll let you off the hook. Tonight. But it's not going to happen again. This is vacation, got it?" She holds my gaze.

"Got it."

I hear liquor pouring and glasses clinking as I make my way down the back stairs, steadying myself with the handrails. I wonder if I'll ever adjust to the yacht's constant rocking.

As I round the stairs to the next level, I approach the hallway that leads to the forward-facing suites. I stop. One of the doors is open a crack, and I catch a glimpse of the massive room on the other side.

Giselle gave us a tour of *The Escape* earlier today after we set sail—previewing the pool and hot tub, the dining lounge, the bars and lounge areas, the mini theater—but we didn't go through the staterooms.

Curiosity gets the better of me.

I check over my shoulder. Nobody is coming. I can hear the girls laughing on the deck above, the sound of the waves crashing against the ship's hull. The staff seems to have cleared out for the evening, and I'm the only one on this deck.

Why not, then? It wouldn't be terrible to take a little peek, would it?

The door is open, after all.

It's practically an invitation.

I walk into the room and am stopped dead in my tracks. It's twice the size of the one I'm staying in. There's a separate bedroom in the back with Vivian's luggage stacked neatly in the corner, and a large sitting area with a sofa covered in fluffy pillows. Two sets of sliding glass doors lead to an enormous balcony where a pair of loungers face the water.

Another door leads to the most unbelievable bathroom I've ever set foot in. There's a huge freestanding tub, a tiled shower with a rainfall showerhead and multiple water jets, and a bowl sink set in a countertop made from sparkling turquoise and blue sea glass. I run my hands over the smooth surface in awe. It's a work of art.

The counter is lined with moisturizers, body sprays, and jars filled with cotton rounds. I uncap a body spray and mist a little on myself, leaving my wrists smelling sweet, like toasted marshmallows. I pretend this is my life, days beginning and ending with a spritz of something refreshing here, a dab of rich lotion there.

If you pretend hard enough, you can make something real, right?

Manifest it right into existence. I bet Vivian would agree.

An overstuffed gold Chanel makeup bag sits to the right of the sink.

Without thinking, I unzip it and peek inside.

Toothpaste, acne cream, toner, a brown prescription bottle.

I pick up the bottle and read the label. My mouth goes dry. I recognize these. Sleeping pills. Strong ones. Dad used to live on them, before his doctor cut him off. Now he goes for the next best thing: cheap whiskey. Guaranteed to leave you slumped in your recliner every night while *Family Feud* plays over and over on the muted television in front of you. Then I read the name on the bottle: Britney Haverford. *What?*

There's a noise behind me. I spin around to see Vivian standing there, eyes wide.

"What are you doing in my room?" she says, blinking.

"Uh." I tuck the bottle behind my back, acutely aware of the fact that in addition to looking guilty as hell, I smell like a s'more. "I, uh . . ."

"You know if you wanted to borrow something, all you needed to do was ask," Vivian says. "It's not like I'd mind."

My face flames. "Yeah, I'm so sorry. The door was open and I got curious to see what the room was like. It was totally wrong of me. I'll go now." My hand fumbles, trying to drop the prescription bottle into the bag without being seen. But the boat tilts as we cross a wave and I miss. The bottle falls to the floor and the cap pops off. Little yellow capsules scatter everywhere, bouncing off the bathtub, skidding into the corners. One rolls to a stop by Vivian's sandaled foot.

Her face pales as she picks up the pill, a burst of yellow between her manicured fingers.

"I can explain," I say. But the truth is, I can't. So I stand here with my mouth hanging open, clammy hands pressed against my sides. Vivian blinks a few times. She looks at the floor and back at me.

"Explain what?" It's Giselle, who has suddenly appeared behind Vivian. "I thought I heard voices. Didn't you come down here to change into your bathing suit, Viv? And weren't you going to bed, Maggie? What's going on?"

I wait for Vivian to rat me out, tell Giselle I was snooping, and my heart races. Not even a day into the trip, and I've already messed things up. Royally.

Instead, Vivian shrugs. "It's nothing," she says. "I told Maggie she could borrow some of my moisturizer. I'm gonna change now and I'll be right up. Maggie's just leaving, aren't you, Maggie?"

I nod, my cheeks still burning with embarrassment.

Giselle doesn't budge. Instead, she snatches the pill from Vivian's fingers.

"Seriously?" she says, her face a combination of anger and pity. "I thought you cared about what you put into your body, Viv. Do you have any idea how dangerous stuff like this can be?"

Vivian stares at Giselle, mouth agape. "Are you being serious right now?"

Giselle stares back, like she's daring her to say something, and pushes her way into the bathroom. I lean against the counter and try to make myself invisible. Giselle grabs the bottle off the floor.

"What are you doing?" Vivian says.

"I'm doing you a favor," Giselle says as she scoops up the pills. Once her hands are full, she walks back through the room and to the balcony. Wind whipping her long auburn hair around her head like Medusa's snakes, she chucks the pills overboard. They fall, yellow confetti landing in the water below.

"You can thank me later," Giselle says.

Vivian takes a deep breath. I try to catch her eye and give her a meaningful look. Something to convey how sorry I am. But she barely glances at me. Just long enough to see the hurt in her tear-stained eyes and a glimmer of anger I've never seen before on her usually serene face.

George Town, Royal Cayman Islands
Police Service (RCIPS)
interview transcript (cont'd)

Subject: VIVIAN PAGE (VP)

Interviewer: Detective Rebecca Bennett, RCIPS

Date: 4/16

RCIPS: Miss Page, I'm going to need you to take a deep breath.

VP: I'm done. I want to leave. You can't keep me here.

RCIPS: No, we can't. You are free to go at any time.

VP: Good. [sound of chair scraping across the floor]

RCIPS: But before you go, I was hoping you could answer just a few more questions. I'll be brief, I promise. It would really help clear a few things up.

VP: [sighs] Okay.

RCIPS: Thank you. [sound of papers shuffling] Ah, yes, here it is! This is the log from *The Escape*'s secure Wi-Fi. Would you like to have a look?

VP: [shakily] I guess. Why?

RCIPS: This line right here. [tapping sound] It's a log-in from your phone's IP address at 1:37 a.m. on the morning of April 15.

VP: Oh, right. I was, uh, scheduling a post. For my Instagram. I do that sometimes.

RCIPS: Huh, that's interesting.

VP: What do you mean?

RCIPS: Interesting that you would bother to schedule a post, using a very expensive at-sea satellite Wi-Fi system that was password protected. Especially when you were going to be onshore in Key West in a few hours.

VP: I knew we were going to be busy, and I didn't want to forget.

RCIPS: I see. So it wasn't because you were contacting someone by the name of Gerard Gallman?

VP: I'm sorry, I don't know who you're talking about.

RCIPS: Let me refresh your memory, then. I have a statement here taken by the Key West Police Department from a Mr. Gerard Gallman, also known as Buddy. Maybe that name rings a bell?

He says the two of you met at Sloppy Joe's.

VP: [softly] I don't know. I meet a lot of people. I actually get stopped by fans sometimes who want to take a selfie with me. Maybe he was one of them.

RCIPS: Well, this particular person says he met you for the purpose of selling you an illicit substance.

VP: I don't know what to tell you about that. It isn't true.

RCIPS: I'd be happy to read you his statement. He provided copies of your text messages as well . . . Guess Mr. Gallman likes to make sure all his transactions are documented. Insurance or something.

VP: [exhales] Fine! I did meet Buddy, or whatever his name is. But I just wanted to get some sleeping pills because it was hard to sleep on the yacht and Giselle threw mine away.

RCIPS: Sleeping pills, you say?

VP: Yes, sleeping pills. I have trouble sleeping sometimes.

RCIPS: Hmm, I find it rather hard to believe that someone who cares what kind of water they drink would buy sleeping pills off the street from a stranger. Would you like to think about your answer?

VP: No.

RCIPS: I mean, I suppose technically Rohypnol is a sleeping pill. Though that's not why most people buy it. Usually they're more interested in knocking someone out. So maybe you'd like to have a seat and explain why a straight-A student like yourself was buying roofies from a strange dealer in a bar?

VP: Roofies? Listen, it's not what you think. She said I owed her one and— [stops abruptly]

RCIPS: Ah, so they were for a friend, is that it? Or maybe you were holding them for someone else? We hear that a lot, from spring breakers especially. Lots of strange things just magically end up in people's pockets on vacation, it seems. Would you like to continue?

VP: No. I wouldn't. I'm not saying another word. Not until I have a lawyer. I'm not stupid. I know my rights.

Dear Mom,

I didn't even bother with the whole weekend pass thing. If Unterman wants to bust me for leaving school, he can go for it. Maybe Dad will actually notice me if I get in trouble again.

By the time I got to Westville it was late. So I went to the chalet and spent a sleepless night staring at the ceiling, listening for the sound of your ghost.

But the only noises were the wind howling outside and the rumble of the heat coming on.

As soon as the sun came up, I showered, had some coffee, and headed into town.

Couture Hardware was already packed with trucks. I went inside and puttered through the aisles, doing my best to look interested in different sized nails and screws. Where was that girl Allison? I hoped it wasn't her day off or something.

Finally, she walked in from a back room, dressed in her blue apron. She was typing on her phone as she went, eyes cast down. When she looked up and saw me, she came to a dead stop.

Hi, I said.

Allison scowled and jammed her phone into her apron pocket.

You lost again? she asked.

No, I said. Actually, I came to see you.

She continued to scowl.

Can we maybe talk for a minute? I asked.

I need to work, Allison said, turning and walking away.

Please, I said to her retreating back. I need your help. It's about Maggie. You tried to warn me about her. I want to know why.

Allison stopped and faced me. What, she screwed you over, too? Not my problem. I don't need to get sucked into her drama again.

PLEASE! I said, letting some well-practiced tears spill down my cheeks. I wiped them away and bit my lower lip. You're the only one I could think of who can help.

Allison exhaled. Fine, she said. But not in here. Meet me in the parking lot out back by the propane filling station in five minutes.

I bought a pack of gum and a Coke and then went outside. It felt like hours, not minutes, before Allison turned up in the snow-covered parking lot. She stopped in front of me, puffy jacket shrugged over her blue apron.

I don't have long, she said, hot breath freezing in little puffs in front of her face. I have to do inventory, and my dad's already on my case. What do you want?

I swallowed hard. You said before I can't trust Maggie. What did you mean by that?

Ha! Allison said with a snort. Maggie cares about one thing, and that's Maggie. Not sure what else you need to know. Seems like you already figured that one out.

And? I asked. Is that it?

Is that it? Allison barked out a laugh. You've been to her house, right? The farm is falling apart. Her dad is all messed up and never leaves the trailer. They're broke as hell. Did you ever stop and ask yourself how someone like Maggie can afford to attend Prep?

There was a lawsuit, I said. She was being bullied and her old school paid her tuition. That's what she told me.

I'm sure she did, Allison said. Got to give her credit for sticking to her story.

So her family didn't sue the school? I asked.

No, they did, Allison answered. Or they threatened to, at least. But Maggie wasn't being bullied. Not like she said.

She wasn't?

Allison shook her head.

I don't get it.

Allison sighed. She blew the whistle on our track coach when she found out he'd been giving supplements to some team members. You know, to enhance performance. They weren't illegal, but they weren't exactly allowed in competition.

Suddenly everything clicked. The newspaper article. The girl next to Maggie in the relay team picture. The one she'd had her arm around. Her name was Allison.

You were friends, weren't you? I said.

Yeah, until Maggie destroyed my life, Allison said.

So you were one of the people using—

Allison cut me off. No! But it didn't matter. The whole team got banned from competition for the rest of the year. And some of us were counting on a win at states for scholarships and college recruiting. That all got shot to hell. So yeah, people got pissed at Maggie and gave her some shit. I did feel bad about that. But you know what? I don't anymore.

Why not?

Because, Allison said, somehow she managed to turn it all around so that SHE was the victim. And the next thing you know, she's got a free ride to your fancy prep school while the rest of us are stuck here.

Didn't she get some sort of death threat, though? I asked.

Allison laughed. You mean the one from that fake Instagram account? I can say with one hundred percent certainty that Maggie made that post herself.

What? I said, taken aback. Why do you think that?

Because the post had a picture in it, Allison said.

Yeah?

I'm the one who took that picture, Allison said. At a party junior year. But I never posted it anywhere. The only person I shared it with was Maggie, because I thought it would make her laugh. I never shared it with anyone else.

I don't understand, I said. If you knew she posted that message herself, why didn't you say anything?

I couldn't, Allison said, tears rimming her eyes. I wasn't supposed to be at the party, okay? And if you knew this town, my PARENTS, God, they shipped me off to Catholic school in sixth grade because . . . She paused and sucked in a deep breath, glancing briefly away. Look, the details don't matter. I don't expect you to understand. Let's just say this isn't your side of the mountain, okay? And Westville High isn't that progressive little school for elite kids you go to. Some of us have to be careful what we do and say.

Do you still have that picture? I asked.

No, I deleted it, Allison said, scoffing. Because MAGGIE asked me to.

Oh, I answered. How about the Instagram post? Do you have that?

Yeah, Allison said. The account was deleted, but I think I have a screenshot of it.

She tapped her phone a few times, spun it around, and showed me. Then she stuffed her phone in her pocket and kicked at the snow-covered gravel. Do you need anything else? My dad will be pissed if he finds me out here taking another break, she said.

No, I said. Thanks.

She started walking away, then turned back.

What is it? I asked.

Just be careful, okay? she said. Don't let Maggie anywhere near your heart. Because if you do, she'll go ahead and stick a knife right into it.

DAY 1

APRIL 12—MIDDAY

Latitude, longitude: 41.093812, -71.926134

1 nautical mile off the coast of Long Island, New York

We pull away from the docks, *The Escape*'s wake churning blue and white as we make our way out to sea. A seagull squawks overhead, the yacht's horn sounds, and Giselle pops the cork from a bottle of champagne. A combination of excitement and terror washes over me as I realize there's no turning back now.

We're on our way into the open ocean.

"To spring break!" Giselle exclaims, handing us each a glass.

"To spring break!"

We raise our champagne flutes and clink them together. I take a sip, my cheeks warming as the bubbles tickle my throat. Giselle brings her glass to her lips, then pauses.

"Oh!" she says. "And to Emi! Who got her acceptance to the University of Southern California on the way here!"

"To Emi!" Vivian and I say.

Vivian hugs her. "Oh. My. God!! Congratulations, Em! That's so amazing."

"Really awesome," I say.

Everyone cheers.

Except Emi.

Instead, she looks stricken.

"What's the matter?" Giselle says, eyebrows pushing together. "I thought you were excited! It's all you could talk about an hour ago."

"I'm not going," Emi mumbles in response.

Giselle lowers her glass, setting it on the bar with such force, I'm surprised it doesn't shatter. "*You're not going?*"

Emi nods slightly and looks away. *The Escape* slices through the waves. The air is briny and warm, with only a hint of cool still lingering in the spring breeze. But the temperature up here has just dropped to freezing. I shiver and wrap my arms around myself.

"Let me guess," Giselle says, biting back the venom in her voice.

Everyone's eyes are fixed on Emi, who is shifting uncomfortably in her chair and not looking at anyone. She chews her lip and twirls a strand of black hair around her finger.

"Zane didn't get in," she says, barely audible.

"Emiene!" Giselle says. "USC has been your dream school since we were little kids! You've been working toward this for years! Seriously, how many months did you put into your film sample?"

I can't even imagine giving up my dream school. Not after working so hard to get in and get a scholarship. I'd light myself on fire before I'd turn that down.

"It's okay," Emi says. "Penn State has a solid film program."

"Not like USC!" Giselle says. "If your relationship with Zane can't survive being at different schools, then—"

"I don't want to go to USC." Emi cuts her off.

"Emi!" Giselle continues. "Since when? Since five minutes ago when that knucklehead didn't get in? You cannot—"

"I'm done talking about it," Emi says. "It's my decision, not yours. Maybe you should be the next Haverford to consider running for president since you enjoy telling other people what to do so much."

The deck falls silent.

"I. Am. Not. My. Father," Giselle says through gritted teeth.

The Escape's engines grind louder as we motor farther into the Atlantic. The coast of Long Island recedes, until all we can see is ocean in every direction. The water below churns like a living thing, undulating, the waves pulsing like heartbeats. It's awesome and terrifying, all at once. Like one of those waves could expand at any moment, reach up, and swallow us whole. The boat rocks beneath us, and I feel the sudden urge to hang on to something for balance.

Emi gets up and walks behind the bar. She pulls out a bottle of rum and four shot glasses, lining them up in a neat little row on the marble top. They slide to the left as the boat tilts. Emi stops them with her hand and fills them with rum.

"How about a game?" she says.

"Oooh!" Giselle says. "I know. How about Truth or Dare?"

Emi glares at her. "Very funny. I was thinking something more like Never Have I Ever."

Giselle shrugs.

"Sounds fun to me," Vivian says. "I haven't played that in forever!"

Emi hands us each a glass. "Who's first?"

"I'll go!" Vivian says, rubbing her hands together.

She twists her mouth to the side, thinking.

"Never have I ever . . . been to a weight-loss spa."

Giselle rolls her eyes. "Oh my God, Viv," she says. "How many times do I have to tell you I wasn't at a weight-loss spa this summer! It was a wellness spa. Big difference! Sorry, but I'm not drinking. You'll have to try harder than that."

"Yeah, yeah. Okay. You still did lose weight, though, but whatever," Vivian says, biting her lip. "Next?"

We go around the circle a few times, the nevers ranging from basic ("Never have I ever snuck out after curfew") to silly ("Never have I ever gone a day without wearing underpants"). Everyone's downed at least one shot.

Except Emi, who's been sitting there pointedly not taking any.

"Hey, how are you not drinking at all?" Vivian says, tilting her empty shot glass toward Emi.

"Hold on. I can make Miss Perfect drink," Giselle says.

The color drains, just a little, from Emi's cheeks.

"Never have I ever . . ." Giselle says, slowly dragging out her words. "Told a lie."

It's supposedly aimed at Emi, but now Giselle is looking directly at me. I reach for a shot glass, hand shaking as I bring it to my lips. The rum burns on its way down, just like Giselle's stare.

Vivian reaches for her glass. Emi leaves hers sitting on the bar.

"Okay, be real," Vivian says, gently setting down her shot glass with a grimace. "You never lie, Emi?"

Emi shakes her head.

"What about when you said those grain-free, egg-free, sugar-free brownies of Vivian's were delicious?" Giselle asks.

"Wait, you guys didn't like my brownies?" Vivian says.

"Sorry, Viv," Giselle says. "They tasted like shoe leather."

"Well, they were delicious . . . to Vivian," Emi says. "I never lie about things that matter."

"Oh?" Giselle says.

Emi scowls at Giselle. "You can't do that, you know."

"Do what?" Giselle says. "Call you out on your bullshit?"

"No," Emi answers. "You can't say something you've actually done. It's against the rules of Never Have I Ever. It's cheating."

"Oh. My. God." Giselle rolls her eyes. "Because you wouldn't know anything about cheating, would you, Em? Go on, then. It's your turn."

Emi sits there a moment, stewing.

"Never have I ever betrayed a friend," she says, barely a whisper.

Her words hang heavy in the air as something unspoken passes between them. Giselle's eyes dart back and forth between Emi and the shot glass before she leans back in her chair, arms crossed.

She doesn't drink.

But I do.

And so does Vivian.

RECOVERED WHATSAPP MESSAGE, 4/15, 8:41 P.M.

HFord25: That's what I can offer. We have a deal, then?

Anon1407: Yes.

HFord25: Okay. I can have the money wired once you've delivered.

Anon1407: No.

HFord25: No? I thought we had a deal?

Anon1407: We do. But I want cash. No digital trail. I'll contact you with a drop-off spot in George Town once the yacht arrives.

Dear Mom,

Well, today's the day. March 21. I'm finally eighteen, and you know what that means.

An enormous red-velvet cake and pair of emerald earrings arrived in my room after dinner, along with a stack of paperwork. My phone rang shortly after.

Happy birthday, Giselle! Dad said. Did you like your present? How was the cake?

The earrings are beautiful, I said. Thank you. A complete surprise. I didn't bother telling him I don't like red velvet cake, because if he didn't know that by now, chances are he never would. And let's not forget he gave me emerald earrings last year, too. Must have a new assistant doing his shopping.

I kept my tone neutral and polite, like I was talking to a teacher I wanted an A from, not my own dad. Because he's never really been much of a father to me, has he?

That huge cake made me the most popular girl in the dorm, I told him.

Oh, I don't think you need a cake to help with that, Dad said in his fake chipper voice, sounding way more like candidate-mode Haverford than dad-mode Haverford. He paused. I waited.

He cleared his throat.

So, what's up? I finally said, unable to take the silence anymore.

Yes, so, exciting news! (There was that fake chipper voice again.) We had an offer. On the yacht . . .

Wait, what? The Escape? I said, letting my voice wobble. Are you serious? I didn't know we were selling her. Why?

Well, it wasn't up for sale, Dad said. But I got a call this morning, unsolicited, from a broker in Grand Cayman. He has a client willing to pay well over market value for it. Seems they saw the write-up in last year's Yachting News and fell in love.

I choked back a sob. No! I said. You can't sell her. I love that boat. I have so many memories on it with Mom.

I know, honey, he said. But it would be crazy to pass this up. We can buy two yachts with what this buyer is offering.

Not one with an interior that Mom designed, I said with a sniffle.

Your mom would understand. You know she valued people more than things.

And you value things more than people, I thought but didn't say. How long would I have to keep up this charade with Dad?

When does the sale go through? I asked.

As soon as possible, he said. The buyer is ready to put down a hefty deposit and is willing to sign off on the deal without a survey or sea trial. The only contingency is satisfactory delivery of the yacht to its home port in Grand Cayman by the end of April.

Then I want to go, I said. To deliver her to the new buyer. One final trip.

Oh, I don't know, Dad said. We can hire someone to do it. You know how Britney is on the water. It's not a short trip to the Cayman Islands.

I cringed at Britney's name. I knew how she was, and I didn't care. The last thing I wanted was to have her along, anyway.

Dad, I said. I'm eighteen now, remember? I don't need a chaperone. I'm an experienced boater. The Escape has a captain and staff on it who take care of everything, so it's not like I have to navigate or cook or clean. Maybe I could take a few friends along. It would be fun. Spring break is coming up soon. It would mean so much to me, I added, swallowing hard and choking back another well-practiced sob.

Dad was quiet. For a moment, I thought maybe he'd change his mind about selling the boat. Or maybe he'd say we would go together, just the two of us, without Britney. Maybe he wanted to spend time with me before I graduated and headed to college. Maybe I still was his daughter, even with you gone and his replacement family in place. It wouldn't make up for all the time he'd missed when I was growing up, not even close. But was it so terrible to hope that he really loved me? That our entire life together, before Britney, had meant something to him?

Okay, Dad said. As long as the buyer agrees, you can bring some friends and deliver The Escape to Grand Cayman. Brit, Knox, and I will take the jet and meet you there. We can spend a couple of days at the Ritz and fly home together after.

I deflated a little, even though I was getting what I asked for.

Maybe, for once, I wanted to get what I needed.

Okay, I'll start planning an itinerary, I said. I want to stop a couple of places on the way down. Is that all right?

That should be fine, Dad said. As long as you remember,

everywhere you go and everything you do, you're a representative of this family.

Yes, sir, I said with a sigh.

Dad cleared his throat. And we should talk soon, too, he said. About how to best manage your inheritance. You got the paperwork I sent?

And there it was. The REAL reason for this call.

I thought about the shock Dad must have felt when he realized, after you died, that you'd rewritten your will. That you'd left everything—except for a few hundred thousand dollars, the Manhattan penthouse, and The Escape—to me.

At first, I wasn't entirely sure why you did it. But when Dad married Britney, I began to understand. Maybe you knew. Maybe you knew all along that it wasn't ME keeping Dad around. It was your MONEY. Maybe you knew Britney was just waiting in the wings to swoop in and take your place. Wear your jewelry. Spend your money. Live YOUR life.

It's really a lot for someone your age to manage, Dad continued. I think my firm is best equipped to handle an account of that size. I think that would be best for everyone, don't you? Let you concentrate on your studies and not the intricacies of a half-billion-dollar estate.

I was done playing nice.

No, I said.

Excuse me? Dad asked. What was that?

NO, I repeated. I am not signing my trust over to your firm. I can manage it just fine on my own.

Now, princess, Dad began. *I think we should talk this over.*

Somewhere in the background, I heard Knox begin to cry.

There's nothing to talk about, I said. *Thanks for the cake. I have homework. And you'd better go. I think your SON needs you.*

Then I hung up.

Subject: EMIENE KAROUSOS (EK)

Interviewer: Detective Rebecca Bennett, RCIPS

Date: 4/16

RCIPS: Thank you, Miss Karousos. I know this is difficult. We're almost done, okay?

EK: Okay. But I'm exhausted. I barely slept last night.

RCIPS: I understand. Just quickly, I've also received a file from the FBI with their initial findings regarding the contents of Miss Haverford's cell phone. [shuffles papers]

EK: Wait, you have her phone?

RCIPS: [pauses] No. We do not. We have the data—text messages, emails, photographs—that the FBI was able to download from the cloud. You look concerned. Are you concerned about what might be in that data? Something you'd like to tell me about?

EK: [clears throat] No. I'm not concerned.

I already told you, I'm tired. This whole thing has been a nightmare.

RCIPS: Yes, I'm sure. Let me find the message from last night that caught my attention . . . [more papers shuffling] Ah, here it is! [sound of paper sliding across table] Do you recognize this photo?

EK: Uhhhhh . . . [blows out heavy breath] Sure, that's me.

RCIPS: And who is the young man you're kissing in the photo? Your boyfriend?

EK: No, that's Max.

RCIPS: Max?

EK: He's nobody. Just a guy we go to school with. But listen, it's not what it looks like, okay? [voice rising]

RCIPS: Perhaps you'd like to explain it, then? The FBI found this photo attached to a draft email Miss Haverford was writing to someone called Zane, who Miss Page tells me is your boyfriend. Why do you suppose she'd do that if it's not what it looks like?

EK: Because she's Giselle! Because she thinks it's hilarious to pull pranks!

It's like her . . . *thing*, playing stupid pranks on people. She does it all the time. Yeah, I kissed Max, but it was on a dare that Giselle made me do at a party a couple of weeks ago. How was I supposed to know she'd be hiding around the corner, taking a picture?

RCIPS: That must have made you mad.

EK: Yes. I mean, no! Ugh, stop putting words in my mouth! I really can't do this anymore. I want to go home. You're wasting your time, talking to me. Maggie is the one who should be sitting here! Where is she?

RCIPS: You are free to go any time. This interview is voluntary, remember? [sound of chair scraping back] But I suggest you sit back down, because I think you'll want a chance to weigh in on what I have to show you next.

DEPARTURE DAY

APRIL 12

The Long Island Coast

I was so afraid of being late, I arrived at the yacht club nearly an hour early. The rest of the girls are still at least a half hour away, judging by their ongoing flurry of group texts. Vivian is somewhere on Route 27 in the back of a town car. Giselle and Emi are en route from Manhattan with Senator and Mrs. Haverford and baby Knox.

I pull into a parking space and hang the visitor pass Giselle gave me from my rearview mirror. You'd think by now I'd be used to driving the crappiest vehicle in the lot. But I still feel out of place here among the Beemers and Mercedes, Mom's old suitcase with the broken wheel propped on the cracked leather passenger seat next to me.

The yacht club sits straight ahead, a gray-shingled Cape Cod–style building attached to an oversized replica of a lighthouse that appears to be a restaurant. Beyond that, I can see pool fencing and a pair of tennis courts.

And past it all, the docks and the open sea.

I take in a deep breath, excited and terrified at the same time.

My phone buzzes and I glance at the screen.

More group texts from the girls.

You packed your silver bikini, right?!

Hahaha, who needs a bathing suit?

OMG, you're nuts. I am not
hot-tubbing with you naked.

I can't believe your parents are
letting us take this trip ALONE!!

Dad and Britney. Not PARENTS. You can
thank the wicked witch for the solo trip.

She gets seasick. Boo-freaking-hoo.

Yo, where's Maggie? How come
she's not saying anything?

She's driving herself, right? Can't text.

Oh yeah, right. Wish I could
drive myself. My chauffeur drives like
an eighty-year-old grandma, groan.

My phone buzzes again. I glance down, thinking I'll find
another message from one of the girls. Except it's from Striker29.
I stiffen as I read.

Maggie, listen, I can't get into the details, but
you have to trust me. I know you think you and
Giselle are close. But she's NOT YOUR FRIEND.
Please, I'm begging you, GO HOME. Forget
about this trip and don't get on that yacht. It's
not too late!

The heat rises on my neck as I let Wyatt's words sink in.

Don't get on that yacht . . .

I appreciate his concern.

But Wyatt's wrong.

It *is* too late.

I have to get on that yacht. The die was cast the day I stole that letter. When I faked my way into Prep. There's no turning back. I'm here, and I'm going to finish what I've started.

I shove my phone away, leaving his message unanswered, and climb from the truck.

The air is salty and warm, a hint—I hope—of things to come. I tilt my face to the sun as the breeze catches my hair. I sling my bag over my shoulder and climb the steps to the yacht club.

The white-painted front porch overlooks the marina. I lower myself into an Adirondack chair and prop my suitcase next to me. There's a huge lounge and sitting area inside the club behind me, filled with overstuffed blue and white furniture and nautical decor, and I imagine people named Biff and Buffy who don't vacation here but "summer" in the massive "cottages" that dot the shoreline. I'm more comfortable outside in the fresh air.

I'm getting ready to pull out my sketchbook when I hear someone shouting my name.

"Maggie!" It's Vivian, dragging an entire set of Gucci luggage behind her. She plops down in the chair next to me and lets out a breath. "We're the first ones here? I'm so excited!"

"Me too." I nod and tilt my head toward the docks that stretch out into Long Island Sound, dotted with yachts and sailboats. It's like a postcard, crisp white masts set against the bright blue sky, clanging in the gentle breeze. "Which one is hers?"

"I can't believe you have to ask," Vivian says. "It's the big one, on the end. *The Escape.*"

Of course it is. I should have known. I've been to her "chalet" in Vermont. Still, when Giselle said yacht, I'd pictured something like a big sailboat. *The Escape* is more like a mini cruise ship, bobbing gently in the water at the very end of the pier, towering over the rest of the boats. Even from here, I can see the crew, polishing windows and shining the deck rails.

Dual waves of excitement and panic wash over me.

You can do this, I tell myself, over and over. *They aren't any better than you.*

I'm like a walking affirmation program. My old guidance counselor would be so proud.

"Hey, what do you think?" Vivian holds up her hands and waggles her long fingers around. Her nails are turquoise blue, with a touch of white feathered at the tips, like a wave.

"Very cool," I say.

"I know, right!" Vivian says. "Thanks! I did them just for the trip. I've already gotten a few thousand likes on Instagram, and I just posted on the way here!"

"That's awesome."

"I brought my polish collection along," she says, leaning back. "It's vegan and cruelty-free. I could do your nails, too. I'm trying to get EMMA Nail to sponsor me."

I hold up my own hands, nails chewed to the quick. "Yeah,

doubt these will help your cause."

Vivian laughs. "Fair enough. I do have some essential oils that might get you to stop doing that. Just make sure to tag me when you post the results, 'kay? Oh, wait, you don't do social media, do you? I forgot."

Before I can answer, my phone buzzes and I glance at the screen, scared to see another warning from Wyatt.

But it's Giselle.

All aboard!!! 🛥️🌴😎

"They're here!" Vivian squeals, looking down at her own phone. "Let's go!"

She pops up and races toward the pier, luggage clunking behind her. I follow. Emi is climbing from the back seat of the Haverfords' Mercedes, wearing oversized black sunglasses, a halter top and light sweater, linen capris, and strappy heels. She looks like a 1940s movie star. I feel woefully underdressed in my denim shorts and simple white tee.

Giselle climbs out next and gives Knox, sleeping in his car seat, a gentle kiss on his round cheek.

"See you soon, buddy," she says to the top of his head.

Vivian runs over to Britney and gives her a hug. Weird. I didn't know they were friends.

Britney coos over the blue streak in Vivian's hair that matches her nails, until Giselle shoots them both a withering look. Vivian backs away, frowning, but not before Britney hands her a small brown paper bag and whispers something in her ear.

Giselle hugs her dad, and it's stiff and awkward, even though

275

it seems she tries, unsuccessfully, to grip him a bit more tightly before he lets her go.

"Have fun, princess," Mr. Haverford says with a pat on her shoulder. "And be good. We'll see you in Cayman."

Giselle nods, tucks a small Louis Vuitton bag over her shoulder, and heads toward the pier. Yacht stewards in crisp white uniforms materialize out of nowhere and collect our luggage to deposit in our staterooms.

I try not to gape as we cross the gangway onto the yacht. Whatever I was picturing back on land is completely blown away by the reality of being on board. The interior gleams, all windows and polished mahogany, cozy loungers and overstuffed pillows in turquoise and blue. Every single view and vista is angled to let the outside in. The crew—a raven-haired captain, chef in a tall hat, and a slew of other staff in white uniforms—stand in a perfect line in the atrium and welcome us aboard with little salutes.

Giselle greets them like they're old friends, even hugging a few. Then she stops toward the end of the line, in front of a woman in her late twenties. Giselle cocks her head to the side, inspecting her name tag, which reads: *Rita, Chief Steward.*

"What happened to Daniel?" Giselle asks. "Dad didn't mention he wasn't going to be here." She seems almost shaken by this fact, though I can't imagine why.

"Last-minute change," the woman answers. "Daniel came down with the flu. I'm Rita. I'll be filling in for him as chief steward on this trip. I know Daniel has been with your family for years. But don't worry, your father hired me personally. I can assure you that you and your guests will be well taken care of."

"Oh. Yes, of course," Giselle answers. "Nice to meet you, then, Rita. I hope Daniel feels better soon. The flu, you say?"

Rita nods, her neck flushing just slightly above the collar of her uniform shirt. Giselle inspects her a moment longer, then smiles breezily and introduces herself to a couple of the other new crew members.

After the introductions are complete, Giselle leads us into the lounge area. A set of clear spiral stairs leads up to the next level. Beyond that, a door opens to a narrow corridor. Giselle directs me toward it.

"You'll be in the guest suite, Maggie," she says, pointing. "Number three on the end. Emi and I are sharing my suite, and Viv will be in the other forward-facing suite on the next deck. Hope you don't mind bunking down here alone."

"No, that's fine," I say, even though I feel like a third wheel all over again, like the first day I met the girls. They were all talking about the exotic and amazing things they'd done over their summer breaks. Bonfires in the Hamptons and trips to Paris and spas.

I was shoveling shit. Literally. I laugh out loud.

"Something funny?" Emi says.

I shake my head.

"Consider yourself lucky," Giselle says. "You don't want to room with Emi anyway. She sleepwalks. I woke up once to find her standing over me. It was creepy as hell!"

"At least I wasn't holding a pillow," Emi says, raising her arms, and they all laugh. I don't. The image of Emi trying to smother me in my sleep is just a bit too realistic. If she had the chance, I think she would.

"Okay!" Giselle claps her hands together. "Here's the plan. Let's head to our rooms, freshen up. Then meet on the top deck for sail-away champagne, 'kay?"

The girls head up the spiral staircase, and I walk down the empty corridor, alone. I can't even begin to imagine what their rooms must be like when I open the door to mine. It's spacious and airy with a wall of windows and glass doors opening to a private balcony. There's a king-sized bed covered with a satiny duvet and fluffy pillows. My suitcase already sits on a rack, next to a built-in closet. Opposite that is a full bathroom with jetted shower, elaborate tile work, and a ceramic bowl sink.

An envelope with my name in calligraphy on the front sits on the table beside my bed. I open it up, slip out the note hand-written on linen card stock, and read:

Dear Miss Mitchell,

On behalf of the Haverford family, Captain Martin Hjelkrem, and the crew of The Escape, it is my pleasure to welcome you aboard! It is our goal to exceed all your expectations on your journey. As your cabin steward, I am at your service if you require anything, no matter how small. Laundry may be put in the bag you'll find in your stateroom closet and placed outside your door by 8:00 p.m., for return the following morning. Meals will be served in the dining lounge on Deck 2, and on the pool deck on Deck 3, weather permitting, according to the attached schedule. If you need to reach me directly, any time of day or night, simply use any of the ship's phones and dial 5.

Have a pleasant voyage!

Marina

Cabin Steward

As I tuck the note back in the envelope, I'm reminded of the letter hidden in my suitcase. The albatross around my neck. I quickly pull it out and stash it in the small room safe, close the metal door, and change the code. The lock clicks shut.

Time to find the other girls.

Back in the corridor, it takes a moment to determine which way to go. When I head right, I end up at a small library, tall shelves stocked with books and board games. I double back and go the other way until I reach the atrium. I climb the spiral staircase, which leads to the pool deck, and then head down another corridor that passes by two sets of closed double doors. Those must be the forward-facing suites. One more flight of stairs brings me to the upper deck, with its bar, hot tub, and oversized loungers all arranged to enjoy the ocean views.

Giselle is already there, stretched on one of the loungers, eyes closed and face tilted toward the sky, serene. She doesn't seem to realize I'm here. I debate clearing my throat or saying something when her eyes abruptly flick open.

"Oh!" she says, sitting up and tucking her hair behind her ear. "You snuck up on me! How long have you been standing there?"

"I just got here," I say. "Didn't want to wake you up. You looked so peaceful."

"Mmmm," she says with a breezy smile. "Just thinking, that's all. This is my favorite part of the journey. Setting sail. So many possibilities. I like beginnings. That's what life should be, don't you think? A bunch of beginnings. Screw endings, am I right?"

I nod, feeling awkward. Everything I've done to get myself here, and I'm still not sure if I can pull this off. Maybe I should just hand her the letter—the one I never should have taken in the first place. Throw the ball in her court and see what she does.

Except, things haven't been the same with Giselle recently. Not since winter break. She's barely spoken to me directly for more than a few minutes. I've had zero chance to get her alone. If I didn't know better, I'd think she'd been actively avoiding me.

But as far as I can tell, she's been avoiding *everyone* lately. She's either been in her room or somewhere in a corner, hunched over her laptop, despite the fact we're in our final quarter before graduation and all our teachers are pretty much giving us fluff work at this point.

And she did invite me on this trip.

Insisted that I come, really.

So perhaps I'm overthinking the whole thing.

Making something out of nothing, like my old friends on the track team said. Maybe she's just been stressed. Preoccupied with school or things that have nothing to do with me. Maybe she's not Allison, who only showed me her true self in secret. Maybe Giselle's simply got her own stuff going on.

The message from Wyatt slides to the front of my mind . . .

She's not your friend.

You know what? That's okay. Friendship's not what I'm here for anyway.

"Yeah, screw endings," I say, returning Giselle's smile.

Emi and Vivian burst onto the deck.

"Omigod, this is soooooo amazing!" Vivian squeals, pointing her phone in every direction and snapping pictures.

"The Swiss chocolates on the pillow were a brilliant touch," Emi says, popping a truffle into her mouth. Chocolates? I remind myself to check my bed when I return to my stateroom.

Giselle climbs off her lounger with a huge grin and grabs an overstuffed bag by her feet.

"Okay, girls, I got us all a little sail-away gift!" she says.

"Ooh! Presents!" Vivian rubs her hands together.

Giselle pulls out four matching plush rainbow-striped hooded cover-ups. "These are to commemorate our trip. Can get a little cold coming out of the pool and hot tub, especially at night, so these should come in handy!"

She gives us each a cover-up. I spin mine around. *#SpringBreak* is embroidered across the back in huge black letters.

"Oh my God, these are so dorky," Vivian says, slipping hers over her head. "And I love it!" She immediately snaps a selfie and I figure it'll be .02 seconds before it's uploaded and liked thousands of times. People can't seem to get enough of beautiful rich girls living their rich and beautiful lives.

"I thought you'd appreciate them most of all, Viv," Giselle says. "You do love a little free swag, isn't that right?"

Vivian's smile falters just a bit. But she recovers, grinning ear to ear as we huddle together in our matching cover-ups and strike a pose for another selfie. A little rush of joy courses its way through my veins. It's thrilling, feeling like an official part of their group, even if it's only temporary. Even if it's utterly meaningless. Even if I'll never truly belong here.

#SpringBreak!

"Yay!" Giselle says. "Also, last thing before we go. Download the SeaChat app and then switch your phones to airplane mode. That way we can communicate with each other, 'kay? There's nothing dear old Dad hates more than wasting money texting at sea. Trust me, I've learned that the hard way, ha ha!"

I tap my phone. A Wi-Fi alert for Escape Guest pops up, but it's password protected. I download the SeaChat app, create a profile, then switch to airplane mode and put my phone away.

"Oh, and one more thing!" Giselle reaches into her bag again and pulls out four sheets of paper. "Our itinerary!"

She hands us each one. I look down and read. Giselle has every day planned out, practically to the hour. Umbrella and drink and sunshine emojis dot the paper, with menus and random bits of info about our port stops. Like the fact the Bahamas is the only country with a marching band on its currency.

"You are seriously the biggest dork," Vivian says. "And I love it!"

"Never hurts to be prepared. Or informed." Giselle grins. Directly at *me*.

I'm trying to figure out what—if anything—she's getting at when there's a clatter and rumble from somewhere down below. The yacht's engines roar to life. More uniformed crew emerge a few decks down, untying *The Escape*.

And we're off.

Nothing but blue sky and open seas ahead; the other girls squealing with excitement, snapping photos and waving back toward the docks like we're celebrities. And I guess, in a way, we are.

Yet I can sense dark clouds, gathering on the horizon. Like back at home when a sudden summer storm would roll in over the hills, obliterating the blue sky. The way the cows would get restless when they felt the shift in weather, the electricity in the air.

I feel that now.

Restless.

Wanting to sit.

To find my dry patch of grass and hunker down before the storm hits.

Dear Mom,

Well, this is it. We're on our way to The Escape. Dad is driving, Britney's in the passenger seat. I'm in the back, Emi on the other side, Knox in his car seat between us. Knox has fallen asleep, with his round cheek smooshed against the side of his seat. I can feel his warm little baby breaths on the side of my arm. I look at him and all I want is to wrap him in a bubble. Keep the world and its poison darts and arrows from ever touching him.

It's been a long few weeks.

I have never felt more alone in my life. It's as though I've lost everyone I ever cared about. You. Emi. Viv. Even Maggie isn't who I thought she was. And Dad? Ha, right. Dad's only goal has been to try and pressure me into signing over my trust to his firm.

He'll have to kill me first.

There's nobody left.

Almost.

I went to see Wyatt last night. One final time before I departed on The Escape. I told him everything I knew about Maggie. How she'd lied and cheated her way into Prep. How he couldn't trust her. How I loved him and always had. I thought if he knew all that, he'd choose me. He'd choose US. Not her.

You want to know what he said?

He told me to go to hell. In those exact words. GO. TO. HELL!

Well, you know what, Mom?

Maggie Mitchell had better WATCH HER BACK . . . because if I'm going to hell, I'm going to take her right along with me.

She can't run anymore.

DAY 5

APRIL 16—PRESENT

Latitude, longitude: 19.278740, -81.429159

1 nautical mile off the coast of Grand Cayman

I slap the journal shut, hands shaking.

Maggie Mitchell had better WATCH HER BACK . . . She can't run anymore.

The SeaChat message from YouCantRun. It was Giselle. That confirms it.

This entire trip, Giselle was seeing how hard she could push me, wasn't she? And for what? To punish me for something she thought I did?

Not that it makes any difference. Because when someone pushes hard enough, apparently I push back.

If everything wasn't so completely messed up—if *I* hadn't so completely and horrifyingly messed up, I'd probably start laughing right now. Because Giselle was wrong. Dead wrong. About so many things. The letter. Me. *Wyatt.*

I was at his house after winter break dropping off his art portfolio. We never kissed. He only hugged me because he was grateful. I was the one person out of that entire school who cared enough to see how he was doing after getting expelled. Maybe because deep down I understood. How it felt to be different. An outcast. Someone's dirty little secret.

I'm so tired of secrets.

My mind races back to Allison. That day in the locker room when we found out our team would be barred from competing in the state finals. Every head in the room had swiveled toward me, faces filled with hatred. I'd caught Allison's eye, hoping she'd say something. *Anything.* Speak up in my defense. I was her other half, right? Her heart. Her *future.*

But all she did was shake her head and walk out.

I raced after her, distraught, catching up with her on the empty track.

"Allison," I'd said, gripping her shoulder, my voice shaking. "Talk to me. *Please!*"

She'd spun around and faced me. For a moment, I saw that girl from the playground, eyes wide with shock. Except this time, tears had replaced the mud streaming down her cheeks.

"I'm going to miss my chance," she said, trembling. "The scout from Michigan is going to be at states, and I won't be running. It's over for me. Do you understand what that means?"

"I'm so sorry," I said. "You have to believe me. *Please.* I was trying to do the right thing."

Allison swiped her cheeks with the back of her hand.

"Yeah, I know," she said. "But why, Maggie? Couldn't you have just turned Coach Whitney down when he offered you that stuff, instead of turning him in?"

"And let him give it to other people on the team? Maybe even get them hooked?" I said. All I could think of was my dad and those sleeping pills. The ones he ate like candy until the doctors

286

cut him off. Then he'd turned to whiskey, straight from the bottle. Anything to blot out the memories that clawed at his brain. The nightmares that wouldn't let him sleep. "No. I couldn't. It's not right, and you know it. I had no way of knowing our whole team would be punished!"

I reached for her. All I wanted to do was pull her close and put my head on her shoulder. Like that night in Kyle Parker's field. Curled up together in my flatbed, sharing a bottle of cheap wine, hands clasped together. Dreaming of a future, together, far away from her closed-minded parents and our tiny town.

Instead, she stepped back and folded her arms across her chest. I dropped my hand.

"Tell me something," she said.

"Anything."

"What *would* you have done?"

"I don't understand."

"If you *had* known," she said. "What would you have done if you had known this would all blow up? That my chance to get a scholarship would be shot to shit? That I'd be stuck working at my parents' store, probably for the rest of my life? Would you still have turned Coach in?"

I hesitated. A moment too long. And it that split second, I lost the only girl I'd ever loved.

Allison shook her head. "That's what I thought. Maybe sometimes being right isn't the most important thing. I have to go or I'll be late for work. Goodbye, Maggie."

She turned and walked away, leaving me on that empty

track, with nowhere to run. My heart shattered.

Not long after, the bullying started. That wasn't the worst of it, though. The worst was Allison, who stood by and didn't do a single thing. Looked the other way when someone stuck their foot out and tripped me in the cafeteria. Pretended not to notice when the air was let out of my truck's tires, leaving me stranded in the parking lot after school. It was amazing how fast they all turned on me, like all along they'd hated me and had just been waiting for any excuse to come in for the kill. Prove that they weren't like me.

The school administration wasn't any better.

If they didn't see it, then it didn't happen.

And bullies are far too smart to get caught in the act, aren't they?

That's when I decided I only had one way out. So yeah, I posted that threat, taped those pictures to my own locker. As long as the evidence was staring them right in the face, the school would have to pay attention. *Allison* would have to pay attention. A part of me even hoped she'd come forward. Rat me out. At least then I'd know she wasn't ashamed. Of us. Of *me*.

When she didn't, I took it as a sign. To run.

Get the hell out of Westville High.

Get to *Giselle*.

What was I thinking?

It made so much sense at the time.

One little lie.

I never believed it would turn me into this.

There's a grinding sound as *The Escape*'s engines shift gears, going slower now. Outside the balcony doors, the coastline of Grand Cayman slides closer into view, all white sand and moored boats and glittering hotels. Sunshine sparkling on the water. A vacation paradise.

My personal hell.

The docks loom in the distance.

Ticktock. Ticktock.

I'm almost out of time.

As soon as I step off this boat, I'll be arrested. I have no defense. No way to explain what happened. I can't fill in the blanks.

I pace the room, thinking.

Maybe I should do what I'm best at: *run*. Play the hand I've been dealt. Isn't that what Dad taught me when we played blackjack at our kitchen table? Isn't that what I did when I transferred to Prep?

I could take the passport and the money. Twenty thousand dollars is enough to get myself far away. We're close to land now. I could jump overboard. Swim to shore. Buy a plane ticket and fly somewhere safe. Take my lies and secrets into the water with me.

Escape.

Maybe if I'm free, there's still hope. I can figure out a way to make things right again. My entire life, I've only wanted to be a decent person. A good one. I've only wanted to do the right thing. Haven't I?

Ah, the lies we tell ourselves are the worst lies of all, aren't they?

Especially when we choose to believe them.

I empty the safe, zipping my phone, the passport, money, and the letter that started this whole mess, into a waterproof pouch. I remember the day it arrived in our mailbox. Mom was at work, pulling yet another double shift. Dad was in Afghanistan. Again. The herd was gone, an empty barn waiting for him when he came home. I know now what I should have done then—I should have set this letter on fire the minute I opened it. But no, I had to start chasing the ghosts of past mistakes that don't even belong to me.

As if I don't have enough of my own.

Hands fumbling with nerves, I pull on a bathing suit, pair of shorts, and T-shirt, and hook the pouch tightly around my waist.

I grab the bright orange life preserver from the back of the closet. Someone might spot me in this thing, but it's a risk I'll have to take. I don't know how far I can swim without it. I yank it on, tighten the straps until it's so snug I can hardly breathe, and try to calm my pounding heart.

The Escape's engines grind even slower, bringing us closer and closer to shore.

I pace the room, the minutes slipping away.

Ticktock. Ticktock.

Can I really do this?

Run, Maggie, run.

You can't fix this. So *run*. Salvage something from this mess. You can't save everyone else anymore, so at least save yourself. You would never set out to hurt anyone on purpose.

Would you?

I can't even answer that question anymore. I grab the journal and slide the balcony door open. The warm, salty air smacks me in the face. I walk to the railing and chuck the journal overboard, watching the pink sequins swirl until they're swallowed by the water. Down, down, down . . .

Gone.

It's now or never.

I suck in a deep breath and jump in after it.

Subject: EMIENE KAROUSOS (EK)

Interviewer: Detective Rebecca Bennett, RCIPS

Date: 4/16

   EK: So what is it that you wanted to show
   me?

RCIPS: Yes, one moment . . . [sound of door
   opening, something rolling across
   the tile floor, muffled voices] Thank
   you, Detective Sheeran. That will be
   all. [footsteps, sound of door clos-
   ing]

   EK: What's with the television?

RCIPS: Our forensics team has been studying
   last night's security footage from
   The Escape. Given your video editing
   skills, I wonder if you might give us
   an opinion on something. Your insight
   could be very helpful. [sound of button clicking, noise coming through
   speakers—female voices, wind whistling and the thrum of waves]

   EK: Do I have to watch this? I don't want

to watch this. I've seen this already and . . . [voice cracks]

RCIPS: Like I said, you are free to go anytime. I was simply hoping you could provide some insight on what our team has found. Let's just have a look, shall we?

[a clicking sound, muted voices from a video, another click, and the voices stop]

RCIPS: Okay, look at that. Right there! That's the thing I want to show you. Let me rewind. [noises repeat, sound of a remote being set on the table] Do you see how the video glitches, just slightly, when the figure that pushes Miss Haverford enters the screen? If you're not looking closely, you might miss it. But watch, there it is. What does it look like to you?

EK: [faintly] I don't know.

RCIPS: Interesting. Because I'm no film expert, but it looks to me like something's been deleted right before we see her enter. And I'm thinking, first we see this girl on the lounger here. [sound of tapping on television screen] But we don't see her get up, and that is odd, isn't it? And then watch, here comes the figure behind Miss Haverford. But we don't see where she has come from. Could be anywhere, no?

[sound of heavy breathing]

RCIPS: Perhaps you have a theory?

[silence]

RCIPS: There's something else. If you look very closely, see where we've zoomed in here. [tapping] This figure who pushed Miss Haverford is wearing shoes. The other girl, Miss Mitchell, was not. And it looks to me like someone would have to walk through broken glass to reach Miss Haverford. I wonder what that would do to a pair of delicate shoes? Say, lambskin? [long silence] Okay. Very well. The FBI is analyzing this video, too, and I'm sure they have forensics experts who are much more skilled than ours. Anyway, thanks for your help today. I am very sorry about your friend. But rest assured, we will get to the bottom of this.

And there will be charges for anyone withholding information pertinent to our investigation.

[another long silence]

RCIPS: The door is there, Miss Karousos. As I said, you are free to go. We will be in contact if there are any other questions. Thank you for your time.

EK: Wait. [high-pitched voice]

RCIPS: Yes? Is there something else? Something you'd like to tell us?

EK: A prank, okay? It was supposed to be a prank!

RCIPS: I'm sorry, what was supposed to be a prank?

EK: Pushing Giselle! It was me, in the video. I pushed her.

RCIPS: So you are admitting, on the record, to pushing Miss Haverford overboard?

EK: Yes. I mean NO! I didn't push her overboard.

RCIPS: I'm afraid I'm not following.

EK: [deep sigh] The whole thing was supposed to be some stupid prank that Giselle wanted to play on Maggie to teach her a lesson. She kept bugging me about it the entire trip. At first I said okay, but then I changed my mind. I didn't want to do it, because what if she really fell into the water, right? But Giselle said not to worry, she was really good at dismounts in cheer and she wouldn't fall. And then she said if I didn't play along, she'd send that stupid picture to Zane.

RCIPS: Excuse me, let's back up. Are you saying she did or didn't go over-board?

EK: Not then, no. She landed on the deck right below, gave me the thumbs-up, and ran away. But . . .

RCIPS: But?

EK: But that's the thing, she never came back to the room. We couldn't find her in the morning, not anywhere. And then the crew found that huge dent on the railing with the blood and her necklace on it, and that's when I knew. Maggie got to her any-way . . . [muffled sobs] I should have been a better friend. I should have done more after her mom died, instead of believing her when she said she was fine. If I'd been there for her, maybe she wouldn't have let Maggie get so close. I should have done more to keep Maggie away . . . [breaks down in sobs]

RCIPS: Miss Karousos, withholding this information could have very seriously impacted our investigation. Why didn't you say anything?

EK: Because what difference did it make? You had the last location of her cell phone. The video was irrelevant. Anyone with a brain can tell that Maggie did it!

RCIPS: Well, from where I'm sitting, you have just admitted to pushing Miss Haverford in that video. You have said you wished you were a better friend. How am I to believe you aren't making up this story about a prank and simply trying to place the blame on Miss Mitchell?

EK: Then where is Maggie, huh? Innocent people don't run away when they get caught. You know who does? GUILTY ONES!

DAY 5

APRIL 16—PRESENT

Latitude, longitude: 19.278740, -81.429159
1 nautical mile off the coast of Grand Cayman

When I hit the water, the first sensation that registers is cold. Like tiny icicles pricking my body as I plummet beneath the waves. Almost instantly, my lifejacket jerks me upward, and I bob to the surface, eyes stinging, adrenaline coursing through my veins. I spit and take a greedy gulp of salty air, and immediately have to catch my breath.

Pain stabs at my right foot and shoots up my leg. I pull my knee toward my chest, wrapping my hand around the soggy bandage while my body lurches in the waves. Tears well in the corners of my eyes. I must have hit the water really hard and opened that cut back up. It's like stepping in that jagged glass all over again.

Something tickles the corner of my brain, pokes at me through the jolts of pain.

Think, Maggie, think.

The glass?

I remember how it felt, slicing my foot. Sharp. Piercing. Blood.

Don't pass out. Don't pass out . . .

Glass. Broken glass. All over the deck this morning.

How did it all get there?

I remember dropping my glass, and then what?

I rewind the security video in my mind and play it back, slowly. There's the image of me approaching Giselle from behind. The bottle, falling from her hand and smashing on the deck as I walk toward her . . .

Straight through broken glass?

Wait, what?

That's not possible. How could I have made it across the deck—with bare feet—and without a single scrape or cut?

The realization hits me, swift and hard: I couldn't have.

Because it wasn't me in that video.

I'm not forgetting anything.

I can't remember because I didn't do it. We all have matching cover-ups. It could have been any one of us, right?

Scratch that, it could have been *anyone* on that boat.

The thought is incredible and terrifying all at once.

Because if it wasn't me, it was someone else pretending to be me.

Someone who wants everyone to think I did it.

Someone who is still on *The Escape*, too far away now to catch, heading straight toward the docks—and the police—in George Town.

I start swimming, as fast as I can. But the shore barely seems to get any closer. I can't give up, though. I need to make it to land. For Sophie. For Dad. For *me*. I put every last bit of effort into moving forward.

By the time I stagger onto the beach, my legs are vibrating with exhaustion. I've moved past the point of pain. Everything—feet, hands, heart—have gone numb. A kid wanders along the sand toward me, plastic pail swinging in his hand.

"Look! A mermaid!" he shouts, pointing at me.

I smile shakily, as though standing here in a puffy orange life jacket, panting for air, is a perfectly normal thing to do. A bit farther up the beach I spot his parents. Watching.

"Connor!" the mom calls out. "Come back here, please!"

There's no concern in her voice for me, the mermaid who has seemingly washed ashore, injured. Just worry for the tow-headed kid. Somehow I'm not surprised. People's first instinct is to sidestep the disaster. Gawk from a distance. Like my former teammates and supposed friends.

But I guess I should be thankful. I don't need to draw any more attention to myself than necessary. What I need is to get out of sight. I stumble away and take refuge beneath a cluster of palm trees, where I shrug off the life vest and collapse in the sand.

I lean back, overcome with fatigue, and tell myself it's okay to close my eyes for a few minutes. Regain my strength. Then I'll get moving. Figure out what to do.

Figure out who set me up.

But when my eyelids flutter back open, I'm surprised to find I must have slept for hours—not minutes. The sun has slipped lower on the horizon. The beach is deserted. I am alone.

I bolt upright, sick with fear.

I've wasted too much time. By now, I'm sure *The Escape* has been thoroughly searched and cleared. The stories have been told. And the authorities have turned their attention to finding their number one suspect.

Me.

The cut on my foot burns. With a shuddery breath, I pull off the bandage. The wound has turned an angry red, throbbing in time with my pulse. At least it's not bleeding anymore. But I'll need to properly bandage it. Buy a pair of shoes. New clothes . . .

I take a deep breath, trying not to let myself get overwhelmed.

One step at a time, Maggie. One step at a time.

I pull my phone from the pouch around my waist. I shouldn't turn it on, because once I do, I'll be trackable. I know all this, logically. But before I make a move, I need to find out what's going on with the investigation.

I push the power button and the screen blows up with messages. My mom, Nana, Wyatt. I quickly read the message I ignored yesterday. Another plea to ditch the trip, get off the yacht, and go home as soon as I can. And then one from this morning. Just two words: *I'm sorry*.

Yeah, so am I, Wyatt. I should have taken your advice when I had the chance.

I scan the latest news updates. Oh, God, they've found a body. Unconfirmed report of a video showing that Giselle was pushed. Blood on the railing. I feel nauseated. Unsurprisingly, they are searching for an "unnamed minor" of interest who was determined to have jumped from the yacht as it approached George Town, and also . . . *Rita*? I keep reading, the hairs pricking up on the back of my neck as I picture Rita skulking around the yacht, spying on us.

A source inside the investigation also tells us that *The Escape*'s chief steward, Rita Gaines, is the sole crew member to not report to the police station and give a statement to law enforcement, and hasn't been seen since she was witnessed walking off the yacht when it docked in Grand Cayman late this morning . . .

I try to make sense of what this means as I watch the waves curl onto the shore and pull back out. A steady rhythm, like the noisy pulsing of blood in my ears. Could Rita have done it? She certainly had access to our cover-ups, the ability to go pretty much anywhere on the yacht. But if she did it, why? Then I remember Giselle's words in Nassau:

I bet my dad hired her to spy on us . . .

What if he'd hired her to do something worse? Ensure he got control of Giselle's fortune so he could keep it. For himself.

I feel light-headed. If that's true, I'm doomed. I can't possibly go up against Senator Haverford and all his resources and connections.

Still, the questions claw at my brain. Why me? Why make it look like *I* pushed her? Because I'm poor and would have a harder time defending myself? That can't be all. There's some key detail I'm missing. This whole thing feels personal, like someone had to hate me enough to set me up. I'm pretty sure Senator Haverford barely knew I existed. And he must be pocketing millions—tens of millions—from the sale of the yacht. Would he really risk his political career to get his hands on more?

Across the cove I can just make out the marina where *The Escape* is docked. What else have they found, I wonder, that the media hasn't reported?

Maybe I should turn myself in. Tell them what I know.

But what is that, really?

That I'm innocent?

Said every criminal ever.

I stare again at the phone in my hand. The lock screen photo flickers to life. A selfie of me and Dad in front of the barn. Three years ago when we'd just finished milking the cows and the sun was creeping over the horizon, bathing our world in a golden glow. I can still smell the hay and the dew on the grass and the earthy scent of the animals. It feels so long ago. Another lifetime.

And I guess in a way, it was.

I was so naive then. Maybe it was all a mirage, but I believed what I saw all the same. That even though we didn't have much, we had each other. We had our family and the farm, the cows and chickens, Dad's woodworking business. The deployments hadn't finished chipping away at his soul. That stupid letter hadn't yet arrived in the mail, threatening to destroy our already fragile family. And Allison was just a girl who made my pulse race when she looked at me from across the room in freshman biology class.

My eyes begin to water. I quickly swipe away the tears and sniffle. There's no time to cry. Feeling sorry for myself won't fix anything. It never has. I need to get out of here.

I power down the phone, stuff it in my pouch, and start walking.

We once had a cow that wandered away from the herd, slipped through a break in the fence, and disappeared. Dad and I searched everywhere. The road, the back field, the forest abutting our property, and no sign of her.

Until that afternoon, when our neighbors noticed they had one extra cow grazing with their herd.

"Hiding in plain sight," Dad had said with a chuckle. "Smart cow."

So that's what I'm doing right now.

Hiding in plain sight.

It's the best course of action to buy myself time while I figure out my next move.

I make my way to the jam-packed cruise port, where passengers crowd along the palm-tree-lined sidewalks. I let myself get swept up in the mass of humanity. Pushing, jostling, pointing, and laughing. I dodge into a pharmacy to get a new bandage for my foot. Then I stop at one of the many kitschy souvenir shops and buy an oversized hat, sunglasses, flip-flops, and sarong, all stamped with *Grand Cayman!* With my hair tucked in the hat and the loud floral print sarong wrapped around my waist, I look like every other sunburned tourist in search of a blender drink.

My parched mouth reminds me that I could, in fact, use a drink. Most definitely not from a blender, though. That nagging feeling that I was more than drunk last night returns. I picture those sleeping pills—the ones that belonged to Britney—scattered in a burst of yellow across Vivian's bathroom floor. All it would take was one, dropped in my champagne, and I'd be out cold. I remember what Vivian said about her friendship with the new Mrs. Haverford. How she owed her. *Everything . . .*

Could Vivian have drugged me?

It fits. Almost. But I have a hard time picturing Vivian, the girl who won't eat anything with a face, being a willing accomplice to murder. And I really thought she liked me, too. Emiene, on the other hand, certainly hates me enough to set me up. Except, she loved Giselle, didn't she? Would she really want to kill her over a stupid fight?

None of this makes sense.

I feel like I'm trying to assemble pieces from ten different puzzles. Ones that fit together but don't form a cohesive picture. I'm still missing something. Because the person who did this either got freakishly lucky, or they had to know that I'd be passed out when Giselle climbed that railing with the security camera filming.

And the question I keep circling back to: *Why?*

I cross the street to an open-air café with a view of the water and a giant cruise ship moored just offshore. I snag the last seat at the bar, wedging myself next to a middle-aged man wearing cargo shorts, sandals, and knee-high black socks. He takes a slurp of his piña colada and glances in my direction.

"You headed back to that ship, too?" *Slurp.*

I nod.

"Boy, those were some rough seas last night, eh?" he continues. *Slurp, slurp.*

I nod again, trying to angle myself away from him. Mercifully, the bartender shows up.

"What can I get you?" she asks.

"Jerk sandwich and a water," I say. "Thank you."

"Sure," she answers. "How's the cruise?"

"An adventure," I say.

"I bet," she says, setting a tall glass of water in front of me. I greedily drink it, almost all in one gulp. The bartender refills the glass and I chug that down, too. "Where have you been?"

My throat tightens. I have no idea. Why did I have to say I came from that cruise ship? And what's with the twenty questions? The news plays on the television above the bartender's head.

"Bahamas," I mumble.

"Bahamas?!" Black Socks next to me shouts. "What are you talking about? Last port stop was Cancun!"

The bartender's eyebrows shoot up. My cheeks burn. "My mistake," I say. "My parents made me come on this trip.

Supposed to be a family bonding thing or something stupid like that."

Suddenly, the scene on the TV shifts to an aerial view of a resort. Here. In Grand Cayman. The name Haverford scrolls across the bottom of the screen.

BREAKING NEWS

I stand abruptly, nearly knocking the barstool over. I need to get out of here before my face shows up on the screen with WANTED stamped right beneath it.

"Wow, is that the time?" I say, trying to sound calm. "I totally lost track. I'm supposed to meet my parents in ten minutes. I'm sorry, I think I'll need to cancel that order. Thanks for the water." I leave a handful of crumpled dollars on the bar top.

"No worries," the bartender says. "Safe travels!" A new customer slips onto my stool almost as quickly as I leave it. I hear the woman next to Black Socks clucking.

"You've always got to be right, Harold!" she says. "And look, you scared that poor girl away."

"What?" he shouts back. "Who can't tell the difference between the Bahamas and Cancun? That's the problem with kids these days, you know! Always got their noses in those damn phones. Could be on the moon and wouldn't know it! Ah, would you look at that . . . more about that senator's kid. Pushed overboard by one of her friends, is what they're saying. See what I mean about kids these days!"

I can't get away from here fast enough.

"What now? I don't believe it!" noisy Harold says behind me. "Not the boy, too. Oh, the poor senator!"

Despite myself, I have to look.

I cast a glance over my shoulder at the television, freezing in shock at the image on the screen and the chyron scrolling beneath it. The missing piece of the puzzle. The *why* of it all.

Suddenly, everything comes into focus and begins to make sense.

Perfect, horrible sense.

And if I don't move quickly, any chance of proving my innocence is about to sail away into the sunset.

BREAKING NEWS ALERT—4/16, 5:59 P.M.

ANCHOR: More at this hour as events rapidly unfold in the disappearance of Knox Haverford from his hotel in Grand Cayman earlier today. Eight-month-old Knox, the son of Senator Robert Haverford and his second wife, Britney Michel Haverford, was last seen on hotel security footage being wheeled in his stroller through the lobby of the Ritz–Carlton by his nanny for a walk around 10:00 a.m. We are joined by retired FBI profiler Kathi Mangold, who is going to share her insights on the case.

KATHI: Good evening, Cameron.

ANCHOR: Thank you for joining us, Kathi. To be clear, you are not directly working on this case, but your years as a profiler in several high-profile kidnapping cases does give you a unique perspective on today's events.

KATHI: That is correct.

ANCHOR: So, help us break this one down. What are investigators up against?

KATHI: Right now, the clock. The first seventy-two hours of a missing persons search are the most critical, and when it comes to a vulnerable person—such as an infant, in this case—I'd say it's more like the first twenty-four. Unfortunately, because Knox's parents were otherwise engaged with authorities in the search for Knox's older half sister, Giselle, and assumed he was safe with his nanny, they did not realize he was actually missing for several hours, losing crucial investigation time they cannot get back.

ANCHOR: Yes, that is tragic. On the subject of Miss Haverford, how do you think her case connects with Knox's—if it does at all?

KATHI: My feeling is that this was an impulsive act. Whoever did it took advantage of the distraction created by the intense focus on Giselle. I'd be looking for someone with access to Knox, or who is close to the family—

ANCHOR: Like the nanny? She has not been located, either.

KATHI: Possibly. Or a hotel employee or perhaps someone who works on the grounds.

ANCHOR: What do you think of a potential motive? Money?

KATHI: Obviously given the Haverfords' immense wealth and influence, money is a definite possibility.

ANCHOR: We haven't heard of any ransom demand at this point, though . . .

KATHI: Exactly. Which brings me back to the fact that I believe this was an impulsive act. And that, sadly, is often more dangerous for the victim because we are dealing with someone who doesn't have a clear plan and may panic at the prospect of getting caught.

ANCHOR: Scary. One minute, Kathi. Sorry for the interruption. Olivia Marlowe, our reporter on the scene in Grand Cayman, has a breaking update. Over to you, Olivia.

OLIVIA: Thanks, Cameron, we've just heard from our source inside the investigation, who tells us they have recovered incriminating phone messages between *The Escape*'s chief steward, Rita Gaines, and an unknown recipient regarding some type of package and a payoff.

ANCHOR: And where is Gaines now?

OLIVIA: That is an excellent question. As you know, Miss Gaines was the only crew member to not give a statement to authorities this morning. She was last seen walking off the yacht when it docked in George Town, after which it seems she vanished into thin air. There has been no sign of her since.

DAY 5

APRIL 16—PRESENT

George Town, Grand Cayman

By the time I reach the docks, my foot is throbbing, and pain shoots up my leg like tiny bolts of lightning. Thankfully, I'm not too late. If my hunch is correct.

And I'm pretty sure it is.

Because I know a thing or two about shaping a narrative to fit the story you want told.

I hang back a moment to catch my breath and figure out a plan, watching as a brand-new set of crew members loads supplies onto *The Escape*.

The yacht couldn't have a more fitting name, now, could it?

I contemplate my approach and decide my best strategy is to move with confidence. Act like I really belong. That's the one thing I've learned hanging out with these girls.

Fake it till you make it, baby.

Squaring my shoulders, I walk down the dock, straight past the crew, and onto the yacht. Before anyone can think to stop me, I've marched up the stairs and am quietly pushing open the door to the primary suite on the right.

She's sitting on the bed with her back to me, staring out the tall windows at the ocean, freshly bleached blond hair arranged in a jagged pixie cut. A stroller sits alongside her. She's lost in thought and doesn't seem to notice me. Or maybe she's chosen not to notice me.

I clear my throat.

"I gave specific orders not to be bothered," she says gruffly without turning. "Now, please, go!"

"Actually, I think I'll stay."

The air goes still, like the calm before a storm.

She turns slowly, newly brown eyes widening in horror.

"Maggie?" she sputters. "What are *you* doing here?"

"Hey, Giselle," I say. "Or whatever name it is you're using now. Maybe you'd like to give 'Beatrice' a try? I think it suits you."

Her mouth opens and closes.

"Yeah, save it," I say. "And here I was supposed to feel sorry for you selling the yacht, when it looks like you're the buyer?"

Giselle doesn't answer. Instead, she watches me like a cornered cat with its hackles raised and claws out, debating whether to flee—or pounce. "How did you know?" she finally asks.

"I didn't. Not at first," I say, trying to keep a measured voice, even though I'm nearly vibrating with anger. I step closer. "Nothing added up, until . . ."

Giselle's hand reaches out protectively toward the stroller.

"Until I saw the news," I continue. "About him. And then it all made sense." I nod at the sleeping baby tucked beneath a hand-looped blue blanket, and flash back to when I first tickled little Knox's feet at the chalet. "He has our toes, you know."

The look on Giselle's face shifts from panic to confusion. "What are you talking about?"

"That gap, between his big and second toe, it's . . . Oh, never mind. I don't feel like explaining. Why don't you see for yourself?"

I pull the letter from my pocket. The once creamy linen envelope is now crinkled and creased, tinged with sand and saltwater. But I know the instant Giselle's eyes rove across the broken wax seal on the back that I don't need to tell her who sent it.

"So you *did* take that from my room," she says, voice turning to steel.

"From *your* room? No, you're wrong about that. Just like you were wrong about me and Wyatt," I say. "I don't know what you think you saw, but we're only friends who had art class together. Nothing more. I never said anything because he told me you guys would be all weird and judgy about it."

"You did find my journal, then, when I sent you to get my phone," Giselle says.

I'm momentarily caught off guard. "Wait, you actually wanted me to take that?"

She shrugs. "I had a feeling you couldn't resist. And it wouldn't look too great for the police to discover you with a journal full of motives, would it?"

I shove the letter toward her, trying to keep my anger from

bubbling over. This whole thing has been one giant setup. And I fell for it, hook, line, and sinker.

She takes the envelope and then blinks with confusion as she reads the name on the front: *Thomas Mitchell*. Hands shaking, she unfolds the paper inside. Her lips move as she silently mouths the words I knew by heart:

Dear Tom,

I know this must seem strange, writing to you after all these years. And I'm sorry. I'm sorry about so many things. Somehow I always believed there would be time to fix my mistakes, to make different choices. But there's not. I'm dying. I don't say that to be dramatic or to ask for sympathy or even forgiveness. It's simply the truth. I have stage 4 breast cancer, and it's metastasized to my brain. The doctors say I have weeks, maybe a few months if I'm lucky. That is why I'm writing.

Because I owe you the truth.

So here it is: You have a daughter. What I mean to say is we have a daughter. Her name is Giselle. And, oh, she's my heart and soul! A gift from the universe. So smart and beautiful and full of life. Like you in so many ways. Sometimes when she laughs in that unabashed way of hers, I hear you—and I'm brought back to the summer we met. When you built my studio at the chalet. I was so young and naive, with my head in the clouds, and I fell for you so hard. Even though I knew it was wrong. Even though I already knew my marriage to Robert was less about love and more about what I could do for him, I had no business letting my heart run away without my head. But I did. Because there you were out on the lawn, sleeves rolled up, carving the beams for my studio's ceiling by hand. When you smiled, it was like the sun came out for me, and me alone. And when your lips met mine, it was like I'd come alive in a way I had never felt with Robert. I watched The Notebook over and over, and you were my Noah in a white shirt and jeans, kissing me in the rain, and I was so sure I'd die as an old lady, lying next to you and holding your hand.

But life is not a movie, is it?

And we can't undo the past.

I have so many regrets about my choices that summer—but she will never be one of them.

I know this all must come as a shock, especially after I'd told you to leave and never come back. There were so many times over the years I thought about telling you the truth. Instead, I made the cowardly choice, if not the easy one.

I heard you joined the Guard and got married and have a family of your own now. And I hope you have found happiness. Truly, I do. The last thing I want is to blow up your life, like I nearly did sixteen years ago. So do with this information as you wish. You know how to reach me. If you don't, I'll take this secret to the grave, and no one will ever need to know.

You'll be in my heart, always.

I'll be seeing you,

Eva

Giselle sucks in a breath. A fat tear rolls down her cheek. She wipes it away with the back of her hand, and looks up at me, eyes wet.

"I can't believe this," she says softly. "She never told me."

"Seems you and your mom have more in common than you realized," I say, nodding toward Knox.

Giselle lets out a small huff. "Right. And Dad knew, didn't he? That I couldn't be his. Maybe he suspected it all along. That's why he forced me to give up Knox. All he cares about is power and money. And taking Knox away from me was the best way to keep control." She laughs bitterly. "But Knox is my son. *Mine*. I can't go back. I WON'T go back. You see that now, don't you, Maggie?"

"So your big idea was to run away and frame me for murder? Did you actually think you'd get away with such a stupid plan? That nobody would figure it out?"

"You mean like Dad—I'm sorry, *Senator Haverford*?" Giselle says with a little snort. "Even if he figures it out—*especially* if he does—he's not going to say anything. Think about it. I've pretty much handed him the presidency on a silver platter. Poor, grieving Robert Haverford, bravely moving forward despite his own personal tragedy, because his country *needs* him. Trust me when I say, he won't be pushing for a more thorough investigation. The last thing he wants is for the truth to come out."

I can't hold back my anger anymore. "Oh yeah? You might want to give me one good reason why I shouldn't go ahead and do it anyway, then. I mean, you can't die twice, can you?"

The briefest hint of fear flicks across Giselle's face. Blink and you'd miss it. Then she juts her chin out in that defiant way of hers. More Haverford than Mitchell, DNA be damned.

"I don't think you'd do that," she says. "You want something.

Otherwise, why not bring the police with you? What is it? You want money, right?" She pulls a stack of cash from her safe and sets it on the table. More money than I've ever seen in one place. More than I have tucked in my pouch from the casino. "Take it. It's yours," Giselle says with a dismissive wave. "I don't need it. I have plenty more in a numbered account I set up in George Town. Oh, and that passport I gave you is real, by the way. You could use it to go anywhere you wanted. Be anyone you wanted. I know you, Maggie, and you'll never be happy stuck on some farm in the middle of nowhere, will you?"

I stare at her in disbelief, and then I burst out laughing. I can't help myself. All the stress from the last few hours—no, make that the last few years—bubbles up to the surface in a fit of uncontrollable laughter. I can hardly breathe through all the laughing, standing here in my ridiculous cruise-ship outfit with my saltwater-matted curls crusted around my face.

"You don't know me at all," I say. "Don't you even care? About the father you've never met? The lives you're destroying? Do you seriously think a pile of money can fix everything?"

"Can't it?" Giselle says. "Christopher didn't mind a few—okay, several thousand—bucks to let me hide in his stateroom this morning when you were all searching for me. I didn't even end up needing that compromising video of him I'd staged. But you know, it never hurts to have a backup plan. Like you did, right? I mean, how long have you kept this letter to yourself? I'm sorry, but my days of wanting an actual father are long gone. What is it, then? What's your price? Everybody has one."

My price. That's a great question. Because when I set out on this journey, I still held on to this tiny bit of hope that Giselle and I had a connection. Something that went deeper than friendship. That we could be true sisters, like me and Soph. That she'd *want* to help our father. Our family. Me. That she'd come down from her castle on the hill and be one of us.

What a crock.

I'm tired. Tired of all the secrets and lies. It's time to let the chips fall where they may.

I'm drawing another card, even if I go bust in the process.

"The truth, Giselle. That's what I want. The truth. *All* of it."

"Suit yourself," Giselle says, and I listen as she spells out how she pulled it off. How she'd spent the last month funneling her inheritance into an untraceable numbered account in Grand Cayman, buying the yacht under a fake name, and paying off Josie with a flight to Guatemala and enough money to give her own family a good life in return for bringing Knox to Giselle this morning. Her bottom lip trembles briefly as she tells me how Senator Haverford forged Knox's birth certificate. How lonely she's been since her mother died, especially as one by one her friends seemed to be slipping away.

I'd almost feel sorry for her—and maybe even a little impressed—except for the part where she explains how she drugged me with pills she made Vivian get from some rando dealer in Key West. Then, while I was passed out, she forced Emi to pretend to push her overboard. Finally, she altered the security video and hid out in Christopher's room until the yacht docked.

When Giselle's finished spilling her guts, she sucks in a little breath and looks at me, eyes wide. I swear I can see the tiniest hint of green flashing beneath her brown contacts.

"There's one thing I don't understand," I say, because there's a critical hole in her story. "Where did you go when *The Escape* docked here in George Town? Surely you didn't just stay in Christopher's room. Someone would have seen you when they searched the yacht."

"Eh, I had a nice little Airbnb set up right around the corner where I could keep an eye on things," she says. "All I had to do was put on that wig I got in Key West, a crew uniform, and a pair of Top-Siders, and then I walked right off the boat. It was chaos. Everyone was pretty busy looking for *you* and not paying much attention to the crew and who was or wasn't there. So thanks for that little stunt of yours, jumping overboard." The corner of her lips twitch into a smirk.

"And nobody recognized you?" I say, incredulous.

"That's the funny thing about people," Giselle says. "They see what they want to see. Like last year when everyone thought I was gaining weight due to stress, not because of him." She tilts her head toward Knox. "Or the police, who didn't need much persuading to release *The Escape* once they'd collected their evidence. That video was pretty damning, after all. Not to mention, the 'new owner's' local attorney is quite well-connected. And convincing. So, you know, when I left the yacht in uniform, everyone just thought I was—"

"*Rita*," I cut in.

Holy crap.

The body.

That's who washed up this morning off the coast of Cuba.

Giselle's expression doesn't change. But the corner of her right eyelid twitches, ever so slightly. "Perhaps they did," she says coolly with a tiny shrug. "Hard to say. I guess it's too bad for her that I dropped my phone on the top deck when I went over the railing. When I ran back upstairs to get it, there was Rita, hiding around the corner and taking pictures. Of course, if Rita didn't spend so much time spying on me and did her job, she'd probably be fine. Instead, she threatened to sell photos of me faking my fall to her friend Harry Fordham at TMZ. Or the highest bidder."

"So you—"

"It's not like I *wanted* to shove her overboard," Giselle says. "But what else could I do? There was no reasoning with her. No dollar figure she'd be satisfied with. So really, that's on her. She should've known I wasn't about to let some conniving thief stand in my way. I don't like to leave any loose ends, sis." She holds my gaze, unflinching. "I just wish she hadn't grabbed my necklace as she fell. That I'm actually sorry about."

The floor beneath my feet begins to vibrate as *The Escape*'s engines power up. Outside, the crew members' shouts grow louder in preparation for departure.

"So, what's it going to be? Time is running out. We'll be underway soon. Or maybe you're planning to sail off into the sunset with me?" Giselle grins in that catlike way of hers and for the first time since we met, I see her for who she really is. Not a sister. Not a friend. Not the girl who would save me.

What was it Giselle said about people? *They see what they want to see . . .*

"Well?" she says impatiently.

"Wait a minute." I stare straight at her, my breath growing shallow. "I never kissed Wyatt."

"So?"

"I. Never. Kissed. Wyatt," I repeat slowly, watching her reaction. She doesn't even bat an eyelash. "But you knew that, didn't you? Which means . . . you lied. YOU LIED! Why? Why invent a kiss that didn't happen?"

I picture Wyatt's messages: she's NOT YOUR FRIEND. Don't get on that yacht. I'M SORRY . . .

"Oh my God," I say, stepping back. "He was part of your plan, wasn't he? You must have edited your journal, after you figured out you were wrong about the two of us. You wanted it to seem like we were together. But for what reason? To punish him, too? I thought you cared about him."

Giselle looks at Knox, tucked in his blue, hand-loop blanket, and that's when it hits me.

"You wanted it to look like Wyatt had a reason to run away, didn't you? Because he felt guilty. Because of me. Getting expelled. Whatever story you told him to tell. Is that it?" I glance around her massive suite. "Where is he, then? Is he in here somewhere, hiding?"

Giselle sighs and gives her head a little shake.

"If he wants to be with his son—like he said he did *after* he told me to go to hell—then he's currently on a one-way flight from Montreal to Havana," she answers. "Sorry, I guess I might have left that part out of my journal. Some things should really never be put in writing. You get that, don't you, Maggie?"

My jaw drops.

"Don't give me that look," Giselle continues. "I'm not a monster. I love Wyatt. I always have. We're going to be a proper family. And I've made sure that Wyatt's mom will never have to clean another room again. Or work at all. Wyatt is a good person. He made the right choice. For his family."

I shake my head in disbelief. I'd hardly call that being given a choice.

"What?" Giselle says. "Like you wouldn't do the same? We're really not that different when it all comes down to it."

I let her words sink in, thinking about everything I've done to get here. Is she right? Are we nothing more than two sides of the same coin, telling ourselves the ends justify our means?

The yacht jerks forward and back again. A horn sounds and lines begin to clunk against the dock.

"Last chance," Giselle says. "Are you staying or going? I have a plane to meet in Cuba."

From the smug look on her face, I can tell she thinks she's already won. She played us all to perfection. I think about what Emi said in the bathroom back in Sloppy Joe's. *The Giselle I know has always gotten her way.*

Oh yeah? We'll see about that.

"I guess you're right," I say, squaring my shoulders. "We're not that different, are we?"

Then, without another word, I scoop up the pile of cash and stride off the yacht—just as the crew unhooks the last line. Maybe money can't fix everything, but it sure can buy a lot of Band-Aids. I can get Dad into a proper treatment program. Mom can get a break for once in her life. Nana can enjoy her retirement. And I can leave for college without having to worry about my little sister, alone in that tiny trailer without me.

When I reach the end of the dock, I turn around and watch as *The Escape* pulls away, slicing like a knife through the turquoise water.

My, how things have changed since we departed New York four days ago, filled with hope and anticipation.

I picture Giselle on that first day, stretched out on her lounger in the sun, the sky blue and the horizon beckoning. Auburn hair spilling across her shoulders, face serene.

I like beginnings is what she'd said. *That's what life should be, don't you think? A bunch of beginnings . . . Screw endings, am I right?*

Yeah, well, screw *that*.

I pull my phone from my pocket and tap the screen to stop the recording I began when I walked into her stateroom a few minutes ago.

Then I stuff the cash into a rented locker at the marina for safekeeping and walk away. Away from the glittering coastline, the tourists with their sunburned noses and blender drinks.

Away from the girl I had wanted so badly to know and toward the police station.

I think I have a story they might be interested in hearing.

Because Giselle isn't the only one around here with a backup plan.

And I don't like to leave any loose ends either, sis.

ACKNOWLEDGMENTS

Writing a book may be a solitary endeavor, but bringing one to publication takes an entire crew. For that, I'm incredibly thankful for the many amazing and talented people who have been on board this journey with me.

Endless gratitude to my incredible agent, Mandy Hubbard. Your ability to get to the heart of a story is unparalleled, your advocacy unmatched. I am so grateful our paths brought us together again. It's fitting that your agency is called Emerald City, because there really is no place like home!

To Erica Sussman and Sara Schonfeld—I couldn't ask for a better pair of editors to steer this story to publication. Thank you for your excellent editorial insights, guidance, and, of course, the yacht puns. It has been an honor to work with you both!

A huge shout-out to the rest of the stellar crew at HarperCollins: managing editor Alexandra Rakaczki, copyeditor Marinda Valenti, and proofreader Lana Barnes; James Neel and Kristen Eckhardt in production; designers Julia Feingold and Alison Donalty; cover artist Leroy Van Drie; publicist Taylan Salvati; and marketing director Audrey Diestelkamp. I can't thank you enough for turning this story into a (beautiful!) book I can hold in my hands, and for helping to get it out in the world! A special thanks, as well, to publicist Megan Beatie of Megan Beatie Communications, and to Kristen Pettit for acquiring this backward tale of a yacht trip turned deadly.

I'd be lost at sea without the love and support of my friends and writing buddies. Thank you, Marina Cohen, for the many beta reads, the phone calls to commiserate, and above all, your friendship! T. P. Jagger, thank you for always agreeing to read my latest wild ideas and for giving me great feedback (along with plenty of your signature humor).

Many thanks to my amazing and talented author colleagues April Henry, Megan Lally, Margot Harrison, Laurie Elizabeth Flynn, Kit Frick, and Marci Lyn Curtis for the blurbs, ARC reads, and promotion.

And love and thanks to all my wonderful friends scattered around the country. I couldn't possibly name you all, but just know—if you're reading this, I love you dearly and am so grateful to have you in my life!

To my readers, thank you for that most precious gift—your time. My books couldn't exist without you!

And last, but most certainly not least, to the people who have been with me from the very start of this journey—my family. All the love and gratitude to my mom, dad, Bev, Greg, Monica, Fiona, Mattea, Celia, my husband and co-captain, Ted, and the lights of my life—Sven and Ava.

Thank you for being my home port, always.